Andy Motson smacked his lips in anticipation - a well deser
X.B would be awaiting him at The White Hart, his local pub
a joke. The idea almost soured the welcoming beery taste in l   ...ought of the place
he euphemistically called '*home*' - a run-down, sleezy bedsit in a grotty part of town, sharing
'*facilities*' with all kinds of low lifes, constant noise, no privacy. God, what had he been reduced to?
No, what had that bitch reduced him to? Crap house, crap job, crap life.

True, he had to acknowledge, he would never have been a high flying entrepreneur, he was no Bill
Gates or Richard Branson, but hadn't he held down a steady job for years as deputy under-manager
in the local branch of a well known insurance company? It wasn't his fault that one of his
underlings had been defrauding the company for a long, long time, and no one had noticed – well,
to be precise, he hadn't noticed. How was he supposed to have known, he couldn't keep track of
everything that went on in the office. They shouldn't have blamed him for not knowing, he wasn't
his brother's keeper. It wasn't fair that he had to pay the price as well.

And didn't he once have a lovely home on a leafy residential street in the suburbs, caring
neighbours, a beautiful wife and two gorgeous children? Andy who was a scrawny, lank haired,
borderline special needs individual, surviving on cunning and primal intuition, actually and totally
misguidedly, regarded himself as a good looking fellow - tall, dark and handsome in a rugged kind
of way - the type of man that any lucky woman should be proud to have at her side.

Through his rose-coloured spectacles, Andy believed he'd had the whole nine yards. Aah, and in
that measured length lay his demise - the gee gees. Not that Andy could even begin to accept his
interest as an addiction - no, he knew he had the gambling well under control, his formula was fool-
proof - a tried and trusted strategy. It was more like a business plan really. What his missus, or
rather ex-missus didn't understand, was that you have to bide your time, roll with the punches, until
- wham! - you hit the jackpot. True, the jackpot was a little late in coming - too late to save his
marriage, but Andy was still convinced his method was spot-on. All he needed was the financial
resources, just like any good businessman requiring investment in a viable project. Why didn't
anyone understand that?

Andy shook his head in disbelief and self pity while he got ready to go. Nothing going on here,
always the same in Winter – as soon as it got dark everyone just wanted to be back in the comfort
and warmth of their own homes. Safe indoors, pulling the curtains tight against the outside world,
living in their own little cocoon - well bully for them. He hated them, he hated the cold and he hated
this job. He could and should be doing something far more profitable like studying the form for
tomorrow's meeting at Haydock Park. Plus, he'd got a mate down at his local who sometimes put
gear his way. It wasn't a reliable income but was often a welcome boost sometimes just when he
needed it most. He didn't see any reason to hang around longer - call it a perk of his crap job that
no-one breathed down his neck telling him what and what not to do. So putting the entrance and

exit barriers *'up'*, he switched off the booth's lights, carefully locked the door behind him and set off for a well earned early pint.

Now, a good thief does his research, and this thief's research had shown that the lazy bastard security guard on the exit always knocked off an hour early. In fact as soon as it got dark - he knew the routine - the guard would leave the barriers up, switch off, lock up and bugger off for the night. A week's discreet surveillance of the site had quickly revealed that this was the perfect time to see to business and the thief was determined to carry out a thorough and professional job. If anyone had been remotely observant, they might have wondered why this well dressed man was lingering so long in the car park on a bitterly cold November's night. But people in a rush rarely take notice of what goes on around them, concerned only with themselves and getting from A to B in the shortest possible time. Moreover, the thief knew well, if you look the part, you'll pass incognito any time.

So he deliberately blocked out the ear-splitting shriek of the car alarm and continued to methodically carry out the job, ignoring the kid's debris – toys, crayons, sweet wrappers. Shame, it was a nice family car, a two year old, top of the range Jaguar XF - bound to put the owner's premiums up quite a bit - but that wasn't his problem and anyway he wasn't about to vandalise it - that wasn't his style. He just used the minimum force to gain access, smashing the passenger-side window and letting himself in. He had read all about the dangers of leaving forensic evidence behind at the scene of a crime and reckoned he'd taken every precaution against it. So, pretty certain there was no chance of being caught, he took his time and searched carefully, pleased with the swag. Still, better make this the last one tonight - no point pushing his luck. He quietly closed the saloon's door, removed his latex gloves and picked up his briefcase, now loaded with goodies and strode purposefully and confidently back through the car park and in to the main building of St Nicholas' hospital, seamlessly blending in with the hustle and bustle around him.

ii.

"Thanks everybody, good job. Time to go home."

There was a collective sigh of relief. It had been a complicated operation on the son of a well-known and demanding celebrity and both the surgeon and his team were exhausted after 5 hours in theatre. The team probably more so than the surgeon who had the highest expectations from those assisting him and little patience with inferior workmanship. He would not tolerate anything but 100% effort and perfect results.

The boy would make an excellent recovery, the scoliosis op had been a complete success. He had no doubt that the quality of the boy's life, which up until now had been severely limited, would change dramatically and definitely for the better. Alistair Neville could imagine the lad playing football, riding a bike, running around just like any boy of his age should be doing - living a normal, happy and carefree life.

Alistair not only took professional pleasure in demonstrating his formidable surgical talent - after all, he was an ambitious man, but also genuinely delighted in being able to make an important difference in his young patients' lives. This rare combination served to make him one of the most sought after paediatric surgeons in the city. He believed and expected his value to be appreciated as well as suitably rewarded, thus guaranteeing him a rapid promotion up the ranks of the elite in his field.

Confident in leaving his staff to finish up, Alistair quickly showered and grabbed a coffee before returning to check on his patient in aftercare. He saw that the lad's parents had been permitted to be by his bedside and were anxious to be fully informed of their son's prognosis. So, Alistair, never one to allow an opportunity to laud his own talents, was happy to outline details of the complex procedure, highlighting his vital contribution and confidently assuring the parents of a total recovery. Leaving the parents happy and satisfied that all was well, he left some final instructions with the intensive care staff and headed off home.

He always walked up and down the stairs, just about the only aerobic exercise he managed to do these days. He wasn't overweight for his 6'2" height and looked after his health pretty well, but his footballing and tennis playing days were far behind and he wasn't remotely interested in golf or jogging. Of course, walking down from the fifth floor paediatric department was a lot easier than going up, but anything was better than nothing he reasoned. As he descended, he considered that maybe he really should consider taking up golf - after all, many a decision was taken on the course rather than in the boardroom and it wouldn't hurt his prospects to insinuate himself into 'The Old Boy Network' now, would it?

Reaching the ground floor, Alistair was surprised to see some kind of commotion going on at the security guard's desk. Several of his colleagues seemed agitated and annoyed, so he wandered over to see what was happening.

"Evening Pete, what's up?"

Peter Forbes, fellow surgeon specializing in orthopaedics, turned to him angrily.

"Some sod's broken in to my car, taken my lap-top and God knows what else. I come back here to report it and find this lot've all had their cars broken-in to as well."

There did indeed seem to be quite a disgruntled crowd and Dave, the security guard at reception was doing his best to calm the situation.

"All right docs, the Old Bill are on their way."

"You said they'd be a half an hour and that was forty five minutes ago," someone complained.

"Well don't blame me, I'm just the messenger," came the tart reply.

"And where's Sid? He wasn't in his booth," asked another.

"Sid?" Dave responded incredulously "Don't you mean Andy? Sid died eight months ago, heart attack. Forty years he worked here and that twat Andy's been here since then. I've been trying to ring him - no reply, so, not surprising he didn't answer then since you say he's not there."

There was a slightly awkward moment of silence as the group realized that not one of them had noticed poor deceased Sid had been replaced.

"Al, I swore to Ann I'd be home on time," Pete said. "She's going to go ballistic. We've got that children's charity function this evening and she's been organizing it for the last three months."

Alistair was well aware of the big event - his own wife, Natalie, was co-arranger - and for weeks had been fending off Pete's pleas to accompany him for moral support.

"Well give her a call and explain what's happened, she'll understand," replied Alistair.

Pete looked embarrassed, "I can't, I left my mobile in the car and it's been nicked as well."

"Here, use mine, you wally." After the call, Alistair was anxious to be off.

"Hey Pete, if I'm not back in the next five minutes, you'll know I've been spared. Let me know how you get on mate."

Alistair quickly made his way to his reserved parking space and took some time to carefully check the vehicle over. Although it was dark, as far as he could see there didn't seem to be any sign of interference or vandalism, no broken windows nor scratches and, thankfully, the doors were still securely locked, not that there was anything worth nicking in it. Maybe his three year old, bog standard Vauxhall Insignia just wasn't snazzy enough to attract a thief's attention. It looked as though he had indeed been spared and with some relief, he got in, started up and set off home.

'Poor Pete, she's going to kill him,' he thought. *'I wouldn' t want to be in his shoes.'*

It wasn't that he actively avoided such events, but rather that he'd had a huge waiting list back-log which had been scheduled for weeks. Well, that's what he had convinced himself was the case - the truth was this type of affair just wasn't his cup of tea. His conscience twinged just a little - he knew he could have had the listing secretary rearrange his workload to free him up in time for this evening, but had persuaded himself that it would be unfair to his patients to have to cancel surgery that they had probably been waiting months for, purely for his own gratification. He had told Nat that it simply wouldn't be fair to commit to the occasion and then find he had to let her down because of over-running in theatre. Typically Nat had not even attempted to over-rule his decision, she hadn't wasted her breath pointing out that Peter Forbes had somehow managed to reorganize his theatre list. Experience had taught her that once her husband's mind was made up there was little she could do to change it, but it was hard to disguise her disappointment when she knew Alistair was well aware of how important this was to her and could almost certainly have rearranged his schedule.

On the journey home, Alistair reflected how it was a pity, but a sad fact of life, that a relatively junior surgeon had to do whatever it took to gain consultant status. Lately he had rarely got home before his kids were in bed and asleep. It was one of his biggest regrets - not being able to devote as much time to his children as he would have liked. They were growing up so fast - where did the time go? He supposed it was the perennial lament and regret of most ambitious working parents - you worked long hours to provide security and stability for your family and, in doing so, missed out on many of the key moments of their childhood. Tonight, however, he had promised Natalie that he would be back as early as possible, send Alison, the baby sitter, home and spend some quality time with the children - they might still be up - whilst his wife enjoyed her evening out with Ann and Pete.

Arriving some thirty minutes later, Alistair was greeted by Natalie who was looking ravishing, her tall, lean figure sheathed in a burgundy velvet long dress which superbly accentuated her russet coloured mane and green eyes. God, she looked like a Victorian romantic heroine from a corny novel, he thought guiltily. He knew he had let her down by swerving tonight's event but, up until that very moment, had felt nothing but relief that she had never commented or insisted he accompany her.

Now and perhaps not surprisingly under the circumstances, he could see that she was harrassed, betrayed by a rosy flush on her freckled cheeks which only highlighted her Celtic origins.

'Get a grip.' He thought a tad remorsefully, the sentiment swiftly banished by Nat announcing briskly,

"Your evening suit's out on the bed, you've got ten minutes to get changed."

"What's going on?" he asked, guessing full-well but obediently setting off upstairs nevertheless, disguising that he was more than a little bit annoyed that his plans for the evening were going to be upset. He supposed he shouldn't be surprised that his little deceit was bound to have failed and would come back to haunt him.

"I've just had Ann on the phone. Evidently Pete's had his car broken in to and is waiting for the police to come, so she's begged you to stand in for him until he can get there. I assured her you'd be happy to. Now hurry up, I promised we wouldn't be late."

"But you told me it was a complete sell out, where will I sit, and what about a baby-sitter?" He whined - trying in vain to delay, visions of having the remote to himself and a night watching boy's stuff on t.v evaporating before his very eyes.

"Don't you worry about that. Ann's going to sort out the table plan and Alison was already coming over from next door to mind the children until you got home anyway, so she'll be looking after them for the whole evening instead. Now move it!"

iii.

Back in his seventh floor flat, the thief changed out of his well-tailored designer suit hanging it carefully in the wardrobe. He was glad, and more than a little relieved, to be back in the comfort of his own home. The place was meticulously and tastefully decorated and furnished, much of which was new but also boasting several painstakingly restored second-hand pieces, every item chosen by himself with huge attention to detail. He'd worked hard and was proud of all he'd achieved. Life hadn't always been easy and still wasn't perfect yet, but he was well on the way to fulfilling his dreams.

He poured himself a large whiskey, serving it in a Waterford cut crystal glass, and reflected upon what had been a successful mission.

'What a bunch of absolute tossers,' he thought. *'so arrogant and superior, think they're invincible, better than the rest of us. Don't even need to lock up their cars.'*

It never ceased to amaze him how casual people were with their belongings, carelessly leaving valuables lying around, often in full view, never thinking that they might be the one to have their car broken into.

Opening the briefcase, he reviewed the evening's haul. A wallet - cash, credit cards, I.D, security pass (could be useful) - a laptop (hidden in the drawer under the driver's seat). It looked like a good make and he knew someone down the market who knew someone who could off-load the goods. He'd recently bought his own laptop, a newer, faster model, so didn't need another one. He was familiar with its systems and reckoned he was getting quite adept at manipulating the programmes, so he'd stick to what he'd got. He'd go down to the second-hand market first thing tomorrow and see what he could get for it. What else? Two memory sticks (keep). Combined cash - not bad - £150 in total, iPhone (same way as the laptop), Kindle (keep). A decent lot of swag considering he'd only broken-in to half a dozen cars.

'Serves the wankers right - they'll never learn.' The thief raised his glass in a silent toast, *'To what you deserve.'*

Downing the remainder of his drink, he headed for the shower. He still had plenty of time but wanted to be well prepared before moving on to the next job.

iv.

Alistair had to admit it - he was having a really good time. Pete had somehow managed to show up only half an hour late, so avoiding the dog-house, arriving, in fact, before they had even sat down to eat after enjoying the pre-dinner drinks and with time enough to relate the wretched car break-in saga to the assembled guests. The food had been better than expected and had actually been quickly served and was hot and tasty. The girls deserved all the credit for their attention to detail and quality.

The companions on their table seemed like a good lot too. Both Natalie and Ann had done a fantastic job in press-ganging their colleagues to attend from their respective work places and everyone was getting along very well indeed. Ann and her fellow teachers had them all in stitches with tales from the classroom whilst Alice, Maria and Simon, who were from Nat's work, kept up a steady and hilarious stream of chit chat recounting office shenanigans about the difficulty of placing clients who often considered themselves way above their true abilities - deluded people who thought they would make good spies or under-cover operatives who were inevitably bitterly disappointed to be placed as security personel in a shopping centre, pub or nightclub. And so the tales continued … The wine and banter were flowing and Alistair allowed the tensions of the week to ease away and began to feel that pleasant, mellow sensation wash over him.

The raffles had taken place and the girls were thrilled with people's generosity, both with the donated prizes and by how many tickets guests had bought. Now it was time for the obligatory auction and they had high hopes of raising a significant amount which they hoped would go some way to alleviate the financial hardship their children's charity was experiencing. They had chosen the guest list carefully - these were professionals or care-givers who all had connections and were, fingers crossed, sympathetic to the cause. Their faith was being rewarded, the generosity was unbounded, the guests were certainly digging deep into their pockets, every item was selling for far more than it's face value. They were absolutely thrilled but Ann and Natalie knew the evening was about to get even better! Alistair could see that they were becoming quite excited - heads together with Pete who leaned across to whisper.

"Al, I'm glad you came, I think you're going to like this!"

A little bemused Alistair said he was glad he'd come too but frankly he really wasn't one for auctions.

"Ladies and gentlemen," announced the auctioneer, "we now come to the main and final lot of the evening. I am pleased to offer this rare Star Trek Original Series medical tricorder used by Dr. Leonard McCoy together with a certificate of authenticity signed by DeForest Kelley, who played the character."

Alistair's jaw dropped, his face a picture of stunned amazement, causing shrieks of delight from the others.

"Told you you'd like it!"

Years before at medical school, on a drunken night out, when a heart to heart seemed like a good idea, Alistair had revealed to Pete that the single most influential reason for him entering the medical profession was his passion for Star Trek. Not only was he the number one fan, but his absolute idol was Dr. McCoy who epitomized the very best of medicine, using futuristic technology, eradicating disease, putting himself in danger for the greater good of his patient. Alistair believed that the future was fast becoming a reality and he wanted to be part of it. Pete had howled with laughter claiming it was the worst reason he'd ever heard for entering the profession - no family history, no calling to the vocation, just the word of a t.v series. Pete wasted no time in broadcasting Alistair's raison d'etre around the faculty and poor Alistair had to suffer his remaining years being greeted with, *'Live long and prosper, doctor.'* However, Alistair had taken the ribbing in good part, their friendship was sealed and, in recent years, had even found themselves working in the same hospital.

He wanted that tricorder but, so it seemed, did several others in the room, including one of the guests at his own table. The bidding rose rapidly but people soon dropped out finding it too rich, leaving just three of them left. The bids had been going up in £10 increments but when the young man on Alistair's own table, Simon, raised this to £50 the third party withdrew.

"Well, what do you want to do, Alistair? Do I win?" Simon seemed thrilled to have secured the bid and Alistair was torn, he coveted that tricorder but, at the end of the day, it wasn't real. He reluctantly nodded defeat and was startled to see an expression of apparent satisfaction cross the man's face.

"Another £50," resounded the clear voice of his wife beside him. Her husband looked as shocked as Simon.

"No! Nat withdraw your bid! Quickly!" exclaimed Alice.

"So, if there are no more bids …?" called out the auctioneer who hadn't heard Alice beseeching Nat, "then, sold to Mrs Neville".

8

After the applause had subsided, Natalie turned angrily towards Simon, Maria and Alice.

"Would you like to tell us what was that all about?"

The three of them looked crestfallen. Their plan had completely back-fired. Maria started to explain.

"Oh Nat, some of the team were disappointed not to be able to come tonight, so they all clubbed together in the office and raised £200 to treat you both to something, and when Pete told us about Dr. Neville's Star Trek obsession we decided to get Simon to bid for it."

Addressing Alistair, Simon, clearly distressed, added, "So, you see, we were always going to make a gift of it to you, Dr. Neville. Natalie, if we've offended you, I sincerely apologize, that was never our intention."

A bit late Natalie realized that Simon and the others had wanted to make a grand gesture on behalf of the team, a contribution to the event. She flushed with embarrassment and had never felt so mean in all her life. She was totally mortified.

"Oh, Simon, I feel like such a berk. What was I thinking? Perhaps you could donate the money to the charity instead? I'm really, really sorry. Can we all still be friends?"

"Always," he and the girls replied generously. But by then the mood of the evening had been a little spoiled and the party broke up shortly after with Ann and Natalie being warmly thanked and congratulated with promises to get together soon.

At home later, with the baby sitter despatched and the children fast asleep, Natalie and Alistair enjoyed one last nightcap before bed.

"An unmitigated success my dear!" Alistair loftily proclaimed raising his glass in salutation to his wife. Laughing, Natalie agreed.

"Why, thank you good sir," adding that it had been a wonderful evening despite the misunderstanding with Simon and the others. Alistair caressed his precious tricorder wryly commenting,

"But buggeration, if we'd only known this could have been ours for free, instead it's cost us an arm and a leg!!"

"I know, painful, but never mind love, it was all for a good cause. You know something? I was determined you were going to have it and quite honestly I'd have gone higher. So count yourself lucky! Come on, let's go to bed, I'm absolutely knackered."

The strident ringing of his mobile slowly dragged the thief to consciousness. Without opening his eyes he reached across to the nightstand and fumbled for his phone. He didn't have to guess who was calling at this far too early an hour.

"Morning Mum, how's things?"

"Fine love." she replied, her lilting brogue as strong today as it had been when she left Ireland all those many years ago. "Just wondering if you'd like to come for your tea tonight?"

He smiled inwardly, she'd asked it as though it were an unexpected invitation, not the same phone call at exactly the same time every Saturday morning.

"Love to. Usual time, six o'clock? Think I'll probably stay the night if that's ok with you?"

He took his mother's sigh of pleasure as agreement. Although he didn't want to make it a habit that his old mum might get used to again, he knew that she loved it when he occasionally stayed over in his old bedroom.

Arrangement sorted, the thief got up and made himself an early morning cuppa which he took back to bed to spend a few minutes savouring the peace and privacy of his own home to review things and make plans for the day.

He loved his mum and it had nearly broken both their hearts when he'd moved out, but a man needed his independence and had to be answerable only to himself. That was a couple of years ago, but nearly four years after the death of his dad. They had both been devastated by the sudden loss and his mum had become so needy – well, not needy exactly, just rather too dependant on him.

His father's death had had profound effects on both of them. He had loved his dad, but he hadn't been an easy man to live with. His constant demands for excellence, *'Never settle for ninety per cent, give it your all or don't bother at all,'* had been his mantra and he had tried to live up to his father's high expectations. Now, he believed, his father would have been proud of him. He was a devoted son, holding down a good job that had real promotion prospects and owned his own home. He now appreciated how right his father had been to advocate not settling for anything but the best. He was well on target to achieve all his goals. Just one hurdle remained and he was well on course to bring that matter to a satisfactory conclusion.

It had been in both their interests for him to move out, though. Actually, it had been the making of his mum, who'd taken up various activities - art classes, yoga, swimming, those kind of things - pursuits she would never have considered had his father still been alive and ruling the roost. In fact, he suspected that his mother had never been so happy and might even have a secret admirer - not that she'd said anything, but he'd noticed that she was taking more care with her appearance and seemed to have a new spring in her step. He'd have to find out for sure this evening. It would be ironic, wouldn't it, if his mother found a partner before he managed to win the girl of his dreams?

'Right, time to get up, things to do, people to see,' he scolded himself.

If he wanted to catch that bloke in the market he'd better get a move on. He quickly got dressed, then ate his usual breakfast of cornflakes and two slices of wholewheat toast and decided he ought to have a quick review of the stuff he'd pinched last night before heading out for the market.

He switched on the kindle while he booted up the stolen laptop. Brilliant, the kindle was loaded with some great crime and thriller books by authors he really enjoyed reading. He'd definitely be keeping that. Wow, would you believe it? The laptop wasn't even password protected - which was actually very convenient for him - it meant he wouldn't have to use his own one to check the gear. He inserted the first memory stick into it, which it seemed, contained nothing but classical music - not really his thing - so he removed it and shoved the stick in to his desk drawer, then put in the second one. Boring … photos of someone's family. He flicked through one or two. Parents and kids at some adventure park, at a party, school play, dad in the bath with the kids, yeah yeah, boring.

"What the fuck?"

Suddenly these weren't your usual family snaps of the perfect domestic idyll. These were graphic images of extreme child pornography, vile and explicit. Stuff you could never imagine in your worst nightmares. Feeling nauseous and with shaking hands, the thief snatched out the stick and slapped down the lid of the laptop. He was shocked to the core and very, very frightened. Flaming hell, what was going on?

"Keep calm, got to think. Think," he said out loud.

He was barely holding it together but he had to get a grip. Shit, had he left any evidence - D.N.A or something - on the vehicles he'd broken into? Could he be implicated in some kind of paedophile ring? Oh God, this was a nightmare. If only he could think clearly. He needed to calm down. He took a deep, steadying breath … No, he'd been careful, worn latex gloves, left as little imprint as possible. And obviously, it wasn't him who featured in those photos, so he couldn't be connected to them, could he? He should be ok. As his breathing returned to normal, clarity returned and a solution began to take shape in his mind. The more he thought about it, the more he realized it was the only way.

Forty minutes later, the thief was parking his pride and joy three year old Audi TT around the corner a few streets away from the police station and far from any prying CCTV. He knew these days surveillance cameras had face recognition ability and could track a person from London to Glasgow, no trouble. Making sure there was no one around, he got out and carefully locked the car. He pulled on some warm gloves, put up the hood of his parka against the steady drizzle and, keeping his head down, made his way to London Road where the main police station which served the hospital could be found. Taking a deep breath he pressed the entry phone button. There was no going back now.

"Can I help you, sir?" came a disembodied voice.

"Yes, I think you can. I understand there was a spate of car break-ins at the hospital yesterday evening. I've got some information which I think you might find interesting."

A moment later the door buzzed open and the thief entered. Still with the hood up and keeping his face obscured, he risked a quick upward glance and located the security camera and then positioned himself with his back to it. The officer behind the reception desk barely acknowledged him.

P.C 206 Richard (Dickie) Brown, a thirty five year veteran, was a stocky, medium built man who had his choice of shifts and these days he enjoyed working the morning one, especially at the weekend. It was nearly always quiet then, a sort of limbo you might say - between the time when the overnight drunks would have been processed and cleared out of the cells by the night shift, but before the football hooligans would be getting arrested later on in the afternoon - by which time, oh yes, he'd be off duty.

He had done his stint on the streets and now preferred the warmth and comfort of a desk job. In his opinion, modern policing should be left to the high fliers - the likes of Sandy Parker and know-it-all Pennock. He'd settled for the more sedentary career. It was a doddle really. It was almost impossible to contact your local nick these days, he often thought. The phone hardly ever rang, and that was simply because the police station no longer had a direct line that the public *could* ring. All calls now went through a central switchboard which seemed highly efficient at deflecting them and never putting them through. The main doors were securely locked to discourage anyone from entering and, God forbid, report a crime (particularly after failing to get through on the phone and being forced to come in person). So, when this unexpected visitor arrived, he found it difficult to muster any enthusiasm. He looked up from his newspaper and enquired without interest,

"So you've got some information, sir?"

"Yes, I'd like to talk to the officer in charge of the case."

"I'm afraid that's not possible, sir. It's his weekend off, he won't be back in till Monday morning."

In fact the constable didn't have the faintest idea who the detective in charge was dealing with the car thefts or even whether he was at work that day or not. Truth be told, it was more than likely no one would be investigating some poxy car thefts but he wasn't about to tell a member of the public that little detail. He just gave the standard response brush off. Apparently unfazed, the thief commented,

"O.k, that's fine."

He then placed a plastic Tesco bag on the counter.

"In which case I just wanted to let you know that I'm returning every last item that was stolen from those cars last night."

That caught the officer's attention.

"In the bag there's a memory stick which, I assure you, has got nothing to do with me, but you should know contains horrible child pornography. I strongly recommend you investigate this."

That said, the thief turned on his heel and exited the building leaving the officer staring, his mouth agape.

He walked speedily back to his car, praying that he'd done the right thing and wouldn't be caught for it. His heart was pounding and he felt clammy and unsteady on his feet. The officer had hardly taken any notice of him, had he? He surely wouldn't be able to give an accurate description. And, honestly, in the scheme of things, how did the crime of a car thief returning a few stolen items compare to the seriousness of child pornography?

Feeling slightly more reassured, the thief set off for home the long way round, obeying the speed limits and making several turns and detours in case he was being tracked by CCTV. He wasn't being paranoid, just being cautious. He parked a half a mile from his flat and doubled back a few times to put anyone off the scent before slipping quickly in to the building's entrance hall, up by lift to the seventh floor and in to the safety of his flat, double locking the door securely behind him.

With still shaking hands, he poured himself a large one and took two quick gulps. It had all gone to plan, he was certain he'd covered all eventualities, so he had to be in the clear. Convincing himself that no more could come of the matter, the thief decided it would be best to spend a quiet afternoon indoors, watch a bit of telly and then go and see his mum later on, spend the night like he said he would - that would please the old girl. Best to keep to a familiar routine.

iii.

Alternating as hosts, the four friends met up as usual on the Saturday evening, this time at Ann and Pete's. The kids were all of a similar age and enjoyed being together, watching films or on the Play Station. They loved being allowed to stay up late and were careful to steer well clear of their parents in case they might remember how late it was and cart them off home and send them to bed. They normally ordered pizza or a Chinese take away which always went down well with everyone.

This evening, however, the adults were still feeling the after effects from the previous night's revelleries and not that much booze was being drunk. But between the many cups of tea, they unanimously agreed that the gala had been an unqualified success and Ann and Natalie thought they'd made in excess of £1500. It was an unbelievably good result. Whilst the girls weren't that keen to repeat the challenge any time soon, it had been a worthwhile effort. They were exhausted and the lives of both families had been dominated by the event for months so they were all looking forward to getting back to a normal way of life.

The house phone rang and Pete went to answer it coming back a few minutes later.

"Miracle of miracles, that was the police. It looks like they've recovered all the gear that was stolen from the cars last night. They want me to go in tomorrow morning at ten to identify my stuff."

"That's great news, Pete," said Natalie.

Alistair was a bit more cynical, "I never thought for a minute you'd ever see those things again. Normally thieves only take the stuff they can quickly off load for cash, way too fast for the Old Bill to stand a chance of getting them. You've been really lucky, Pete. Usually the police can't be arsed to investigate petty crimes these days."

"Well maybe it's because it happened to doctors at the hospital, not the general public," suggested Ann.

"Yeah," agreed Pete, "It must be '*quid pro quo*', the Old Bill probably figure that if they don't produce results for us, then we might not do our best for them on the operating table!!"

They all had a good laugh at Pete's feeble attempt at witty repartee and proposed that in future it should be made hospital policy, clinking tea cups in a toast.

"You know what?" said Alistair. "It's been a great weekend. All's well that ends well. Cheers everybody!"

3

Just before 10 a.m the following morning, Pete presented himself at the London Road police station. There was an extremely helpful and efficient constable on the front desk, an older fellow who was obviously extremely experienced.

"Good morning, sir," the officer said politely. "Dr. Forbes? Please come with me. D.I Pennock and D.S Parnell are waiting for you in Interview Room 2."

P.C Brown had been brutally savaged by his superiors the previous afternoon. They'd absolutely flogged him for his failure to detain the thief, for his inability to give a decent description of him and for his total ineptitude as a police officer. Dick by name and dick by nature they'd said.

He thought they were being a bit harsh. He shouldn't be blamed that there weren't any helpful security camera images, that the man had managed to keep his face pretty much unseen. He'd hardly had the chance to get a good look at the bloke before he was out of the door.

He realized his career might be hanging by a thread if this case were as serious as it seemed. In his own defence though, he hadn't delayed in delivering the bag upstairs to C.I.D. He'd only got a few years left before retirement on a final salary pension - there was no way he was going to jeopardize that, he couldn't risk some kind of demotion or official reprimand, so was making every effort at amends as best he could now.

P.C Brown was given a curt but frosty acknowledgement as he showed Pete in to the interview room. It was the first time Pete had ever been in one and it was exactly like on t.v right down to the two way mirrors.

"Thanks for coming Dr. Forbes. I'm D.I Pennock and this is D.S Parnell. Please sit down. Before we return your items sir, we'd like you to tell us what happened on Friday evening."

"Well, there's not much to tell really," Pete replied. "I finished work just before 5pm because I needed to get home early. When I got to my car, I realized it had been broken in to. It looked like my laptop and mobile phone had been stolen, so I went back in to the hospital to report it and discovered a queue of other staff who'd also had stuff pinched."

D.S Parnell was taking notes while Pete was speaking.

"Then what happened?" he asked.

"Well, the police took ages to come and when they did finally show up, they told each of us to write down on a piece of paper the damage that had been done to our cars, what had been taken, then put our name, address and contact number on, sign and date it. They warned us that there would be hardly any chance of getting our stuff back but that they'd be on to it straight away. But you know all this, right?"

Ignoring the question D.I Pennock asked.

"So, Dr. Forbes, the only things you had taken were a laptop and your mobile phone?"

"Yes, that's correct."

"Not your wallet or maybe a memory stick?"

Pete looked a little confused, "No, I've got my wallet on me now and I don't have a memory stick in the car."

"O.k then, thanks very much. If you'll just wait here for a moment, Dr Forbes we'll be right back with your things."

Both Pennock and Parnell left Pete alone in the room and observed him through the two-way mirror.

D.I Richard Pennock was an ambitious career officer. He had entered the force some sixteen years earlier as a naive, fresh-faced young graduate entrant. Of course he had encountered the usual hostility and snide comments that most fast track entrants suffer from their fellow officers, but time and steady results had gained him respect and popularity among his colleagues. Now, into his late thirties, he still retained a youthful appearance although his light brown hair had recently become streaked with the first strands of grey and the frown lines on his forehead had, without him noticing, become permanent wrinkles.

Moreover and as importantly, he was a husband and a father as well. It was no wonder this latest case was already having a profound psychological effect on him - one that he admitted probably wouldn't have occurred if he hadn't been a parent himself. He wouldn't have had quite the empathy he now felt if he were still single. But at work he was a detective first and foremost, and a damn good one too and if parenthood had added anything to the equation, it was that it made him all the more determined to nail the sick bastard and put him away for a very long time.

D.S Harry Parnell, on the other hand, was an excellent foil to his boss. A seasoned officer who had never aspired to the higher ranks - Parnell had been content to remain a P.C. He had enjoyed being on the beat - till the powers-that-be decided to yank policemen off the streets and made them go around in pairs in cars instead.

The job had changed over the years, he had still enjoyed it but it was no longer as satisfying, so he had taken the advice his superiors had been giving him for years and sat the sergeant exams, which to his surprise, but no one else's, he comfortably passed. So, he had swapped the trade mark P.C's black uniform for well worn jackets and slacks. And as a result he'd put on a few (o.k quite a few) extra pounds over time due to, he tried to convince himself, the sedentary nature of the job. Time had been kind to Harry - nearly bald men, he was told, tend to look old when they're young but young when they're older. Harry fell into this category, never seeming to age much - just maturing like a fine wine as he was fond of saying.

Now, several years later, he was glad he had moved on and happy to know he was well suited to the job. He was a people's man, his forte was reading body language, facial expressions, tone of voice. No university had taught him these skills, this was gleaned from long experience learned out on the streets, hands-on in the front line when instantaneous decisions and arrests had to be made.

By comparison, Pennock was more cerebral, more scientific; he sifted painstakingly through evidence and followed up even the most tenuous leads. Armed with a dogged determination, he had a nose for the job and his instincts were spot on more often than not.

They made a great team, one that had got them the monniker of *'The 2 P's'* from their colleagues - not only because of their combined initials but because of the reputation they had gained for their fast clear-up rate and how cheap that made them in terms of money saved by the taxpayer.

Professionally they complemented each other's talents enormously, but socially, apart from the odd beer together, they didn't have much in common outside of work. What drew them together now though was the fact they were both fathers - a grandfather in Parnell's case - and what they had seen on that memory stick had sickened and galvanized them to catch the evil paedo.

"So what do you think, Harry?" asked Pennock

"Too early to say for certain, Gov. Let's shake the tree and see what falls out," replied Parnell.

ii.

Some ten minutes later, Pete was still waiting for the officers to return and, when they did he detected a subtle change in their attitude. When D.S Parnell had switched on a recording machine D.I Pennock began,

"Thank you for your patience Dr. Forbes. I have to advise you that we are going to tape what is said from now on and continue this interview under caution. You do not have to say anything. But, it may harm your defence if you do not mention when questioned something which you later rely on in court. Anything you do say may be given in evidence."

"I don't understand," said Pete.

"You don't understand the caution Dr. Forbes?" Parnell questioned.

"No, I understand what a caution is, what I don't understand is why you're cautioning me."

"Don't worry Dr. Forbes, at this time you are helping us with our enquiries. Like we always say, if you haven't done anything wrong, then you've got nothing to worry about," said Pennock.

Slightly reassured, Pete said he was happy to help in any way he could. Donning latex gloves Pennock withdrew a mobile phone from an evidence bag.

"Is this your mobile, Dr. Forbes?"

Pete confirmed that it was.

"How do you know it's yours?"

Disconcerted, he answered, "Well, obviously I can't be a hundred per cent sure, but it looks exactly like mine. If you switch it on you should see a picture of my family as the screen-saver."

"Is it ok if we do that? Is it password protected?"

Pete told them there was no password and agreed they could look at the phone. A moment later, a family photo appeared on the screen. Parnell asked if Pete could identify the people in the photo.

"Yes, that's Ann, my wife, on the left and the two children are my daughter, Millie and my son, Max with me on the right."

"Thank you." Pennock returned the phone to the evidence bag and, from another, withdrew a laptop. "So, Dr. Forbes, is this your laptop?"

Pete was a fast learner.

"It certainly looks like my laptop," he replied.

"How could you verify whether it's yours or not?"

"The same way actually, I've got the identical photo as my screen saver on this as well."

Pete agreed they could boot up the machine and told them that this device wasn't password protected either. Soon the family portrait appeared on the screen and Parnell asked Pete to confirm that it was, indeed his laptop. Pennock repeated the procedure, returning the device to the evidence bag before removing an item from a third bag.

"Finally, Dr. Forbes can you confirm this is your memory stick?"

Pete was confused,

"No, that's not mine. Like I said, I don't have a memory stick in the car."

"Dr. Forbes, just to reiterate - you're absolutely certain that this isn't your memory stick?" Pennock pressed.

"I'm absolutely sure it's not mine," Pete insisted.

"Okay," Pennock said slowly, "in which case Dr Forbes, could you please explain to us how exactly the same material on this memory stick can be found duplicated on your laptop?"

Pete was nonplussed.

"I have absolutely no idea," he said beginning to become agitated, "but, listen here, this is starting to sound more like an interrogation than an interview. Tell me, do I need a solicitor?"

"We don't know Dr. Forbes. Do you?"

iii.

Parnell and Pennock suspended the interview to allow Pete to consider his options and it resumed after a much needed cup of tea and a comfort break. They returned with a laptop. Although Pete didn't feel totally at ease, he was quite intrigued, knowing he had done nothing wrong therefore, according to the police, had nothing to fear and so agreed to carry on the interview unrepresented. Pennock began,

"So, Dr. Forbes, just to recap and for the tape - you say that this is not your memory stick?"

"That's correct." Pete confirmed.

Gloved up, Pennock removed Pete's laptop and, once again, asked if it was ok to boot it up. Meanwhile, Parnell had set up the police laptop and inserted the unidentified memory stick.

Clicking on Pete's photo gallery, Pennock brought up the first image - a family photo showing two parents and two children at, what seemed to be, a theme park.

"Do you recognize this photo?" he asked. Pete's look of recognition quickly turned to one of confusion.

"No, I've never seen this photo before, but I do know the people in it."

"Really?" said Pennock doubtfully. "What about this one?"

Pete was shown an image of a party, followed by children in a school play and finally a photo of a man in the bath with some kids.

"As I say, I know this family very well but I haven't the slightest idea what their photos are doing on my laptop."

"So you claim. Dr. Forbes, could you tell us who these people are and what type of relationship you have with them?" said Parnell.

Back on solid ground, Pete gave the officers details of the names and address of the Nevilles and told them that he and Alistair had been friends since medical school as well as colleagues for the last few years. He confirmed that the woman was Natalie Neville, Alistair's wife and the two youngsters in the bath were Dr. Neville's children, Martin and Juliet.

Parnell spoke for the benefit of the tape as he inserted the memory stick in to the police laptop.

"Dr. Forbes, we are now going to show you some images from this memory stick." Parnell scrolled through the same four photos that had appeared on Pete's device.

"Well that explains it," Pete said with some relief, "it's got to be Alistair's stick." But then he paused, perplexed, "But he told me he hadn't had anything taken from his car. So how did these photos get on my laptop then?"

Parnell shrugged.

"Well, that's what we're investigating, sir."

At this point, Pennock took over the interview.

"Dr. Forbes, there are further images which are the same on this memory stick and on your laptop. We'd like you to take a look at them now."

Pete recoiled in absolute horror as the obscene images were presented first on the police's, then on his own laptop.

"Now you understand our dilemma Dr. Forbes," commented Pennock dispassionately.

Shaken to the core, Pete said,

"I think I'd like to phone my solicitor now."

4

Monday mornings inevitably came around all too quickly and with it, the usual chaos of lost/forgotten/not done homework, P.E kit and school uniform. It didn't matter how often Natalie warned the children to be organized on a Sunday night, she always ended up screaming like a banshee at them to hurry up or they'd be late and this particular Monday was no exception. No doubt the same scenario was being played out in many households across the country, but that was of no concern to Natalie - getting her own kids off to school was. Juliet, your typical 10 year old going on 18 came strolling down the stairs as though she had all the time in the world and Natalie hadn't seen any sign of 11 and a half year old Martin at all yet this morning.

She took a double take of her daughter. Was she wearing make-up and mascara?

"What?" said Juliet insolently, hoping her mother hadn't noticed she was wearing mascara and a touch of clear lippie. Her mum didn't usually notice anything much.

"Nothing, love." She really didn't have time for any show-downs this morning. It would keep till this evening.

"Right, you lot. If you're not in the car in the next 30 seconds, I'm going without you."

One of these days she actually would, she vowed.

"I'm going then," she yelled and it wasn't until she had reversed halfway down the drive that Martin came hurtling out of the front door and threw himself in to the front seat.

"All right, keep your hair on," he shouted.

"Hair! Don't talk to me about hair! It's a flipping miracle I'm not bald with the way you two carry on," she bellowed tyres squealing as she put her foot down in the vain hope of avoiding yet more detentions and sarky letters home from the school secretary, exhorting students to arrive punctually.

It was an absolute logistical nightmare holding down a full-time job as well as being a hands-on mother and a generally ok wife. Although full of good intentions, Alistair was hardly any help at all. She couldn't blame him really, what with early starts and a heavy work load, frankly the situation was only likely to get worse not better, especially as he was determined to forge a name for himself and was working all hours to achieve that goal.

With the children safely delivered to school, Natalie continued on her fifteen minute drive to work, savouring the peace and quiet. She loved her job and her family and wouldn't trade them for the world. But work was where she retained her sanity, a place where she was no-one's wife or mother, but an efficient line manager who was well liked and respected by her work mates.

The company, a careers advice and job placement agency had only been around for the last seven years but had been growing steadily within a niche market and Natalie had been with them from the start. She was now head of a talented eclectic team which placed workers in jobs ranging from the highly skilled technology field, to telecommunications and media, as well as security.

As soon as Juliet had begun nursery school Natalie was raring to be back in the work-place, she'd served her time as a stay-at-home mother and felt she'd got plenty to offer to a potential employer. Luckily for both parties, Natalie had proven to be a valuable asset to the firm and they'd rewarded her with rapid promotion and substantial salary increases. She recognized that she wasn't in Alistair's league, she wasn't interested in that kind of driving ambition, but her career was progressing nicely thank you very much. It had even been hinted that a directorship could soon be on the cards.

'Actually, bring it on,' she re-evaluated. She was ready, willing and more than able. Maybe she should seriously consider giving Alistair a run for his money in the career stakes after all.

The office was already humming by the time she got to her desk. Most people, including her own team, came in early to get a head start but that was impossible for Nat, so she tended to make up the time by cutting out her lunch break and staying on an hour or so later in the evening. Both children did after school activities and were dropped off by a friend afterwards, so were only home for a short time before she got back herself. The time difference was covered by Alison, their very kind and obliging neighbour who was always on stand-by in case of emergency. They were truly lucky to have her living next door. She was an unmarried woman - or single, as it was more p.c to say these days she supposed, who lived with her elderly mother. As far as Nat knew, Alison had never held down a full time paid job. She had devoted her entire life to the care of her mother. And both women loved Martin and Juliet as if they were their own family, and they could always be relied on to lend a hand at short notice.

This was a real blessing for Nat. Her household had to function with military precision or there would soon be anarchy and Nat was the general who assured its smooth operation. Frankly it was an on-going nightmare to stop all the spinning plates from coming crashing down. The calendar on the fridge, dog-eared from continuous consultation, outlined everyone's activities and whereabouts, so *'no excuses'* she would tell them. They each knew what the others were doing, and who had to be where and at what time. Fortunately there was nothing scheduled for this evening thank goodness, because she still felt shattered from the weekend's events and simply couldn't face any more running around.

She was cornered by the three colleagues who'd been with her at the charity event and they all agreed it had been great fun with good food and even better company. Laughing, Nat assured them that the next occasion they would be called upon would be some time away - mainly because they were all now skint and she was exhausted. They all needed some time to recover.

Nat stopped Simon before he went back to his desk.

"Simon, hold on. I'm still so embarrassed about the auction. I virtually accused you of trying to do Alistair over. I don't know what came over me. I suppose it was because I wanted him to win it so much, I didn't pick up on the signals you were giving me. I just wanted to say I'm really, really sorry once again."

Putting his arm round her shoulders, he gave Nat a quick hug.

"Nat, forget it. I already have. It was a lovely evening and you made loads of money. All credit to you. Well done."

"Thanks, Simon. I appreciate that."

'He's such a nice fella,' thought Nat. "Now come on, let's get going, there's work to be done."

ii.

Alistair's day had started off badly and had got progressively worse. The parents of the lad whose back operation he had performed on Friday were moaning that they hadn't seen him for the whole weekend, that it just wasn't good enough, that he should be available, that he wasn't doing his job properly, threatened to take the matter higher. Christ almighty, what was he, a slave or something? He might as well be chained to the place. He already worked over and above the call of duty. He couldn't believe he was getting this grief when the op had been a complete success. His assurances that he would have been called should it have been necessary and that their son was recovering very well, fell on deaf ears. Alistair had remained civil but had taken about as much as he could put up with and had to remove himself before he said something he might later regret.

At coffee time he set off in search of Pete to let off steam. Pete was nowhere to be found and his secretary informed him that Mrs Forbes had phoned in saying that her husband was sick. Alistair called his friend on the newly returned mobile, to find out what was up with him but the call went straight to voice mail.

"Hi Pete, understand you're under the weather. Hope it isn't food poisoning! I was wondering why you hadn't phoned after your visit to the local nick and if you got your stuff back ok. You'd better not be skiving you lazy dog! Anyway, wish you better. See you later."

He had ten tons of paper work to get through, so made his way back to his office to knuckle down to the drudgery. He'd been at it for about an hour when his secretary knocked and entered saying that the police wished to see him. Not unduly concerned, Alistair told her to show them in. He often had to liaise with the police under various circumstances and had formed a pretty good relationship with them. However, he didn't recognize the two officers who entered and introduced themselves as D.I Pennock and D.S Parnell.

In advance, the two detectives had decided to present themselves unexpectedly and interview Dr. Neville at his place of work, thus catching him unawares. They wanted to assess his initial reaction to their arrival and questions.

Alistair stood up to welcome them.

"Good morning, gentlemen. What can I do for you?"

Parnell took the lead.

"Good morning Dr. Neville, we'd like to talk to you about the car break-ins that occured here at the hospital on Friday evening."

"Yes, I know about that. Actually, I was lucky. My car wasn't touched, thank God. Please, sit down. Can I get you anything - coffee, tea?"

Pennock ignored the attempt at courtesy and asked,

"And why do you think that was, Dr. Neville?"

Alistair thought for a moment.

"I have absolutely no idea. Maybe they got interrupted, maybe they couldn't get my car open. More likely though is because it isn't exactly a top of the range motor. But it could be any number of other reasons I suppose."

"Quite right," said Pennock. "So, you're sure that nothing was stolen from your vehicle then?"

"No, not as far as I am aware," Alistair affirmed.

"Dr. Neville, do you recognize this memory stick?"

Alistair took the sealed plastic evidence bag and looked carefully.

"Yes, I do. My daughter gave it to me last year."

"You're sure?" This from Parnell.

"Well yes. Unless there are other pink memory sticks covered in pig transfers out there, I'd say this was mine."

"But you say that nothing was taken from your car that night."

"That's correct." Alistair looked a little confused. "This memory stick wasn't in my car. I had it in my computer at home. I was transferring some photos on to it."

Pennock and Parnell exchanged a significant look.

"Dr. Neville, we'd like you to accompany us and continue this conversation down at the station. You may wish to have your solicitor present." said Pennock.

"Sorry, I don't understand. What's this all about? The car break-ins haven't got anything to do with me."

"Well let's just say you'd be helping us with our enquiries, shall we?"

"But why do I need a solicitor present?" Alistair pressed.

"Dr. Neville, those car thefts have uncovered other matters of great concern and we believe you can assist us in our investigation. Now, if you could get your things together please, we'll get going."

After hurriedly contacting his solicitor's office, Alistair had been allowed to phone Nat from his office and told her, tongue in cheek, that he was helping the police with their enquiries regarding the car break-ins and that he'd be in touch later on. As he left, he gave his secretary the same bemused line, telling her he'd see her later.

Of course Alistair's solicitor couldn't extricate himself on a moment's notice, so it was several hours before he arrived at the London Road police station. Nigel Crowley, a rather nervous, bookish type of man arrived somewhat breathless and was shown in to the interview room where Alistair had been left to stew and, by this time was fuming at the inconvenience of it all. Up until a couple of hours ago, it had seemed quite exciting, helping the police with their enquiries but the feeling had long since worn off. Nigel asked Alistair to explain what was going on to which he snapped that he hadn't the slightest idea - it was all to do with some cars that had been broken in to at the hospital on Friday evening and a memory stick Juliet had given him. That was all he been told.

"Good," said Crowley optimistically, "hopefully we can get this sorted out asap and be home in time for dinner."

iii.

Pennock and Parnell swept in a few moments later all business - their intention to present a formidable and intimidating front - they didn't hold with the good cop/bad cop routine - they were both the types of detectives who neither gave nor took any bull. After the introductions had been made, Parnell got straight to the point.

"I hope you've had enough time to brief your solicitor, Dr. Neville."

Alistair replied icily,

"It's difficult to brief someone when you don't know what the hell's going on or the reason why you're here."

Pennock responded.

"Well before we get down to it, we'd like to take your finger prints to help us in the process of elimination."

With a nod of ok from Nigel, Alistair reluctantly agreed, although what they were eliminating he still hadn't got a clue. He was assured that the prints would be destroyed if they proved to be unrelated to the investigation.

Alistair and the solicitor accompanied Parnell down a corridor and in to an office where there was a constable waiting with the finger printing kit which was swiftly administered. Alistair was then asked if he would be willing to give a D.N.A sample with the same proviso of it's destruction should it be considered unconnected to the case. A swab of the inside of his mouth was taken on what appeared to be a cotton bud stick, it was all efficiently done in a matter of seconds, the samples bagged and tagged for processing.

Back in the interview room, Parnell continued,

"Now, Dr. Neville you are going to be interviewed under caution which will be taped and recorded on video."

He read Alistair the Miranda warning and asked if he understood, to which Alistair replied that he did.

Pennock began.

"Dr. Neville, after Friday night's car thefts certain matters which concern yourself have come to light."

"What matters?" asked Alistair curtly.

"All in good time, sir," he continued, ignoring the interruption. "I am pleased to report that, as a result of good policing, all the items stolen on Friday evening have been recovered and accounted for via the lists signed by the parties involved. The only outstanding item left is a memory stick, which Dr. Neville, you claim is almost certainly yours and wasn't in your car at the time. Is that correct so far?"

Alistair acknowledged his agreement.

"Now we understand that your colleague, Dr. Forbes, had a couple of items stolen - namely a lap-top and a mobile phone."

"Yes that's correct," responded Alistair, "I believe he had an appointment to come here yesterday morning to collect his things, but he wasn't at work today and I haven't had a chance to speak to him, so I don't know how he got on."

"Quite so." said Parnell, "For your information, Dr. Forbes is still assisting us with our enquiries."

Alistair was perplexed, "Enquiries, but what enquiries? I thought you said you'd got everything back."

"Well, Dr. Neville that's true. But, as a result of those enquiries, some disturbing new evidence has come to light. Matters which we'd like to review with you now."

Pennock took up the thread, leaving Parnell to gauge Alistair's body-language and responses.

"With your permission, I'm going to insert your memory stick into our police laptop."

Alistair agreed his assent.

"We've had the stick tested for prints and we're still waiting for the results. But obviously there should only be yours and perhaps your daughter's on it."

The image of the family at a theme park appeared.

"Do you recognize this photo?"

Yes, Alistair did. And yes to the party, school play, and in the bath.

Pennock clicked on to the next image and Alistair's chair nearly tipped over as he lurched violently backwards.

"Jesus Christ!" he yelled, "What the hell is this?!"

The photo showed his little daughter splayed naked on a bed pleasuring herself. The next one was even worse - an obscene image of his daughter engaged in an act of fallatio with someone who appeared to be … Oh my God ... it was himself. Then one with Martin, equally horrific. The images became progressively more vile and more explicit.

"Stop!" shouted Alistair, "Stop, stop! I think I'm going to be sick!"

The interview was suspended with Pennock and Parnell leaving the room. Alistair turned to Nigel, his face ashen, a mask of anguish, tears streaming.

"My God, what's happening? What's this all about? Nigel, you've got to believe me, I know nothing about these photos, I've never seen them before. I wouldn't ... I couldn't do anything like ... Please, please, you've got to believe me." Alistair said desperately.

Indeed, Nigel was trying very hard to believe Alistair but he was out of his depth here and badly shaken by the evidence he had seen with his very own eyes. Although they had known each other for years and could be said to be friends of sorts, there was no way Nigel wanted to be involved in a matter like this. He needed to extricate himself forthwith.

"Listen Alistair, obviously we had no idea that this is what they were going to spring upon you but I'm way out of my league here. I can't represent you professionally. It's impossible. I haven't got the skills or experience, you know that. I specialize in family law and that's a million miles away from this type of criminal law. That's what I do and what I'm good at but that's as far as I go. It would be totally negligent of me to continue representing you."

Nigel stopped and thought for a minute - his legal cogs whirring laboriously. Finally, he ventured,

"If you instruct me, I can put you in contact with a barrister of the highest repute who's Police Station Accredited and well regarded in the criminal law field. He gets some good results. If anyone can help you, I am certain that he can."

Outside the two officers reviewed the progress of the interview so far. Parnell commented.

"He's good, Gov - quite convincing. Just the right amount of shock and disgust you'd expect. But I don't know ... it's like he's almost too pat, too horrified, you know."

"You're right," agreed Pennock, "he's not being totally up front, he's hiding something. Let's keep at him a bit longer, see if we can drag something useful out."

Unfortunately for them, Nigel was more than anxious to be on his way and he was the one to call Pennock and Parnell back in. He explained that, should his client be charged, these were indictable offences to be heard in the Crown Court and so he would necessarily be recusing himself for professional reasons and that a barrister, to be confirmed, would soon be representing Dr. Neville. Could they now please bail his client in order for him to seek further legal advice.

The expressions on both officers faces was a picture. Did Mr. Crowley really think for a second that they were going to grant Neville bail? They had barely scratched the surface of the investigation and, as was perfectly obvious, Neville was a person of considerable interest. So no, the solicitor was informed in no uncertain terms, his client would not be granted bail - he would be held for up to 24 hours, plus the 12 hours Chief Superintendent Worth had already agreed to, before bringing charges pending their on-going enquiries. Moreover, and that at this very moment, an application was being made for listing at the local magistrates court to extend that time limit to its maximum.

Nigel tried fiercely to fight for Alistair, proclaiming that he was a family man, a pillar of society, no threat that he might flee and would answer to bail on any conditions the police might wish to impose. It all fell on deaf ears and Nigel was forced to concede that the police were well within their rights to hold Alistair for up to and well beyond the 24 hours. If he were honest with himself and in the light of the evidence, it was a perfectly reasonable decision. He felt it judicious not to draw his client's attention to the fact that the police could hold a suspect for a considerable number of days without charge if the magistrates were satisfied that they were acting expeditiously and diligently. He didn't think his client could take that possibility on board at this moment in time. With some considerable relief, he left a distraught Alistair with promises to phone Nat immediately and to arrange a barrister to attend at his earliest convenience.

5

It had to have been one of the worst nights of Alistair's life. The police informed him that due to the seriousness of the allegations and because he was technically no longer represented, they could not continue interviewing him any further that evening. He had been unceremoniously and silently escorted to the holding area where his tie, belt, watch, laces, and personal effects had been removed and bagged. Alistair sensed the antipathy and revulsion of the custody officer, who with a jerk of his head indicated that Alistair should enter the cell. He was then left alone in the 8'x 6' box, the door clanging and locking behind him.

The breeze block walls were painted the usual institutional grey. There was a dubious looking toilet bowl on the left side and a small bunk-style bed, with the thinnest of coverings, on the right. Miserably he sat down on the bed and waited. He had absolutely no idea what to expect.

He was brought a withered ham sandwich and a cup of tea after some indeterminate length of time and a short while after that, when his plate and mug had been removed, the lights in the cell were extinguished without warning. Just a small outline of illumination filtered through the gaps around the door frame eventually allowing his eyes to adjust to the gloom.

He sat trying to calm himself, to be rational but it was proving impossible to still his mind. It was churning in a turmoil of harrowing images, repeating over and over again on a never ending loop. Even when he shut his eyes tightly, they were still there - his children, himself - no way to delete them, so instead, he sat wide eyed staring straight ahead.

More than fear, more than anger, Alistair felt confusion. His world had been turned upside down in the blink of an eye. He had been confronted with, but not yet accused of, what had to be, every parent's nightmare. But worst of all, he appeared to be the main protagonist.

Pennock and Parnell had not been idle while Alistair was being booked into the custody suite. It was disappointing that they had had to break off the interview prematurely - in their experience, they found that they often squeezed the most valuable information out of suspects in the early stages of the interrogation, before they got properly lawyered up and told to shut up. But maybe, it was no bad thing. Neville had been caught unawares, he was vulnerable, plus the fact his brief had abandoned him pretty sharpish, that must be pretty demoralizing, and he was going to stew in a cell overnight. It should all add up to a more productive interview tomorrow morning.

However, the two detectives still had plenty to keep them occupied for the next couple of hours and they were now busy applying for a further warrant to search the office of Dr. Neville. Under S.18

of The Police and Criminal Evidence Act 1984, Chief Superintendent Worth had earlier authorized in writing the search of both Neville's and Forbes' homes and the chairman of the local magistrate's bench, who by now had some inkling about the investigation, had earlier agreed to be on call should it be required. So now, when they informed him that the need for expediency could not be stressed strongly enough - that the suspect had admitted under caution that he had been in the process of transferring images from the computer using the memory stick and that they couldn't afford the risk of losing that evidence through any delays, the warrant was promptly granted.

Yesterday, in fact, the two officers had persuaded that same magistrate of the urgency to grant an emergency warrant application to search the office of a certain Dr. Forbes. They had been informed however, that the likelihood of the warrant being executed on a Sunday was extremely remote - there simply weren't enough officers on duty at the weekend. That had proved to be a frustrating delay for Pennock and Parnell, but there was nothing they could do about it. At least they had Forbes safely tucked away for the time being, until late Monday morning in fact. It was no wonder Alistair had been unable to get in contact with him.

Peter Forbes too, had spent an uncomfortable night in the cells. His solicitor, an experienced criminal lawyer had employed every trick in the book, but had been no more successful than Alistair's in securing his client's release. But at least Pete had been fortunate to locate his brief at home that afternoon and that he was prepared to attend on a Sunday. In the presence of his solicitor, the police had taken samples of his finger-prints and saliva for D.N.A . The interview had resumed but had taken the investigation no further forward. Pennock's re-questioning had thrown up no discrepancies nor trip-ups in Pete's version of events, which left both detectives frustrated and annoyed. They knew they would have to cut him loose pending the results of the search warrant but dragged it out until the last possible moment. Pete was reluctantly granted conditional bail after the 24 hours were up - the conditions being - 1) to have no contact with Dr. Alistair Neville or his family, and 2) to report to the police station every day at 6 p.m. Pete had swiftly agreed to the conditions and had stumbled out of the rear exit of the police station and into the car where a tearful and anxious Ann was waiting for him.

Their short drive back had passed largely in shocked silence. She had not been able to speak to her husband since he had left to go to the station yesterday morning. Her repeated calls entreating the police to allow her to talk to him were all politely declined. They had said it was out of the question unless it was an absolute emergency. Now they were together again, it was difficult to know where to begin, so they agreed to wait and talk in the privacy of their own home.

Ann, who was a secondary school French teacher, had phoned in sick that morning claiming a mystery bug and promising to be back as soon as possible. She had then phoned Pete's secretary at the hospital telling her much the same thing about him. Fortunately both children had happily gone off to their primary school today and were none the wiser of the truth of what had been going on.

The evening before, Ann had concocted a story that their Daddy had been called in to do emergency surgery because of a pile up on the motorway and that the hospital needed all hands on deck.

32

Typically, and to Ann's huge relief, neither child was remotely curious and had accepted the reason for Pete's absence without question nor real interest.

The couple had scarcely got through the front door before there was a knock and Pete, going to open it, was confronted with four officers disgorging from a couple of patrol vehicles and an unmarked car all prominently parked in front of the house. He recognized D.I Pennock instantly.

Actually, the delay in executing the warrants had meant an added bonus that both officers could be present during the two searches - Pennock at the house, and Parnell at the hospital. Pennock informed them of the reason for their presence showing them the written approval. Pete was absolutely livid.

"There is no way you're coming in to this house. You damn well wait there while I phone my solicitor," and slammed the door shut in his face.

This was not an uncommon reaction and, unperturbed, Pennock waited patiently whilst Pete received instructions from his law-firm. A few minutes later, the door reopened and a defeated but still angry Pete allowed them reluctantly in.

"Perhaps it would be best if you and Mrs Forbes went through to the kitchen while the search is being carried out. Make a nice cup of tea. This shouldn't take too long."

Pennock stepped forward, subtly forcing the couple to back-track in to the kitchen where a constable was then posted to watch over them. The team that had accompanied him were old hands at searching. The brief from their boss today was to secure all mobile phones, P.Cs, laptops, iPads, memory sticks or other electronic equipment, whilst keeping alert for anything odd, suspicious or out of place. Experience had proved time and again that a diary, a family portrait on the side-board, the type of clothes in a wardrobe, stuff under the bed could all be relevant to an investigation.

Indeed the search was soon completed. Pennock was informed that the team believed 3 mobiles were unaccounted for - Mrs Forbes', and the two children's. Ann reluctantly handed over the mobile from her handbag telling Pennock the password and that the children were still too young to have their own phones. Satisfied that this was probably true, Pennock asked them both to sign and acknowledge that they understood that all the items were being removed as evidence. He wasted no further time on pleasantaries, reminded Pete of his bail conditions and left with his team.

ii.

Meanwhile, Nigel Crowley had been true to his word. He had been badly shaken up by what he had witnessed at the police station and was relieved he would be able to divest himself of such a distasteful client. He had contacted the barrister immediately upon his return to the office and apprised him of the situation. The barrister, Charles Kingsley Q.C was, quite honestly, very excited to get his teeth in to such a juicy case and thanking Nigel for the referral, promised to attend the London Road police station as quickly as possible.

As Nigel made his way home that evening, and much as he loathed the idea, he thought that rather than merely informing her by phone, it was only fair to go round in person to fill Nat in on what had been happening so far. When he arrived, the children were in their rooms doing their homework, which allowed him to come straight to the point. Predictably, and to Nigel's extreme discomfort, Nat was horrified.

"There must be some kind of mistake. No, no way in a million years. Tell me exactly what happened."

The lawyer composed himself, disguising his revulsion, before furnishing her with a succinct resume of all that had transpired. Finally he concluded.

"All I can tell you is what I saw with my own eyes. It would seem that the evidence is most compelling. However ..." Nigel stated, though more for Natalie's benefit than not, his tone of voice somewhat dubious. "... However, there are always two sides to every story and all may not be what it seems. There may well be some perfectly innocent explanation. As you will appreciate, this is obviously outside my field of expertise and therefore I've recommended your husband a thoroughly reputable barrister and Alistair has instructed counsel to represent him."

He handed Nat Charles Kingsley's business card.

Nigel had been debating with himself on the way over but now the moment had arrived, he found himself awkward about what he was going to suggest.

"Natalie, I think it would be for the best if the children went to stay with their grandparents for a few days. Give you time to focus on this without any distractions."

"Listen to yourself! It's as though you think he's guilty. He's their father, he loves them." she responded furiously. "It's out of the question to even suggest it. What's Al going to say when he comes home and finds his children gone? He's going to imagine that we think he's guilty too."

Although Nigel had not spent much time advocating in the criminal courts, he knew he was offering good counsel.

"You could be quite right my dear. Let's hope so. I'm merely recommending you consider the possibility. But, make no mistake, there are going to be some difficult times ahead. To be brutally honest, Alistair will not be permitted to see his children, certainly not in the short term whilst the police are still investigating. And you are going to have to be available 100% to support Alistair.

So, I feel that it might be prudent to free yourself up as much as possible, perhaps take some time off work, and, if the children were with their grandparents, you could do this."

Nigel could see that he had not yet convinced Nat and so was forced to bite the bullet and reveal the true reason for his recommendation, however uncomfortable it made him feel.

"Furthermore, Natalie, the court has a legal obligation with regard to the protection and well-fare of juveniles and will insist that the children should be removed to reside in a place of safety until you, as their mother can be eliminated from the police enquiries and they can be returned to you. They will probably do this quite quickly. But by sending them to their grandparents in the meantime, the court may be satisfied as to their well-being and you will hopefully avoid them being sent to a children's home during the police investigation."

It took several moments for Nat to assimilate what she had just heard and her jaw fell open in shocked disbelief as she realized the implication of Nigel's words. It seemed that she too was under investigation, suspected of actively colluding with or simply ignoring the possible child abuse taking place under her own roof.

"Oh my God, Nigel. How can this be happening?"

Of course Nigel could offer no explanation and therefore remained silent. Nat nodded her reluctant agreement as she processed the wisdom of his advice.

"But how am I going to explain it to my Mum and Dad?" she worried tearfully.

Nigel answered with great compassion.

"My dear, I shall leave that with you. You could invent some innocuous reason for their visit or, as you may eventually have to do, tell them the truth."

Nigel took his leave with a heavy heart. He didn't need to be a top criminal lawyer to know that this family was about to face the most challenging and awful future, one which they might not survive intact.

As it turned out, the decision was taken out of Nat's hands. Shortly after Nigel had left, Nat received a call from the London Road police station. The officer identified himself as D.S Parnell and she was told that this was a courtesy call to inform her that her husband was going to be appearing at the London Road Magistate's court tomorrow afternoon if she wished to be present.

"Can you tell me what's going on? I know it's all a dreadful mistake. My husband hasn't done anything wrong, he's a good man."

"I'm sorry Mrs Neville, I can't really divulge very much. As you can appreciate, these are early days in an on-going investigation. However, I believe your husband has instructed a barrister. Perhaps you should contact him, he may be of more help."

Nat felt like she was spinning out of control. She had a splitting headache and was in a state of shock, barely able to function. She needed to get a grip, so trying hard to compose herself and taking the detective's advice, she put through a call to Charles Kingsley.

"Ah, Mrs Neville, just the person I wanted to speak to. You probably have a hundred and one questions. Would it be acceptable for me to pop round for a few minutes or you could come to my office first thing in the morning if you prefer. However, as I understand it, time is of the essence."

Nat was relieved that Mr. Kingsley had suggested coming to the house and agreed to see him within the hour. It would give her time to sort out a plan of action. Depending on what the barrister had to say, she would contact her parents to come and pick up the children. She would keep the details to the bare minimum without lying directly, after all these were outrageous allegations not proven facts. She would phone both their offices and the school tomorrow with a plausible reason for their absence and would take it from there. Yes, she felt a little more in control now, knowing she was doing something positive and helpful.

Charles Kingsley was also relieved that Mrs Neville had invited him round to her house. He knew it would be hugely beneficial to experience first hand the dynamics of the Neville family before they inevitably became more reticent and suspicious as time wore on. The children would both be at home and he planned to take the opportunity to covertly observe their behaviour and that of the mother. He might even be able to go round the house and get a feel for the place and the family that lived there.

He had spent an unpleasant afternoon with Dr. Neville at the police station. They were granted time for a private discussion before the police interview resumed. First things had to be dealt with first though and all business, Kingsley had produced a contract of engagement to be signed. He was obliged to warn his client that his fees, whilst not the highest in the profession, would be substantial and that the case was likely to be quite protracted - would Alistair be able to cover the costs and the and initial retainer? Satisfied that Dr. Neville did in fact have the resources albeit perhaps by credit card, Charles laid out the rules of how they would proceed, warning Alistair to keep his answers brief and to listen to the advice of his counsel at all times with regard to his responses, in case there should be any ambiguous or compromising questions.

Initially, his new client had seemed genuine and most convincing - he believed this was just the type of case that would enhance his reputation no end. That was until he had seen the first of the evidence. Charles Kingsley thought he had seen it all in the course of his career and that nothing remained that could still shock him - but apparently not. Were there no lengths some people would stoop to in order to gratify their own depravity? He had just witnessed how Man's basest instincts had just sunk to a new and odious low. Of course, he had to admonish himself, that was not the case with his client - his client was innocent and it would be his job to prove it, despite whatever personal misgivings he might harbour. It would be a great challenge, one that he was more than worthy of - but Charles Kingsley was finding it difficult to shake off a strong feeling of doubt regarding Alistair Neville and was experiencing a visceral and, in his experience, generally trustworthy sensation against his client, developed over many years of advocating in the legal profession. He sincerely hoped that this visit to the family home might go some way to allay those fears.

iii.

As he drew up at the Neville's, Kingsley was dismayed to see two patrol cars and an unmarked police car in front of the house. Damn, they'd managed to execute that warrant very speedily. It would spoil his plan to some extent. Not so surprising though, time really was of the essence here - for both parties it would seem. Opening the door to his firm knock, Nat couldn't disguise her relief at his arrival.

"They've got a search warrant and just came barging in. They're upstairs now."

"Don't worry Mrs. Neville. We'll soon have this sorted out. Where are the children?"

"They're in the kitchen. They're upset and very frightened. The police told us to wait together and have a cup of tea."

Spotting D.I Pennock in the hall, Kingsley pompously demanded the reason for this intrusion and gross violation of privacy. Pennock wasn't in the mood for the Q.C's excessive posturing and uncompromisingly retorted that there were significant grounds to believe that evidence existed at the address and that they would be removing all the Neville's electronic devices, plus any other material which might be relevant to the enquiry. Pennock then firmly invited Kingsley to join the others and wait in the kitchen until the search was concluded and the team had left.

Some time later, Pennock came in to the kitchen. As requested, Nat told him the password to her mobile, confirmed that the children didn't have phones and signed for the removal of the devices.

"I'm glad you're still here Mr. Kingsley. You'll be able to clarify any questions Mrs Neville may have."

He turned to Nat and said quite kindly.

"Mrs. Neville, could you ask the children to go to their rooms while we talk? Thank you. Now, I know this is difficult but I want to be transparent with you. Tomorrow we are going to ask the court to extend the length of time we can hold your husband for questioning in order for us to continue our enquiries. Unfortunately this does mean he will probably be remanded to a prison pending our enquiries."

Nat fought back a sob. "No, no," she wailed, "I need to see him."

"Well you will certainly see him tomorrow in court. There may be a chance for you to have a quick word then when they bring him in. Now, Mrs. Neville, listen carefully. I want you to come down to the police station tomorrow first thing and be interviewed under caution."

Exchanging a significant look with Kingsley, Pennock continued gently,

"I must warn you, Natalie that, as our investigation proceeds, we will certainly also need to interview Martin and Juliet. Obviously that interview will be conducted with rigorous attention to child safety in accordance with police protocols and in the presence of appropriate professionals. They will be seen by a female police officer from RASA - The Rape and Sexual Assault - Unit. Do you understand?"

Nat had thought it couldn't get any worse, but it just had. Pennock's words brought her almost to the brink of collapse. With tears flowing unchecked, she nodded resignedly. Kingsley assured Pennock that she understood and Pennock took his leave with his gut telling him that Mrs Neville was innocent in all of this but that he simply couldn't afford to be wrong. He would keep an open mind and carry on treating both parents - as well as Peter Forbes - as suspects.

Meanwhile, Juliet sat huddled, wrapped in the 'Star Wars' duvet on Martin's bed. He never usually let her into his room, in fact rarely even acknowledged her existence these days. He couldn't be bothered with his annoying pain-in-the arse little sister, but now they needed to talk, to put up a united front. Lip wobbling and eyes brimming over with tears, she asked.

"Mart, d'you understand what's happening?"

For her part, Juliet didn't often look up to her older brother for advice or information, that wouldn't be cool at all. But even she could tell he was worried. Martin didn't want to show weakness in front of his sister, but, he too, was scarcely holding back the tears. Something very serious had happened. The police didn't search people's houses for nothing, did they? It all had to do with their dad. What could he have done that was so awful?

Martin had been eavesdropping from the landing and had tried to catch what the policeman was saying to his mum, but the only bit he was able to hear clearly was *'remanded to prison'*. He didn't know what *'remanded'* meant but he did know what prison was.

38

He didn't want to frighten his sister, so he made up an answer that seemed to make the most sense to him.

"I think Dad's got involved with something to do with those cars being broken into. Mum's had to get a lawyer to sort things out."

Juliet didn't look convinced.

"But Daddy's not a car thief."

"Duh! I didn't say he was a car thief, you idiot. Just that it's connected to what the police are investigating and they need Dad's help. Maybe he's a witness or something." He wouldn't tell her what he had heard. He'd spare her the need to hear mention of prison. And in an uncharacteristic gesture of solidarity, Martin shrugged up beside his sister beneath the duvet as they both waited for their mum to call them.

Downstairs Charles was telling Nat that she would need to bring some fresh clothes for her husband's appearance in court the next day and also that he concurred with Nigel's advice regarding the children, informing her that he would seek approval from the agencies involved. He left soon after, agreeing to meet with Nat in the morning at the police station.

Before she could change her mind, Nat picked up the house phone and called her parents, briefly outlining what she needed of them and why. As expected they were utterly horrified and disbelieving, full of questions - to which Nat had no answers - but promising to arrive as quickly as possible. They agreed it would be best to spend the night and set off early the next morning with the children. On top of everything that was going on, Nat felt particularly awful for her parents - they weren't young any more and lived a 150 miles away. They were understandably upset by the little she had revealed but family, loyalty and love for their daughter had overcome, or at least temporarily suppressed their shock. They would talk more when they arrived.

Dealing with the children was going to be a bit more complicated. They knew something bad was going on and she was going to have to handle this carefully and, she decided, with a small degree of honesty. Calling them down, she sat at the kitchen table and looked in to their scared white little faces.

"Mummy, what's going on? Is Daddy going to be sent to prison? That policeman said he was."

Martin's lip trembled as he spoke for the pair of them.

"No darlings, he isn't going to be sent to prison, I promise."

She stroked their two precious heads. God love them, what were they all letting themselves in for? But right now, her main focus had to be for the well-being and safety of her children.

"Do you remember Uncle Pete's car got broken in to at the hospital the other evening?" Both children nodded. "Well, it turns out that there was some evidence - some stuff - left behind from the theft that might involve your father and the police want Daddy to help them sort it out. He'll be back before you know it, I promise."

The children didn't looked convinced, particularly Martin, who, not ten minutes ago, had just made up the exact same story to pacify his sister. They were definitely even less so when Nat explained that Granny and Granddad were coming to take them off for a few days.

They begged not to be sent away. Please Mummy, they promised, they'd be really, really good - be quiet and not argue. Then. that she'd miss them too much, and, finally, desperate. that they couldn't afford to miss any school. Nat had to smile at this final gambit - the truth was they loved staying with their grandparents who always spoiled them rotten, and would normally jump at the chance of bunking off school for a bit.

"Listen, it's only for a couple of days, treat it like a mini-break. I'll come down at the weekend and we'll have a great time, do some really fun things."

"Really?" said Martin dubiously.

"Can we go to Harry Potter World then, Mummy?" piped up Juliet optimistically.

"What a great idea. That's exactly what we'll do!" Nat promised, relieved that the children could be deflected so easily. "Let's get your bags packed and then off to bed. You'll need to get cracking first thing in the morning to fit in all the lovely things you'll be doing."

6

The next morning Nat's parents had reluctantly set off home with the children, extracting promises from their daughter to keep them in the loop . They had talked long in to the night but achieved very little. At this point there wasn't much to go on but undoubtedly, what had been suggested by the police, was patently impossible and untrue. They were all physically and mentally exhausted.

Nat had tossed and turned all night, tormented with sinister images, accusations and denials and - in the darkest hour of the night, for the merest nanosecond - the possibility that it could all be true. God, she despised herself for that unbidden thought - how could she ever, ever doubt him? No, she needed to pull herself together if she were going to be of any help to her husband. He would need and get, her unwavering loyalty and support. She swore to herself that she would fight till the ends of the earth to clear his name and bring him home to the bosom of his family. How unaware was Nat, that her ability to fulfil her vow would so soon be tested to the limit.

First she would phone the hospital - shit, what was the number? All her contacts were on her mobile or else backed-up on the computer. Thank goodness they hadn't got rid of the land line as Alistair had wanted, often saying it was a waste of money and that they never used it anymore. How did you find out a number these days? Did Directory Enquiries even still exist? They didn't even possess a phone book, the only number she knew off by heart was her Mum and Dad's. She suddenly remembered the little contacts diary she'd had for years. Searching around she eventually found it shoved in the back of the sideboard drawer. Grateful to find the number and the fact that she'd obviously taken the time - when for the life of her she couldn't remember - to keep it updated, she was soon put through to Alistair's secretary.

"Oh hello Janet, it's Nat here. I'm so sorry but Dr. Neville won't be in today. He's come down with a nasty bug. I'm sure it's nothing serious but it's probably best if he doesn't come in for a few days."

"Really?" came rather a frosty, unconvinced-sounding reply.

Janet had been present when the police had arrived and whilst not party to the details or reason for the search warrant, she was no fool.

"It's probably the same bug that Dr Forbes is suffering from I expect."

She and Pete's secretary were close friends as well as colleagues and both would do their utmost to protect their bosses, but rumours were beginning to spread and Janet didn't like what she was hearing.

"Keep me informed Mrs Neville. Goodbye."

Disconcerted by Janet's brusqueness, Nat wondered what she had meant about Pete but didn't have time to dwell on it. She had to phone the school to apologize for the children's absence and then her office. Simon answered. He was really such a decent bloke, quite distressed that she was under the weather. Completely different from Janet.

"Take your time, get yourself better. We can manage fine here. You've definitely been overdoing things."

She could hear the rest of the group shouting out for her to make a speedy recovery and that, believe it or not, the place would survive for a few days without her. They were a great bunch - a solid and dependable team. She'd be back soon she told them.

She'd better give Ann a quick ring too. Find out what was going on.

"Hello Ann, it's Nat. I hoped I might catch you before you go off to work."

There was a long, silence before Ann replied.

"I'm sorry Nat, I really don't want to talk to you and would prefer you not to call again."

Nat was flabbergasted.

"What do you mean? What on earth's the matter?"

"I think you know perfectly well what's the matter, Nat. And to have involved Pete and my family is beyond obscene. How could he, Nat? How could he?"

"Ann, you're wrong. It's not true, it's all a big mistake. I swear he's done nothing wrong. Come on Ann, you've known Alistair for years, we're best friends, we see each other all the time. You and Pete know him better than anyone. How could you even believe for a minute that he's capable of what they're saying? Please, please Ann, don't condemn him out of hand."

The silence continued once more, but to her credit Ann was considering what Nat had said. It was true, they had been friends forever. If she had ever been asked the possibility of this happening before, she wouldn't have hesitated to defend their friend to the hilt. Of course not. But her own family had now been implicated, Pete had seen some of the evidence and what he had told her had altered her perspective significantly. She wouldn't, couldn't, allow themselves to become further embroiled in this mess. It was bad enough already. Her sole priority now was to protect her husband and her family.

Finally she responded,

"I hope for yours and the children's sakes that he is innocent, Natalie, I really, really do. But from the little Pete's told me, they've got a lot of evidence against him. I don't suppose you're aware of this but they kept Pete in the cells all night and they're still investigating his connection to Al. He's had to take a leave of absence from work and we've had search warrants. He's got bail conditions - to stay away from Alistair. Nat, I think it's for the best if you don't contact us again till this has all been sorted out. I'm sorry for you Nat. I'm sorry for all of us."

ii.

The previous evening Parnell had supervised the search of Alistair's office and the computer they had removed had been added to the evidence taken from both the Neville's and the Forbes' properties and sent for analysis. Now both officers were anxious to move the investigation forward. It would take some days for forensics to work their magic, but there was still plenty to be getting on with.

In the Incident Room, the evidence board and log book had been set up and the preliminary findings entered. The first days of an investigation were always frenetic - the race would be on to collect as much evidence as possible as fast as possible whilst the Chief Super was still on board and prepared to throw resources and man-power behind the investigation. There was scant information as yet, but a strong case took time to build up. Photos of both the Nevilles and Forbes, as well as blank space for the unknown car thief, had been attached and the first of the notes added. Not a bad start.

Accompanied by Charles, Nat had presented herself at the London Road police station as agreed. The interview with Mrs Neville, had been unsurprisingly but thankfully disappointing. Whichever angle their questioning came from regarding her involvement, it was clear that she had no prior knowledge nor any connection with the evidence they possessed. So Pennock and Parnell decided to spare her the details and horrific images of her children - certainly for the time being. They didn't know how long they would be able to shield Mrs Neville, or even if they should, but the important thing was that those little kiddies wouldn't have to be taken into care just yet and, hopefully never would be. Moreover, they both anticipated that the specialist RASA unit would soon give them all the information they would need to bring charges.

Whilst they both agreed that Mrs Neville was more than likely innocent, they reiterated to her, in the strongest possible terms, the seriousness of the accusations against her husband. For the time being, Mrs Neville didn't need to be interviewed any further. It seemed that line of enquiry was now exhausted and she was released on unconditional bail.

Charles too felt some considerable relief - it would have been heinous if Nat were involved. It was a pity that she had to go through the trauma and suspicion but apparently the police were satisfied and that was an excellent result. They left the police station and made their way to the magistrates court.

They had agreed that Nat should have a few moments with her husband first, to be able to talk together privately and to make sure he looked suitably smart for his attendance in court. Charles had advised Nat that, in his experience, it was sad but true, that there was only one chance to make a first impression and those initial impressions with the magistrates were of paramount importance in which the element of doubt regarding a defendant's culpability could be decided merely from their appearance and demeanour.

Seeing her husband shocked Nat to the core. He seemed to have aged ten years, his face was sallow and haunted, his body hunched over as though in self-protection. It was a tearful and unhappy reunion. Alistair could do nothing but swear over and over that he was innocent, and Nat, that she believed him, that they would sort it out, and he would soon be home.

Details of discovery so far were read out and the Crown Prosecution put forward compelling reasons why Alistair should be remanded overnight - primarily that the evidence collected so far was of the most serious nature, and should Alistair be charged and found guilty at trial, he could expect a very lengthy custodial sentence indeed. In addition, it was also most important to remember that because the investigation was in its early stages, not all the evidence had yet been collated and there was a strong likelihood of more evidence coming to light and further charges being pressed. And finally, but most significantly, the accused lived under the same roof as the two alleged child victims, and was, in fact, their father.

The revulsion was clear to see on the magistrates' faces as well as their inclination to agree with the prosecution, but Charles was an old hand at bail applications in difficult circumstances. Years of experience had honed his skills and he relished the opportunity to demonstrate his considerable talents.

"Your Worships, I have to agree with my learned friend - these charges are of the gravest nature."

The magistrates on the bench looked startled that the defence barrister should be concurring so readily. Charles nodded his agreement and continued.

"But I would like you to seriously consider if remanding my client into custody is entirely necessary. You have heard the prosecution outlining the reasons why bail should be denied and, I agree those reasons are quite valid. However, I believe that we can satisfy the court that it would be completely appropriate to grant Dr Neville bail today, albeit with rigorous conditions.

I shall be brief. Dr Neville is an upstanding pillar of the community who has done much good in the medical field. You may even have heard of him by reputation, Your Worships. He is a local man, born and raised within a few miles of here, from a close and caring family, and should considered an unlikely flight risk. He is a dedicated and loving husband and father and is of previous good character.

He vehemently denies these accusations, and as the court is well aware and as the prosecution has mentioned, this case is in its earliest stages and is likely to drag on for quite some considerable time. This will undoubtedly have a considerable negative impact on Dr. Neville and his family. Your Worships, Dr Neville's reputation is in extreme jeopardy at this time as well as his career. It is imperative that he should be allowed to return to work as soon as possible in order to be able to continue to provide for his family."

Charles could see that the bench wasn't being persuaded. They were sitting stony faced, they'd heard these same arguments in other cases many times before.

"Therefore," he continued, undaunted, "I should like to put forward a proposal, which I hope will meet with your approval. As we are all fully aware, the overriding duty of the court and its officers is to guarantee the safety and protection of the children involved in a case such as this. To that end, I have been in dialogue with the CPS and Social Services who are content that the well-being of Martin and Juliet is being adequately safe-guarded at this time. The children, Your Worships, are currently staying with their maternal grandparents some 150 miles away and are welcome to remain there ad infinitum. Both Dr. and Mrs Neville understand that this is a legal obligation in a case of this nature and agree to fully cooperate with the agencies involved.

Furthermore, I have today met with Mr and Mrs Neville senior, the accused's parents, who are here in court now if you should wish to speak to them, and they have offered their son a home for as long as he should need to stay. Dr. Neville's wife, Natalie, who as you know, is also present, informs me that she supports her husband 100% and whilst she would prefer him to come home, fully understands and is content for her husband to reside with her in-laws with whom she has an excellent relationship.

Your Worships, if you see fit to grant Dr Neville bail, he will be able to continue to support his family and keep his job secure. He is prepared to report daily or twice daily to the London Road police station and understands that one of the stringent conditions you will impose for his bail, I am sure, will be to have no contact with his children until this matter is resolved. He also understands that Your Worships may wish to impose further bail conditions which he assures you he will fully comply with. Thank you."

Charles thought Alistair's chances were touch and go. The bench had retired for an awfully long time. It was a difficult call, but their lengthy absence surely meant they were considering all the options. When the magistrates returned, the chairman announced that they would indeed require confirmation from Mr and Mrs Neville that their son would be able to stay at their address for, what could be a lengthy period. They also wished to speak to Nat and Social Services.

Eventually it seemed they were satisfied measures had been put in place to protect the children but included the aforementioned order of no contact with the young Nevilles either in person or by phone, and not to approach nor enter the marital home as well as adding twice daily reporting restrictions. Bail was granted and a date was set for the case to be heard at the Crown Court some 28 days later. Charles was delighted with the result and Alistair's teary relief was clearly evident. Now the battle to clear his client's name would really begin. Alistair and Nat hugged tightly and turned to shake hands with Charles, thanking him repeatedly for securing Alistair's release.

iii.

Both Pennock and Parnell had attended the hearing at court that afternoon. They believed that when the magistrates noted the presence of senior police officers, it would lend weight to the seriousness of the charges and reduce Neville's chances of being released. Although they were disappointed at the outcome, there wasn't any point in dwelling upon it for too long. Long experience proved that eventually he would have been given bail anyway. The Nevilles, on the other hand were massively relieved.

Back at Mr and Mrs Neville seniors' house, they heard from Alistair exactly what had been alleged and what evidence the police had to support the charges. It made for grim listening. Alistair's parents were beside themselves as their son outlined the content of the images. Nat, having been spared the lurid details by the police, was pale with shock and distraught both for her husband and her family. On top of it all, she was then obliged to compound their horror by telling them of the warning Pennock had given her - that the children would need to be interviewed and most certainly, medically examined.

The prolonged silence after this revelation was shattering. With his head in his hands, Alistair wept. They all wept, it was too much to bear, too much to comprehend. They were overwhelmed and exhausted, too numb to fully begin to absorb the ghastly implications. They should try to sleep on it and work on a plan the next day when they would meet with Charles. Nat promised to return tomorrow with a suitcase of clothes for Alistair. She would phone work again with apologies for their absence, but tell their respective employers they would certainly be fit to come back the following day. They knew it was vital to return to a normal routine, to be seen to have nothing to hide and nothing to be ashamed of. They hugged tightly, whispering their love and support for each other. This would be their second consecutive night apart, the first time in their fourteen-year marriage, but sadly, it would not be the last.

7

So in the interim, while Pennock and Parnell were waiting for the forensics to come back, they considered themselves better employed in tying up all the loose ends and making sure the evidence was iron-clad in order to guarantee a conviction before submitting it to the C.P.S. They were redoubling their efforts to track down the bloke who had brought in the Tesco bag the previous Saturday morning and find out if he had any more sinister connection to the case than being just your run of the mill car thief.

It was proving to be a laborious task. He obviously wasn't one of the usual and well-known local scrotes that they might have had some chance of recognizing. P.C Brown distinctly remembered that the man had been wearing gloves which effectively ruled out the possibility of finger-print identification on the plastic bag and retrieved items. There had been no helpful CCTV in the station waiting room. The unsub had deliberately kept his face averted from the camera, and disguised his shape and height by wearing a bulky parka coat with the hood up. The brief glimpse the camera captured of him as he entered simply wasn't sufficiently clear to make any kind of identification. All very suspicious, well planned and a bit too professional they both agreed.

They had been even less fortunate in tracking his movements after he left the station. They caught him on a couple of the station's cameras as he left, but the images were too grainy to be of any use. After that he seemed to have disappeared in to thin air. They widened the search area but no joy. For God's sake, a terrorist could be tracked step by step from the Middle East in HD resolution but they couldn't even follow a suspect for two hundred yards. It confirmed in the detectives' opinion that this man should be considered of interest, he was just too slick. But how to track him down was evidently outside of their limited abilities and they were reluctantly going to be forced to turn the search over to the technology pros.

However, the following morning did bring some good news. Pennock and Parnell were delighted to get the first forensics back from the Forbes's electronic devices. The nature of the investigation had pushed their case to the top of the pile. Luckily for them, anything that involved minors in perilous situations like this immediately got prioritized. They weren't about to let the techies rest on their laurels though, insisting that they really needed the Neville forensics back pronto, like now, immediately, preferably even sooner than that. The tecchie guys got the message and promised to get straight on to it. Finally the two detectives had got some material they could begin to get their teeth in to.

The forensic report stated the facts clearly enough but, in all truth, it didn't push the case any more solidly forward. Dr Forbes' hospital computer was clean, there was no evidence of it ever having held any images either still present or deleted, which the report promised, they would have been able to recover nevertheless. Both detectives agreed that Forbes would never be stupid or reckless enough to leave evidence on his work computer which could be easily accessed by anyone, and so were not disheartened.

They moved on to the report regarding the computer taken from the office in the family home. Now this should be more promising - but, once again, the computer was clean of any compromising images. Nor was there any evidence that Dr Forbes had ever accessed any websites, including the dark web, searching for paedophilia or anything similar. There was no sign via his emails that he was in contact with like-minded perverts - the forensic team had gone through all the correspondence and confirmed that there were no coded messages, no sign whatsoever of criminal activity, either current or historic. Parnell and Pennock were annoyed but, once again, concurred that it was unlikely that Forbes would leave incriminating material on a computer that wasn't even password protected and available for all the family to use.

Mrs Forbes' mobile phone was also declared to be free of any illegal activity. This was a relief to the two officers rather than a frustration. They now believed it was safe to conclude that she had no connection to the matter and they could eliminate her from their enquiries. Only the analysis of the laptop remained. Once again, the emails contained nothing of a sinister nature. They read that Forbes' browsing history was innocuous and raised no red flags. The only inconsistency was the images - matching those on the memory stick - of which Pennock and Parnell were already aware. This really threw the two men. They had fully expected to be presented with more conclusive evidence. Where did that leave them, and what was Forbes' involvement?

Later on, doing the grunt work going over the first interview tapes, Parnell began to formulate a working theory. He was now almost certain that Forbes' responses and appropriate shock were genuine despite his initial impression when, if he were honest with himself, he had wanted Forbes to be guilty. If not, he was one hell of an actor. He wasn't in the job to release guilty men, but neither was here there to detain innocent ones. The explanation, when he realised it, was obvious.

He put forward his theory to Pennock. The unknown car thief takes the stolen gear back - probably to his home. He begins to look through the haul and comes across a memory stick. He has already got the stolen laptop which, he discovers isn't password protected. So rather risk putting a USB stick in his own P.C - assuming he has one - he puts it into the one he's pinched. He scrolls through the content and comes across the images. He's shocked by what he sees but needs time to decide what to do. Going through his options he concludes that the risks of being caught or implicated in kiddie porn outweigh the benefits of the theft. So, he wipes everything clean and makes a plan. Incognito, he'll return everything to the local police station, so divesting himself of any connection. He'll plan his route there and back to avoid surveillance cameras, he'll obscure his face by wearing a bulky jacket with a hood and by keeping his back to the CCTV and then - he'll hope for the best.

Pennock knew straight away that his partner was right. The explanation made perfect sense. Damn, there was no longer any point in continuing wasting time and resources pursuing the car thief any more, so that was now another dead end. What had started as a promising investigation with several suspects emerging was fast whittling down to only one. Both Dr and Mrs Forbes were out of the frame, as was Mrs Neville, which only left Alistair Neville as the prime mover unless, of course, there was some other accomplice they were unaware of at the moment.

ii.

Alistair was beyond grateful to his parents for taking him in. They had given him the chance to breathe and take stock of the situation while offering him all the unconditional love and support they possessed. They couldn't actually do anything to help clear his name, but the very fact that they believed in him and loved him was enough to sustain him for the time being.

He was sleeping back in his old bedroom - it still looked and smelled the same, as though it had been waiting for him to return some day. He realized he hadn't stayed at his parent's house since he'd finished university. He had gone straight in to his first medical job which came with accommodation provided. Soon after, he and Nat had decided to get married and they had bought their first house together. Of course, he came home regularly to see his mum and dad but as a visitor these days. But for now it was good to be home, to be nurtured and feel secure, protected by his parents just as he had been when he was a boy.

He and Nat had agreed that getting back to work would be for the best, hiding away and fretting would achieve nothing. It was decided that he should return and seek an appointment with the board to explain the events of the last few days. They felt that he shouldn't be accompanied by his lawyer at this stage in order to keep things low key. Returning to some kind of normality was exactly what Alistair needed right now.

By the end of the week both he and Pete were back at work. Not only were tensions running high between the two men, but the rumour mill was working overtime among their colleagues and fellow workers who were agog with gossip and speculation. They fell squarely in to two camps - those that always knew there was something dodgy about the two men and those that firmly believed they were both decent, innocent blokes, wrongfully accused. Whenever either of them passed by, however, an uncomfortable silence would fall, and all eyes would follow them along - critically assessing.

Pete's bail conditions had been lifted but he still had absolutely no intention of speaking to Alistair ever again. He was angry and embarrassed, knowing full-well that mud sticks even though the police had publically exonerated him of any wrong-doing. For all of that, he wasn't blind - he could see what his colleagues were thinking - that there was 'no smoke without fire'. They were sentencing him without trial, without hearing the evidence or allowing him the right to defend himself.

Furthermore, the curt summons to an extraordinary meeting of the board had left him mortified. Word had reached them with incredible speed and the interview was more of a cross examination than an endorsement of his innocence, wholly lacking in the support they should really be offering a respected and innocent colleague. Even with their assurances that they fully accepted the police's findings and that he should resume his duties forthwith, Pete was left with the overwhelming feeling that his career at the hospital was over. He was in no doubt he would now be passed over for promotion and side-lined, he had brought shame and embarrassment to the hospital, something his prospects couldn't survive.

In his moments of anger, Pete began to hate Alistair for what he had wreaked upon him. It was a monumental disaster and the truly unbelievable part was that he was in no way to blame. His job was in ruins and his marriage was suffering incredible strain. He would have to begin looking for a new post immediately and pray that the rumours hadn't reached the board of the next hospital. The family would have to be uprooted, they would have to move, change the children's schools and Ann would need to find new work somewhere else. Everything they had worked so hard for, everything they had achieved was crumbling before his eyes. He simply couldn't believe it. In a mere couple of days he had gone from being a happy and fulfilled surgeon to an outcast. From his perspective, it frankly didn't matter whether Alistair was guilty or innocent because, at the end of the day Pete's reputation and his future were in tatters - collateral damage to the whole sordid business.

Alistair too felt the furtive glances of his co-workers burning into him. He tried to keep his head held high and carry on like a man with nothing to be ashamed of. All he really wanted to do was run away and hide, or fall asleep and wake up to discover it had all been a terrible nightmare, a dreadful mistake and that everything was going to be ok. But it wasn't going to be ok and when the order to present himself before the board came, he knew the worst was about to befall him. He had hardly been back a morning and thought he would have had a little more time to prepare himself and his arguments before the summons came.

He was never even given the chance to present the plan he and Nat had anticipated the governors would need to be apprised and reassured of, in the hope of keeping his position secure. He never even opened his mouth.

Entering the board room, Alistair was not invited to sit down. The chairman launched straight in to the attack with a pre-prepared statement.

"Dr Neville, certain accusations against you have been brought to the board's attention, namely that you have been interviewed in connection with offences of paedophilia. We have been deliberating at length regarding this state of affairs and have unanimously agreed that, at least in the first instance, you should take a three month paid sabbatical from St Nicholas'. Whilst we accept that one is innocent until proven guilty, this hospital cannot afford to be tainted by association with such a scandal. Moreover, as a paediatric practitioner, it would be wholly inappropriate for you to continue working with children whilst such charges are still pending. We have consulted with our law department who endorse this recommendation and who believe it to be a responsible as well as legally acceptable solution.

You may wish to consult with your own counsel or union rep, as is your right. You will now be escorted off the premises. Good day Dr. Neville."

The chairman signalled to the waiting security officers, who closed in on Alistair. Shell-shocked, he accompanied them with no resistance and without uttering a word of what he had planned to say. They didn't even give him the chance to go into his office to say goodbye to his secretary. A few minutes later he found himself dumped unceremoniously outside the hospital with his possessions handed to him in a plastic bag. Numb and disbelieving, he returned to his car and headed towards the exit booth where he was stopped by Andy Motson.

"I'll need you to return your security pass and car-parking permit, Dr Neville," said Andy, with relish. It seemed the hospital grape vine functioned with amazing swiftness. Alistair handed them over and the barrier went up.

"Have a nice day, doctor," Motson called after him cheerfully.

8

Later on that evening Alistair and Nat went down to the White Hart for a drink. They didn't feel comfortable being squeezed in to Alistair's little bedroom or at ease talking in front of his parents downstairs, so they resorted to the local pub. The temptation to get totally smashed and obliterate their worries for a couple of hours was almost overwhelmingly inviting, but they knew it really wasn't a great idea and that they'd only regret it the next day.

Even here though, there was no real escape - they were either imagining the curious, sometimes hostile looks cast in their direction, or word had already reached this small community. Alistair realized it was the latter when he spotted that greasy haired, lanky shyster, Andy Motson propping up the bar surrounded by an enrapt group, seemingly pontificating on, what Alistair was sure of, was the latest scandal from the hospital.

They quickly downed their drinks and decided to move on to the other pub in the village. As they left, there was no doubt that the mutterings they were meant to overhear were menacing. *'Sick paedo'* and *'Kiddie abuser'*. They got out as fast as they could, badly shaken by people's automatic ability to believe the worst of something - that people were happy to believe Andy Motson's wharped version of gossip as gospel truth.

They couldn't face the possibility that the same thing might happen in the other pub, so they ended up sitting on a bench in the freezing cold in the playground. Alistair had never been more wretched or more frightened in his life.

"They all think it's true. They think the police wouldn't have arrested me if they weren't sure I was guilty. God, what am I going to do? Nat, how are we going to get through this?"

Nat was nearly as distraught as her husband, but had realized from bitter experience earlier on, that going to pieces wouldn't help their predicament much. If Alistair couldn't, then she needed to keep her wits about her.

"Well, calm down for one thing and try to think straight. It doesn't matter what those tossers think. They're a load of nobodies. The truth will come out soon enough and then we'll be able to put this nightmare behind us and get on with our lives. What we've got to do now is put up a united front and then find out why those pictures were on your memory stick and laptop and how they got there. Right?"

"… Right."

"Well ...? Any theories?"

"No, not really. I genuinely have no idea how they could have got there. I accept I'm a bit casual about leaving it lying around but, I've been wracking my brains for the last few days, and the only explanation I can come up with is that the computer was interfered with and they were transferred remotely, like electronically."

"Is that actually possible?" said Nat doubtfully.

"I've got absolutely no idea. I don't even know how we'd go about finding out if such a thing is possible. I suppose we'd need to find some computer whizz who'd know about this kind of stuff."

"Well, our lot in the office are pretty sharp when it comes to technology. I'll ask around and see if any one's got any bright ideas or knows of anyone else who might have."

"No Nat, I don't think so. That sounds all well and good, but it means you'd have to explain the reasons why you'd want to know something like that and they'd get curious."

"Oh, Al. It's a bit late to worry about them finding out. You've just seen them in the pub... everyone already knows."

ii.

Nat was absolutely correct - whoever didn't know before, now had all the gory details. The next morning Alistair was sitting dismally at the kitchen table trying to force down a couple of slices of toast, when his dad walked in through the back door with a copy of the local weekly Gazette. His father looked shaken and upset as he spread the paper open on the table. There, emblazoned on the front page was the screaming headline,

'Children's surgeon centre of paedo ring.'

It was accompanied by a full size photo taken of Alistair attending a children's charity event last year where he was presenting prizes to children who had suffered and overcome the most horrible medical conditions and were being rewarded for their bravery and stoicism. The words blurred before Alistair's eyes. He shook his head violently partially to clear his vision and partially in denial of the content of what he was reading.

'Dr. Alistair Neville, the well respected and talented surgeon at St. Nicholas's Children's hospital, was recently taken in for questioning, along with an unnamed colleague from the same hospital, and has since been charged with paedophile offences and released on conditional bail. Local police report that this is an on-going investigation and have declined to say whether Dr. Neville is part of a larger paedophile ring and whether they intend to charge any other suspects.

Dr. Neville (37) resides with his wife Natalie (36) and two children M.N (11) and J.N (10), who both attend London Road Primary School. The family lives in the desirable Newbridge area of the city. Dr. Neville has been working at St Nicholas's for the last five years. The hospital yesterday issued a brief statement.

"The board of St. Nicholas's can confirm that it is aware that one of its hospital's doctors is currently the subject of a police investigation. By mutual agreement and in full consultation, the doctor in question has been granted a leave of absence while the legal process runs its course. The board will not be issuing any further comment in this matter."

Neither Dr. Neville nor his wife were available yesterday for comment.

This paper asks if it is right that paedophiles should be given bail and be allowed to roam our streets preying on our vulnerable children?'

Alistair was ashen and trembling as he finished reading the piece. His father was the same. So much for reporting restrictions.

"Dad, how can they get away with this kind of sensationalist reporting? They've virtually made up the whole story. It's a pack of speculation and lies. They've printed private stuff about where the kids go to school and our address. What the hell? They know they're not allowed to do that, they just don't give a damn whose lives they destroy."

Mr Neville could offer his son no answer, but he did have some practical advice.

"Listen son. You should get on to Nat right now and warn her the wolves are going to be at the door baying for blood. The only reason they haven't got to her before now is because she slept here last night. Tell her not to go home - come straight here. We won't be able to keep them away for long, they'll soon work out where you're staying. Then we'll decide what to do."

iii.

The Neville's phone rang at that very moment. It was Nat, nearly hysterical.

"Al, there's reporters and t.v cameras everywhere - all over the car park, they're trying to get into reception. The phone's never stopped, we're not even answering it now. They're shouting for me to come down and give my side of things ..."

Alistair could hear the noise in the background, it sounded exactly as his father had described - a pack of baying wolves.

"Listen Nat. Can you get out of there unseen? I don't know - maybe get someone who looks like you or who looks like they might give them an insider scoop - get them to go out as a decoy while you escape out the back or something. Can you do that? Don't go home. Its bound to be the same there. Come straight to my parents."

"Yeah, I think so. They're not letting up, I can't see any other way. I'll be there as soon as I can."

Nat's colleagues were distressed for her but the directors were certainly even more embarrassed and upset by what was happening on their property. When she went to ask if she could be allowed to make her escape, they were more than relieved to let her go. Full of concern, they told her not to worry, to go and look after her family and husband, get things sorted out. Take as long as she needed. Privately though, the two founder members had already anticipated her request and decided to grant her time off. In fact, they would have insisted on it if she hadn't asked first. However, this whole business was in danger of bringing the company into serious disrepute and they could ill-afford to be associated with criminal goings-on in their line of work. They were not happy, not happy at all. And, unbeknown to Nat, they had agreed that the recommendation for a directorship - well that was no longer on the table, she could forget about it, she was never going to be offered it now.

They quickly drew up a plan of campaign. Alice said she would act as the decoy. She had parked her car at the far end of the car park and said she would walk towards the pack of hyenas as though planning to talk to them but then veer off at the last moment, get into her car and drive away. The distraction should give Simon long enough to get Nat out of the rear exit and into a taxi. That is, if it all went to plan.

"Hang on," said Nat, "I just need to get my things from my office."

"Don't worry, I'll get your handbag. I know where you keep it," replied Simon, "you just get ready to race out the back door."

Alice's part went perfectly. What they hadn't anticipated though, was that seasoned journos know all those old tricks and there was a small bunch out the back waiting to ambush her as she came out. The waiting taxi was like a red flag signalling to them. Nat emerged into an explosion of flashing cameras, blinding and disorientating her. Microphones were thrust into her face, shouts for her comments deafened her.

"Natalie, how are you bearing up?"

"Mrs Neville. Is your husband guilty?"

"Are you going to stand by your man?"

"Mrs Neville, what's it like being married to a paedo?"

She was overwhelmed, but Simon had taken control and with one arm around Nat's shoulders guiding her firmly along and the other pushing the journalists roughly out of the way, they cut their way through the throng with Simon shouting,

"Mrs Neville has no comment. I said *'No comment.'* Please respect Mrs. Neville's privacy at this time."

He pushed and jostled the press out of their path and virtually shoved Nat into the taxi before jumping in beside her. There was absolutely no way he could let her go alone, they would devour her.

"Put your foot down, get us out of here now," he yelled.

The taxi driver didn't need to be told twice. He accelerated away leaving the reporters angrily disappointed.

Twenty minutes later, the taxi dropped Nat at the Neville's. Simon declined her invitation to come in. He told her she needed privacy to sort matters out with her husband, and returned to the office in the waiting taxi. By now, the taxi driver had worked out who his fare was and was soon enjoying his moment in the limelight revealing Mr and Mrs Neville's exact address to the hungry hacks.

Alistair held Nat tightly, she was anxious and tearful. It tore him apart to see his wife so unfairly distressed. He told her that he and his parents had been speaking and thought it would be for the best if she and the children all stayed with her own parents till things blew over. He swore that the press would soon get fed up of waiting outside empty houses and when the police realized it was all a ghastly mistake and exonerated him, they would eventually leave them alone.

She hoped to God he was right. She hated to leave him when he needed her most, but she had responsibilty for her children as well and had promised to be with them and take them on some outings at the weekend.

"What are we going to tell them about why you won't be able to see them for a while? We're going to have to come up with something convincing."

"Let's just get over the next few days. Hopefully after the weekend, this nightmare will be over. The police aren't stupid and the forensics will prove there's been some kind of malicious software planted, then they'll have to find the real culprits."

Nat took heart from his positivity.

"Yeah, of course you're right. I'll tell them you've got to work this weekend and that we're going to have a little holiday while you're busy. Martin's got to be back next week, he's got SATs exams coming up. Please God it'll be over soon. We'll get through this, won't we Al?"

"I swear we will, Nat. Now listen love, the sooner you get going, the better. Let me know when you get there and give the kids big kisses and hugs from me."

So, with nothing more than her handbag and the clothes she was wearing, Nat took Alistair's car, leaving him to retrieve her's from work, and set off for her Mum and Dad's.

When the doorbell rang a few moments later, Mrs Neville thought Nat had returned for something she'd forgotten. She opened the door with a strained smile and was greeted with a barrage of flashing bulbs and microphones thrust into her face. It hadn't taken the wolves long to track them down and this time they weren't going away.

9

Pennock and Parnell knew no progress would be made over that weekend but hoped, by Monday, some forensics might be back and that they would be able to move the investigation significantly forward and be able to charge the bastard. They were in luck. The tech team had really come through speedily as promised. Now the results would need to be carefully analyzed.

They decided to look at the reports in reverse order - the least likely to surprise to be looked at first. As expected, Mrs Neville's mobile showed no evidence of a suspicious nature - nothing current nor anything that may have been deleted in the past. It seemed that she hardly used any of the apps available to her - her phone appeared to be merely a tool for communication and all of her contacts were either friends, family or business associates. Her photo gallery was full of images of the family and social occasions, nothing that would even remotely set off warning signals. Although her mobile was capable of receiving and sending emails as well as having internet access, it seemed that Mrs. Neville rarely, if ever, used those functions.

The two officers were genuinely relieved that she wasn't implicated. Nat too, it seemed, could now be definitively eliminated from their enquiries. It was clear that she had not been an accomplice nor been neglectful in turning a blind eye to what had been going on in her household. They were certain that she would be relieved to be permitted to bring her children home.

Dr Neville's work computer was next on the list. Essentially, there was nothing of any interest to the current case contained on it. Apparently, the computer had been solely used as a work-tool, holding a data-base of patients who had or would be undergoing medical procedures with notes attached to each one. There were a few internal memos and some correspondence with fellow professionals. Dr Neville had accessed on-line medical journals pertinent to his speciality - nothing untoward in the least, the report was forced to conclude. A pity, but after seeing how Forbes used his work computer, it was pretty much what the two men were expecting.

The report confirmed that Dr Neville's use of his mobile phone was unremarkable. It was an old model which had internet access but which was never used. The call-log showed activity with known associates, family and friends. It was clear that the device was nothing more than a tool for communication, like his wife's. Yet another dead end waste of time.

Next they reviewed the memory stick. They were already aware of the images on the pen drive and learned that there was very little new to offer there. The analysis confirmed that the only adult suspect appeared to be Alistair Neville and the only victims, his two children. The images were fairly recent, the report concluded, because the children's physical appearance corresponded, possibly to within six to nine months, to their current ages. Therefore, the report suggested, the alleged abuse had not been taking place over a long period of time but was of a more recent nature.

The two men wondered whether it was unusual for sexual interference to occur when a child was slightly older or was it more typical for molestation to begin in infancy. Neither man had much experience of investigating crimes of this nature, thank God, so they really didn't know the answer. The psychology and impetus for this kind of deviance was something they needed to discuss with a professional, someone who undoubtedly would have to be brought on board now.

For the time being, Pennock hazarded his own cynical interpretation which he shared with Parnell. He put forward his theory that babies and toddlers would hold little appeal for a bloke like Alistair Neville. What he reckoned was that Neville would only get total gratification when his child could communicate, fully participate and be able to *'enjoy'* the experience with him. What a sick bastard. However, not totally convinced, Parnell wasn't prepared to commit or pass judgement just yet, although he had to concede that the theory held more than a ring of truth about it. He needed to keep all the options open and counselled his superior to do the same. He fervently hoped his boss was wrong but, deep down, feared he might have hit the nail on the head.

They moved on to the laptop which also contained exactly the same images as the pen drive. The report stated that other than that, the device appeared to have been used for all the typical things one would expect from a personal computer - emails (nothing dodgy or suspicious contained therein) - the usual correspondence for business or social situations, a few banking/savings entries - apparently there were no extraordinary deposits or withdrawals to be noted, no perusals on the internet which threw up any red flags. All in all another disappointing outcome.

Finally, they got to the analysis of the family's desktop computer. They read that further but similar domestic transactions were to be found - weekly Tesco orders, details of up coming events, emails, photographs, music and so on. It was noted that both Mrs Neville as well as her husband were regular users of the machine but that Mrs Neville was probably the primary user keeping records of domestic accounts and outgoings, bills and standing orders etc. Nothing out of the ordinary, in fact, it should be noted, perfectly ordinary and completely to be expected content in a domestic environment.

This was very disheartening for the two detectives. They had been banking that the P.C would provide the final seal to secure a guaranteed conviction. But those tech boys knew how to string out a good story. They had saved the best until last and finally offered something worthwhile. The report observed, in it's unemotional but critical way, that whilst the same images that could be found on the laptop were also to be found on the P.C, there were a considerable number more of a similar nature on this computer, all showing Dr. Neville engaged with his children in compromising situations or with the children individually exposed.

Bingo, they'd got him, they'd nailed the sick bastard banged to rights. Their gut feeling and experience had been vindicated at last. They now realized that Neville had actually implicated himself - he had previously told them, under caution, that he had been in the process of transferring the images. Clearly he hadn't had the chance to complete the job. Pennock made a jubilant call to the C.P.S who concurred that, based on the evidence from the laptop and memory stick, Alistair Neville should be charged at the earliest opportunity with Sec.5 Rape of a child under 13 (Sexual Offences Act 2003), Sexual Assault (Sec 25 Sexual activity with a child family member), and Making Child Pornography (Sec 1 Protection of Children Act 1978 F1-4) and that the children should also be interviewed by a RASA officer and examined by the F.M.E. as a matter of urgency. The two officers were ecstatic that the C.P.S had agreed to throw the full weight of the law into the charges against their man.

They were exceptionally fortunate to discover that one of their very own colleagues, D.S Sandy Parker was a trained Rape and Sexual Assault Unit officer and was keen to come on board with the investigation. She outlined how the interviews would proceed, and how the strict protocols would be followed. She explained that neither parent would be permitted to be present during the interviews. The children would be seen separately and it would be her function, she told them, to ascertain each child's level of understanding of the difference between right and wrong. She described how this would take place with the use of dolls to investigate the sexual touching/contact which was alleged to have taken place in accordance with an ABE interview.

Neither Pennock nor Parnell had a clue what Sandy was talking about - this was well outside of their field of expertise - all these new acronyms that they couldn't begin to comprehend. Sandy looked at their blank faces and decided she would have to treat them like her child interviewees.

"Ok Gov, Harry, I'll explain. You now know who RASA is. An ABE is our primary aim... Achieving Best Evidence. Familiarizing ourselves with the content of the evidential images plus using the dolls to elicit what may have occurred is the way we accomplish this. Understand now?"

The two men nodded in unison, still somewhat baffled but definitely in awe of their colleague.

"Right then, I'll get straight on to it and arrange for the children to attend and get our report to you asap."

Although the core evidence was incredibly strong the two men were still not totally satisfied and needed the case to be absolutely air tight. So they thrashed out a plan for the next steps of the investigation which would consolidate and reinforce everything they had so far and then brought the evidence board and log right up to date. They were determined there would be no way some slimy, smooth talking brief was going to get his client off on a technicality or on questionable/unused disclosure. A productive day all in all, deserving of a celebration with a couple of pints down at the local, they both agreed.

ii.

The White Hart wasn't busy early on a Monday evening, and they both quickly picked out the gangly hospital car-park attendant who was holding court at the bar. The few drinkers in, the usual regular die-hards, were all ears, agog to hear Andy's summary of how he had always known that Dr. Neville was a paedo and how he, humble Andy Motson, had personally steered the police in the right direction. Stood to reason, didn't it, that any bloke who wanted to operate on little kids all the time, was bound to be a bit peculiar.

The two men listened briefly but then tuned the moron out. They needed to organize how they would handle the results of the Neville children's interviews and then their medical examination. There was no avoiding it now, and they had no doubt that Mrs Neville would be traumatized by the whole process. The important thing though was to deal with the children as sensitively and carefully as possible but - and they had to acknowledge this unpleasant truth - the very satisfying icing on the cake would be the physical evidence of abuse which would be the final clincher of the case.

As it was quiet in the bar and private where they were sitting, Parnell phoned the Neville's home, but got no reply. He tried her work number but was informed by some late stayer-on that Nat had taken a few days leave. They had her mobile down at the station, so there was no point in trying that. In order to locate her current whereabouts they were forced to contact Alistair at his parent's house. Might as well kill two birds with one stone. Having briefly spoken to Alistair and been given Nat's parents' number, they then informed him, as a matter of courtesy, that his children would be required to attend for interview and medical examination on a date soon to be arranged.

Dear God almighty, that was the worst possible news. Alistair had taken the phone, answered by his mother, optimistic that there might be some good news at last - maybe even that the whole thing had been sorted out. And so, Alistair was left absolutely bereft at the prospect of the ordeal his poor children would have to undergo. At that moment, he was almost incapable of any coherent thought, his brain was refusing to cope with, or even acknowledge what Juliet and Martin would have to endure. His heart was cut to the quick as he thought about his children being intimately examined by some stranger, how frightened, humiliated and confused they would be. Moreover, he knew he wouldn't be permitted to attend to provide moral support for his wife and family.

Eventually he realised he had better pull himself together sharpish and get on to Nat to warn her what the police had in mind. She'd be totally crushed. But when he called, using his father's mobile, all he got was an engaged tone and he knew he was too late.

By now the strain was starting to tell on them all. Mr and Mrs Neville were bewildered and overwhelmed by the whole nightmare. They were still fiercely loyal in their faith in their son's innocence, but the pressure was just getting too much for them to bear and this latest news about their grandchildren was truly unbelievable. Furthermore, the press was still camped outside, waiting and jockeying like scavengers for some juicy morsel. It seemed that the local papers had been joined by the national press and even some t.v stations. These were people who wouldn't take *'no comment'* for an answer - they were there to get results, the more sensational the better - and didn't care less about the distress they were causing. The Neville's were prisoners in their own home and the phone hadn't stopped ringing morning, noon and night, so they had eventually been forced to unplug it in order to get a moment's peace.

Nat got in contact immediately after the call from the police. Of them all, she proved to be the most positive - amazingly composed and stoic. She had been pre-warned of this possibility by D.I Pennock and had had time to think the whole gruesome business through. Because of being given that advance notice, she hated herself all the more for the festering kernel of doubt that lingered in her mind over her husband's innocence. She too had fervently prayed that the police would drop the case for want of evidence, but the fact that they were prepared to subject the children to this horrendous invasion kept the bitter flicker of doubt alive in the recesses of her psyche - a doubt that was becoming more and more difficult to extinguish. But it was her duty and her solemn promise to support her husband and she was determined to be positive. There was only one way to dispel the suspicion completely.

She told Alistair to listen carefully and then said, firmly.

"Al, when, and not if, the examination shows that the children haven't been sexually molested, the whole case will collapse for lack of physical evidence. Do you understand?

"Yes, I hear what you're saying. But Nat, there's no way we can let the kids go through that. I've told the police, till I'm blue in the face, they should be investigating some other explanation. We've got to spare the children from being put through it."

She agreed that the whole situation was horrendous, but it was going to happen whether they liked it or not. She pressed on.

"Alistair, don't delude yourself for a second that the police are looking for anyone else in this investigation. They're not. They couldn't give a damn whether you swear you're innocent till you're blue in the face, like you keep on saying and that there must be some other explanation. All they know is the evidence speaks for itself and what they want is the examination to prove it once and for all. But, on the other hand, if it vindicates you, it will have been worthwhile. They'll have to drop the case then. And we'll be there to pick up the pieces. The children will recover and eventually put it behind them. We'll certainly have to get them specialist counselling, I know that. But they're young, they'll bounce back. Keeping the family together is what's important now. So we've got to take the positive out of this and prove you're innocent. Right?"

"I suppose so, but I hate it - that they'll have to go through it for me."

"It is what it is and we'll survive. That's what counts."

Nat was trying hard to convince herself that what she was saying was true. If their children's ordeal led to her husband's proof of innocence, it would have been worth it, wouldn't it? But that niggling question continued to nag her - but what if it didn't?

Alistair, mercifully ignorant of his wife's deepest fears, was stunned by Nat's strength of character and beyond relieved she was on his side. She truly was his rock. Nat said she would come home the next day, get the children back into school and, together they'd face whatever challenges would come their way over the following few days and weeks.

Feeling more buoyed up and optimistic than he had been for quite a while, Alistair went in to the kitchen to tell his mother what he and Nat had been discussing, but was horrified to find her slumped and glassy-eyed at the kitchen table, a small trail of green vomit trickling from the side of her mouth. Her face was chalky white and clammy with a fine sheen of sweat coating her skin. Instinctively, he grabbed her wrist - her pulse was weak and thready.

"Mum, Mum can you hear me?"

No response. He shouted for his dad to come quickly. He still had his dad's mobile in his hand. He pressed 999, called for an ambulance and informed the dispatcher that he was a doctor and his mother had suffered a stroke.

Alistair raced upstairs to get his mother's medication. He used the angina spray liberally under her tongue and did everything he could medically think of to save her life. He prayed she was going to be ok because, even though she appeared to have started to regain consciousness, she remained confused and disorientated, her words slurred and uttered without any meaning.

The arrival of an ambulance forced the press to scramble out of the way, sending them in to a frenzy of unexpected excitement and speculation. Several minutes later, Mrs Neville was taken out on a stretcher, followed by her husband. Alistair remained behind to gather his mother's bits together. He promised his father he would escape out the back way and join him at the hospital as quickly as he could.

The journalists couldn't tell in the dark who was under the sheet. They jostled and scrabbled to get the best shots of the drama.

"Can you tell us what's happened, Mr Neville?"

"Has someone died, Mr Neville?"

" Is it Dr. Neville? Was it suicide?"

10

By the middle of the week, the children were back at school. Nat had seen no option but to inform the head teacher that her husband was under investigation. She suspected that he was already well aware of the allegations against Alistair, after all they had been broadcast all over the newspapers and was humiliated to have to reveal some of the details - especially the bail condition for her husband to have no contact with the children - but she felt the school should be aware of it. She was as economical with the details as she dared be. She warned the head master that there might be some disruption to the children's schooling which she hoped to keep to a minimum because, as they all knew, Martin was at a crucial stage in his education.

The head's response was a combination of compassion for Mrs Neville and evident distaste for her husband. He promised to keep the children under close observation and wished Mrs Neville all the best. He had always felt a sneaking admiration for Mrs. Neville and regretted the circumstances she now found herself in.

The school run had always seemed like ground-hog day to Nat and in some ways it continued to be. But that morning, late and frantic as usual, she glimpsed her daughter flying out of the front door, and suddenly observed her in a new light. She may have only been 10 years old but she was growing tall and there were definitely signs of her budding womanhood. Nat felt a visceral pang of fear. She desperately hoped it was an irrational fear - she prayed it was merely the same anxiety every mother experiences when they see their baby developing.

For her part, Juliet thought she had been super discreet - the mascara was a colourless liquid that lengthened and separated the lashes without being too obvious and the lippie was a clear (well maybe slightly rosy) gel. She didn't wear foundation on a school day preferring to save it for the weekend when she might be allowed to go to the shopping centre or cinema with her mates - or if she was extremely fortunate - get invited to a sleep-over at a friend's.

"What you staring at, Mum?" Juliet asked a little nervously. Had she over-done the slap this morning and been caught out?

"No, it's nothing love. Just thinking what a beautiful young lady you're turning into. Not such a nipper any more, are you my girl? Oh, for God's sake, where's your brother? He's really going to get us all into big trouble today."

On cue, Martin sauntered out. Nat eyed him closely - well, at least, he looked the same as ever. Sloppily dressed, lank hair too long and shaggy and a surly face sporting the first signs of acne. He wasn't anywhere near as well groomed as his sister. 'Groomed'. Oh sweet Jesus. Nat shuddered as she realized the connotation of the word that had sprung into her mind.

It was as though she were seeing her children for the first time. Had she become so accustomed to them always being there, that she had forgotten what they really looked like? Or, she asked herself, was she seeing them for the first time through fresh eyes, someone else's eyes - a predator's eyes?

She berated herself for allowing such disloyal thoughts to enter her mind unbidden once again. It seemed her psyche had a way of re-evaluating and processing information and bringing it to the forefront of her mind but not producing the answers she was hoping for. She scolded herself sternly. No one knew her husband as well as she did, psyche or no psyche, her common sense told her that Alistair must be innocent - mustn't he?

Dropping them at the school gates, Nat considered how all of this was affecting the children themselves? The poor things - both Martin and Juliet had been fretful and anxious that they hadn't seen their Daddy for ages and that Granny was very ill in the hospital but they weren't allowed into the heart attack unit to visit her. They were confused and distressed knowing the bad stuff that had been happening to Dad wasn't sorted out yet. At home they wouldn't let Nat out of their sight, trailing after her like puppies, afraid that she too might suddenly be taken away from them.

A couple of days ago, Nat had bought two new pay as you go mobiles and at last she and Alistair were able to talk privately. During their often stilted and awkward conversations they had decided to tell the children an abbreviated but truthful version of what was going on and prepare them to some extent for what the police had in store for them. And at least now Alistair was able to have supervised chats with his children. Up until that moment, despite his continuous requests, Nat had not permitted Alistair to speak to Martin and Juliet citing the police bail conditions. Now it seemed she had thawed somewhat and allowed him to talk to the children on speaker-phone so she could participate-in, as well as monitor the conversations. Actually, Nat wasn't doing it for Alistair's benefit at all but for the children's. Martin and Juliet had pleaded so piteously to speak to their father that she had finally relented - the calls clearly providing them with some small amount of comfort. Her act of defiance had gone down well with a very relieved Alistair, who took it as a good sign that his wife still had full faith in his innocence.

He had given them an update on Granny's progress, assuring them that she was doing well and was likely to make a full recovery. They were going to keep her in coronary care for a few days more to monitor her condition, but all being well, she should be home by the weekend and they could come and see her then provided they were on their best behaviour and promised to keep the noise down. But no, he had told them, unfortunately he wouldn't be able to see them then.

He had attempted to put their minds at rest and reassure them that everything was going to be alright, but it might take a little time, they'd all have to be patient. They'd have to be really good for Mummy now, help her as much as they could. They had promised him they would be as good as gold and he, in return, promised them faithfully that he'd be home soon and that he loved them very, very much. For Alistair too, it was some small consolation to be able to speak to the children again - now that he wasn't allowed to see them in person.

ii.

Pennock and Parnell had been put in contact with a Dr. Elizabeth Tomasson - designated to be their expert witness. She came highly recommended and, according to her resume, was, amongst other talents, a specialist in child abuse cases, particularly those of a sexual nature. It seemed that she was experienced at giving evidence in court, sometimes for the prosecution - this was very good news - and sometimes for the defence - not so good. She agreed to meet them at her offices at the end of the week for a discussion and pre-evaluation of the case.

Dr. Tomasson was not what they had anticipated. They had expected to meet the typical stereotype psychiatrist - some crusty, wiry grey-haired, serious woman, devoid of any humour or humanity, totally and exclusively passionate about her field of expertise. The woman who greeted them that Friday afternoon was far removed from that. She was a vibrant, vivacious, middle-aged woman, who had clearly developed an excellent life/work balance. Not that she wasn't passionate about her speciality, as she explained, but the only way for her to retain her sanity when confronted by such monstrous stories, was to maintain a sense of proportion in her work-space and separate her private life completely from it.

She told the two officers that she had asked them to meet in her offices so that they could see first-hand the importance of the children's interviews being held in neutral surroundings. She showed them in to a room painted in soft pastel colours full of toys and puzzles with a comfy bean bag area. This is where she proposed to conduct the interviews with both children at the same time. She believed they would be more relaxed and responsive in there, especially if Mrs. Neville were allowed to be present as an observer and accompanying adult - but not as a participant under any circumstances, she insisted. She indicated the discreet recording and microphone devices located within the room to capure the whole session and assured them that a transcription of the interviews would be provided to them soon after.

The whole set-up seemed perfect and they agreed to schedule the meeting for Wednesday of the following week in order to give Dr. Tomasson time to review the evidence, read the report to be submitted by D.S Parker from the RASA unit and get a clear grasp of the complexities of the allegations and prepare her line of questioning. Mrs. Neville would also need some time to make arrangements to attend.

Dr. Tomasson told the officers that she was obliged to inform them both morally and ethically, that she and Dr. Neville had met on several occasions, not only professionally but socially as well. Whilst they had probably exchanged no more than a few casual greetings, and they certainly were not on first name terms, their worlds sometimes intersected - as a result of them both being paediatric practitioners.

Dr. Neville, she told them, was considered to be a rising star in his field and there would be very few colleagues in the surrounding area who would be unaware of his reputation. Other than that observation, she made no further personal comment about their suspect. She told them that situations like this had arisen before when giving evidence which sometimes caused a bit of a mine-field but which hadn't caused any major problems for her so far. It was recognized that the medical profession was a small world and, it was understood, practitioners would be aware of each other. She guaranteed that this would not impact on her impartiality. She confirmed that she had never met Mrs Neville and her sole interest now lay with Juliet and Martin who were to be considered by everyone as her patients and who could perhaps, be victims of a very serious crime.

Natalie and Alistair were informed of the pending appointment arranged for the following week. They had naively believed that the interview with D.S Parker and her team would be the end of the children's ordeal. Deeply concerned, they immediately contacted Charles Kingsley. Charles was disappointed that the police had beaten him off the mark - he too would have engaged Dr. Tomasson to represent his client. However upon reflection, he decided, the fact that the police had engaged an expert witness at this point in the enquiry seemed to indicate that the results of their RASA unit's interview might be ambiguous or inconclusive. This might not prove all bad after all.

He suggested that they should all keep calm, Dr. Tomasson was a thorough and fair psychiatrist. She would not compromise her ethics simply to satisfy her employer in order to gain a conviction, that was not her style. He had come up against her in court once or twice and really rather admired her professionalism. Furthermore, he understood that Natalie would be allowed to sit-in on the session and, therefore would be able to give a full and frank assessment of the meeting. This could be very good for them, give them the heads up, well before the police even got sight of Dr. Tomasson's report. In the mean-time he would make provisional arrangements for the children to be seen by their own psychiatrist, should the evidence presented by Dr. Tomasson need to be repudiated - which was commonly the case with expert witnesses - he informed them. Additionally, he would set about organizing their own medical examination, should that too be required.

Relations between husband and wife were straining to breaking point. Their entire family was being systematically destroyed, eroded catastrophically it seemed, and there was nothing they could do about it. It was becoming increasingly difficult for the couple to maintain a positive attitude, and speaking to Charles was not much consolation. They both felt he wasn't pulling his weight as much as he could. But, as he was at pains to point out to them, under English jurisprudence law, there is a presumption of innocence and it is the duty of the prosecutor to prove beyond reasonable doubt that the accused is, indeed, guilty. Until, the full disclosure became available, and the impounded devices released, there was little more that could be done. They could then request their own analysis of the computer and he had already alerted a technical team to be on stand-by. He had some top notch and very experienced contacts, he told them, and the moment they knew the strength of the prosecution case they could put measures in place to counteract it.

iii.

Alistair was devastated that he wouldn't be permitted to support his wife and family. He knew Dr. Tomasson slightly and was aware of her excellent reputation and was glad, if it had to be anyone, that it was she. He and Nat had prepared the children as thoroughly as they dared. They could not tell them what to say, they would not coach the children too much but it had inevitably been necessary to hint at what the doctor they would be visiting would probably want to ask them. Juliet appeared none-the-wiser by what her parents were implying, but Martin, a little older and on the cusp of adolescence, got the message loud and clear. He wasn't best pleased.

Dr. Tomasson introduced herself as Dr Lizzie when she showed the children through to the play area. She told them to relax while she talked to Mummy outside for a few minutes.

"Mrs Neville, I know this must be very difficult for you and I promise I'll be as sensitive as possible. Just for your information, I'll quickly outline how I intend to proceed ... My first aim is to relax the children and make them understand that they have done nothing wrong and are not in any trouble. We must make that abundantly clear. I usually observe through play in the first instance and then, perhaps follow up with some questions. I assure you, I'm very experienced with this type of situation, and I promise you that I will treat the children with the utmost dignity and cause the least upset possible. I cannot stress strongly enough that your children are now my patients and, although I have been engaged on behalf of the police, my primary concern is for their well-being and theirs alone. Alright? You are welcome to interact with the children while they are playing if you wish, but must not, I repeat, must not interrupt or prime the children in any way when I question them later. Do you understand?"

Nat reluctantly nodded and the two women entered the room. Juliet was already busy playing with the toys but Martin was standing stubbornly against the wall. Dr. Lizzie pointedly ignored Martin and approached Juliet asking her which kind of toys she preferred - she had already noticed the child was surrounded by books and puzzles. They chatted for several minutes and Juliet told her that dolls were for little kids but she admitted she still occasionally played with her old favourites at home, but generally she liked reading and board games. Dr. Lizzie pointed out one or two and asked if her brother sometimes played with her. Yes, he sometimes did but he was usually busy on the Play Station when Mum and Dad allowed them free-time to do what they wanted. She said Martin was only allowed to play for an hour a day.

Dr. Lizzie turned to Martin as if noticing him for the first time.

"So Martin, what's your favourite computer game?"

Martin looked away, ignoring her completely.

"I wonder if I can guess?"

"That'll be the day," said Martin rudely.

"Well, let me have a go anyway ... Mmmm, if you're anything like my grandson, and I'd say he's about your age, I'd have to guess at 'Fortnite.' Am I right?"

A reluctant Martin was impressed. It was his number one all-time favourite.

"Unfortunately, that's as far as it goes. I know absolutely nothing else about it. My grandson is far too busy to fill in an old codger like me. Do you think you could you tell me a bit about it so I can surprise him with my new found knowledge?"

Despite himself, Martin was drawn-in. Dr. Lizzie listened attentively, occasionally asking a question about the tactics and battles. Martin was animated and engaged. She then showed him some of the computer games she had there, which she invited him to try, apologizing for them being so ancient. But Martin was enthralled. He told her there was a big market these days for retro games. He'd heard about Gameboys and Wii's but had never played with them. Mum and Dad had them when they were young but they had got lost or broken. He was soon absorbed with Super Mario but, Dr. Tomasson noted, he was keeping a surreptitious and wary eye on his mother and herself from across the room.

Dr. Tomasson and Nat sat quietly watching the children. She gently probed Nat about herself, then asked some general questions about their family life, hobbies, holidays, but nothing specific or intrusive. Everything she had seen and heard so far seemed to indicate a well-balanced family unit which was undergoing significant major upheaval at the moment. Juliet was responding as would be expected from a ten year old, with compliance and a desire to please, whereas Martin was showing classic signs of fear/uncertainty demonstrated by mild aggression and apparent unwillingness to co-operate. So far, there was nothing obvious or untoward in their demeanour to indicate that anything was seriously awry.

She then told Nat that she intended to ask the children some preliminary questions. She assured their mother that she would not be devious nor put words in to the children's mouths, nor try to catch them out. Her sole intention was to allow the children to open up to her in their own time and in their own way.

Natalie closed her eyes and tried to will her mind to escape to another place, run away to somewhere they could all be happy, where they could be left alone to get on with their lives and just be a family again. A desert island where nobody could find them and they could be themselves once more. But that heavenly place didn't exist and this living hell did. She knew that the real interrogation was about to begin and there wasn't a damned thing she could do to shield her children, herself or Alistair.

iv.

Dr. Tomasson's report to the police was short and succinct - but not helpful. She stated that - yes, both children confirmed that their father often bathed them, dressed and undressed them. Both Martin and Juliet agreed that their father frequently washed them all over with a flannel or sponge including the genital area. Among other physical/ intimate interactions she mentioned was that they came in to bed with him for cuddles and tickles in the mornings at the weekend but, it should be noted, Mrs. Neville was nearly always there too. Finally and most overwhelmingly apparent was the fact that the children missed and loved their father very much indeed.

Dr Tomasson concluded that she broadly concurred with the report recently furnished by the R.A.S.A unit, that while Dr. Neville's behaviour and actions towards his children could be construed, in this modern day and age, as inappropriate and perhaps seen to be unwise, particularly with regard to their ages, there was no definitive evidence that either child had been sexually penetrated nor interfered with.

Her recommendation, therefore was two-fold. First, and her preferred option, was that she should interview each child individually and in greater depth, employing hypnosis techniques. This would be less invasive, and if successful, could elicit positive results. (However, Dr. Tommasson noted that if such a session did produce a firm belief that sexual interference had occurred, then naturally a medical examination would have to be carried out anyway for verification.) Or second - proceed straight to medical examination which would provide irrefutable evidence but would result in more stress and trauma to the children, who it should be remembered, were considered to be the victims in the scenario.

After reading the report, Pennock and Parnell felt that it would most likely be pointless to continue with Dr. Tomasson, especially, as she herself pointed out, it would probably come down to physical medical evidence anyway. So they decided to set the wheels in motion to arrange an appointment with the Force Medical Examiner. Apparently, they were told, that wasn't going to take place any time soon, priority or no priority, it didn't matter. They would have to wait their turn and it could take some time to be seen.

Meanwhile Pennock was beginning to experience an increasing sense of unease regarding the findings.

"Those images on the pen drive and P.C looked pretty convincing to me. I really thought it was just a question of confirmation from Dr. Tomasson, dotting the i's and crossing the t's...but Sandy and that bloody woman have thrown a bloody big spanner in the works."

"What're you saying, Gov? You starting to have doubts about Neville? Think he might be innocent after all?"

"No, it's not that at all, Harry. I still think he's as guilty as hell. But I also think there's got to be more to this than meets the eye."

"Such as what?"

"True, we've got loads of evidence but the fact is, it's all on two devices. And equally there are loads of contradictions - like there's nothing on his personal laptop or mobile, things he keeps with him all the time and other people don't have access to. You'd think that's where he'd stash the images, not on the family computer where everyone can get their hands on it."

"Yeah, but like he said himself ... he was in the process of transferring the images. Maybe he would have deleted everything from the P.C once it was on the pen drive and then put them on to his laptop."

"That may well be the case. Let's hope so. But it's an inconsistency, Harry and I hate inconsistencies. There's too much ambiguity, and if the defence get their teeth in to it and start to persuade reasonable doubt to a jury, I think there's a real possibility he might get off. Harry, I think maybe we've missed something. Maybe there's more evidence at the house but we ignored it or didn't see it because we only targeted the obvious stuff, because it seemed like an open and shut case. I think we need to go back, get another warrant and go over that house with a fine tooth comb, tear the place apart if we have to. It'll be there, we just have to find it."

"Fine by me, Gov. But it's not me you have to persuade, it's the Super who'll say yay or nay to the warrant. Better make your argument convincing though, he won't be happy about granting another warrant without exceptional reasons. For what it's worth, I agree with you - we need it be cast iron, no stone left unturned and all that. There's no way Neville's going to wriggle out of it, whether he's got the best lawyers in the world or not."

11

Mrs Neville senior was now back at home and resting. The poor woman was weak and frail-looking and her husband was determined to keep her away from as much stress and unpleasantness as possible. He had been terribly upset by his wife's stroke and it had really brought it home to him that they were getting no younger and they'd need to look after each other properly. She had always been the strong one in their marriage, he assumed that she would outlive him by many years, it was only now that he realized how precious she was to him.

That didn't make what he had to do any easier. He loved Alistair with all his heart - they both did - and was incredibly proud of his achievements. But his main concern now would have to be for his wife and their own mutual well-being. He regretfully told his son that he would have to find an alternative place to stay, his mother needed calm and peace now. Alistair, who was already drowning in guilt, was horrified at the shock-effects that everyone around him was suffering - they were like dominoes falling uncontrollably one after the other or a tsunami crashing down and destroying everything in its path. He couldn't blame his father, his request was perfectly reasonable, but he had to beg him for a couple of days to find somewhere else to live and then get the court's approval for a change of address.

There was no way he could afford to consider staying in a hotel on an indefinite basis and still be expected to hand over the bulk of what the hospital was still paying him to Nat and the rest to his lawyer, so was forced to look for cheaper rooms somewhere fairly close by. He trawled through the listings in the estate agents, but all the decent accomodation had minimum contracts of a year - he had to have faith that this would all be resolved long before then. He eventually resorted to the small ads in the local paper.

The flatlet in the hostel he was finally shown barely met health and safety requirements but, he accepted, it would have to do for now. It comprised, what was rather euphemistically described as, a single-person-occupancy professional residence. For a surgeon accustomed to working in the most hygienic and sanitary of conditions, the shock was considerable. Beneath the feeble glow of its single, inadequate light bulb, the dingy kitchen was nauseatingly vile. Crumbs still stuck to the grease-laden counters and floor. The cooker hob and oven were covered with an indeterminate residual grime and the fridge was green with mould. All the mis-matched crockery, cutlery, cups, glasses, pots and pans would have to go. The lounge and bathroom offered more of the same substandard, disease-promoting furnishings, but the bedroom was the final straw, with several mouse traps and foul smelling droppings liberally strewn around the caked and cracked cheap lino floor.

Alistair had to steel himself to take the positive from the situation. It wouldn't be for long, maybe days or a couple of weeks rather than months. The first thing he would do would be to buy a new mattress and pillows. A good scrub and a clean and it would be ok, he was sure. However, the other, even more depressing down-side, he soon learned, came when he met his first neighbour, that sod, Andy Motson who, he discovered, also lived in the hostel. The smarmy git could barely contain his delight when he saw the high and mighty Dr Neville viewing one of the flats.

"Welcome to the dump," he called gleefully. "Now we're neighbours, we'll have to go out for a pint, eh doc? Catch up on the gossip."

No way would he ever be seen dead with Motson. He totally ignored him and told the agent he'd take the flat.

So, a day or two later, accompanied by his father to provide corroboration, the court heard the circumstances of the application - in short, how his mother had suffered a stroke and how his presence in the family home was no longer welcome due to the stress on his parents caused by these ongoing proceedings. The bench was satisfied and, oddly enough, seemed to be familiar with the address he gave them and with no police objections, granted him leave to move there.

He had hoped Nat would give him a hand to move in and clean up a bit once she'd calmed down but he hadn't been able to contact her, nor had she phoned him, since the day his mother came home. By mutual agreement, Alistair had been hidden from view when the children had run happily inside their grandparent's house only reappearing when they had disappeared within. Then the two of them had snatched a tense couple of minutes to catch up.

Of course he, perforce, had been doing nothing very much and was going demented as a result he told her, full of self pity. And to top it all, was going to have to move out in the next couple of days to give his mother a chance to recuperate quietly at home. One small mercy was that the press seemed to have had enough and buzzed off for the time-being. Nat, on the other hand, he was sharply reminded, was single-handedly running the family home, taking the kids to and fro to school and their various clubs, whilst holding down her own job and ... oh yes, being compelled to attend a psychiatrist's office to endure the torture and humiliation of her children being grilled about their sexual activity.

No wonder she refused to talk to him for the last few days since his mother's home-coming. He was the sole cause of the chaos their lives had been reduced to. He was impotent to help in any way being the catalyst of all their woes - all he could do was provide support and love, but Nat seemed to have rejected the little he had to offer. He was deeply concerned that she was beginning to feel alienated from him, just when he needed her most. He knew there was no point hassling her, she would hate it. He prayed that she would reconsider and would soon get in touch.

She did. To inform him that the police had phoned to say they had a warrant to further search the property and that she should make herself available that evening to grant them access and perhaps ensure that the children would be with a neighbour while they conducted the search - *'To minimize the upheaval'* she quoted.

She didn't know how much more she could take, she told him. She had thought the police would have backed off once Dr. Tomasson's report had been submitted. There was clearly no case to answer, not a shred of evidence. The children had given absolutely no sign whatsoever that anything was wrong. Why were they still persisting? Did they have other evidence, something they hadn't been told about yet? What hadn't he told her? She had demanded.

Alistair swore they had nothing - there was nothing - he hadn't done anything wrong. It was victimization pure and simple. He begged his wife to stand by him, carry on believing in him, please, please. It would all be ok. She hesitantly agreed but at that moment, the thought crossed his mind that she didn't sound totally convinced.

Pennock had been told by his boss that he had better make damned sure he turned up some vital evidence if the Inspector expected him to put his neck on the line and issue another warrant - it was all highly irregular he had grumbled. Now, Pennock and Parnell, accompanied by an experienced team arrived at the Neville's at the agreed time. By now Nat knew the drill - she retreated, silently to the kitchen and made herself a cup of tea. She confirmed that the children were at Alison's house and she would pick them up after the police had gone. The team's brief this time was to leave no stone unturned - consult, photograph, then bag and tag anything that might be relevant. Nothing was to be overlooked. They didn't know specifically what they were searching for, but knew they would recognize it when they came across it.

The search was painstakingly slow and thorough. The house was a typical modern family home, comfortably furnished and child-proof, a house that was lived in rather than being a show home. There were four bedrooms, one with a master en suite. The children each had their own room and there was a small spare guest room. The lounge, kitchen/diner and office were reasonably clean and tidy but not excessively so, with evidence of their everyday lives all around. They started in the loft - but that produced nothing of any interest to them, just the usual boxes and unneeded paraphernalia that had been dumped up there and never looked at again until that very evening - and continued to work their way down, floor by floor, room by room, inch by inch. Bits and pieces of potential evidence were consulted upon, photographed and bagged but nothing concrete was being unearthed, nothing damning. It was all a bit frustrating and unsatisfactory. Pennock was starting to feel anxious - they had hoped to have found more by now.

Then a voice called out.

"Over here, Gov. Think I might've got something interesting."

The two men went in to Juliet's bedroom and looked towards where the officer was pointing.

"What are we looking at? I don't see anything," said Pennock.

"Me neither," from Parnell.

"In the middle, just above the wardrobe," said the officer indicating where to focus.

"Ok, now I see it. What is it? It looks like part of the pattern of the wall-paper. Just a dot."

"It is a dot of sorts, Sir. It's a dot camera. Called that because it's so small. Actually Gov, it's a wireless surveillance webcam. Very neat and very discreet. This one is particularly miniature. Can be accessed remotely from downstairs say or even from a long distance away, in case the parents want to keep tabs on the kids - see what they're up to in their rooms and so on. A bit strange though, if you ask me, if that's the reason why it's here. But that apart, a lot of people have them these days to keep an eye on the house while they're away. You can see what's going on in real-time and that gives the home owner peace of mind."

"Blimey, what will they come up with next?" said Parnell.

"I don't know much about all this technology stuff, but from what you showing and saying we could be on to something big here," replied Pennock who was becoming quietly excited by the revelation. "Well done Officer. Good work. There's no way I would have ever spotted it. Right, let's see if there are any more hidden around the house."

The search resumed with new vigour. Another one was found in Martin's room, so well hidden that it was practically invisible, but which, nevertheless, afforded the secret camera a good wide angle towards the boy's bed and desk, just as it had in Juliet's room. Pennock once more instructed his men to photograph everything in situ before removing it as evidence.

Pennock decided to call Mrs. Neville upstairs at this point to ascertain whether she was aware of these webcams or if, indeed she had installed them herself. Nat was confounded by what they had to show her, and horrified when they discovered another one hidden in her own bedroom. She was confused, and ... no, she knew nothing about them, she hadn't fitted them, and was completely unaware of their existence until that very moment. They believed her.

The woman looked like she had been punched by a heavy-weight in the belly – totally pole-axed. She suddenly stooped over, unable to breathe, desperately trying to draw air into her lungs as the implication of what these spy cameras really meant dawned on her. Her fragile world had finally come crashing down, smashing into smithereens as she realized the lengths of depravity her husband had gone to satisfy his vile deviance. Parnell gently told her that he would have to take a statement from her, but that they could do it downstairs where it would be more comfortable, after they had concluded the search.

Two more cameras had been located, one in the lounge - which offered a wide-angled view of the whole room and one in the kitchen which was mounted directly across from the fridge and which also provided a good field of vision of the entire room. The forensics teams were using futuristic instruments not unlike the fake tricorder Alistair had bid on at the auction, and their final sweeps around the house also unearthed two tiny audio devices, again located near the fridge in the kitchen and in the lounge. The property had been very professionally bugged, it seemed.

Mrs Neville was sitting almost catatonic at the kitchen table. There was no way she was fit to be interviewed, nor could they leave her in this state. She eventually roused herself and turned to them wailing,

"How could I have been so blind? How is it that I didn't even know what was going on under my own roof?" She cried out in anguish and self recrimination. "A mother is supposed to protect her children, keep them safe from harm. I never suspected a thing, never thought for an instant ... I loved him ..."

The victory and vindication felt a little hollow as the two embarrassed men witnessed the outpouring of grief and misery that Mrs Neville was feeling. But at the same time, it had to be admitted, they felt an overwhelming sense of achievement, an intense satisfaction that Dr. Neville had been stopped in his tracks and they had spared those two innocent children any more untold hurt and abuse.

Parnell explained to Nat slowly and clearly that they believed she was too distressed to give a statement that evening and would she please attend the police station tomorrow afternoon with Mr. Kingsley. Nat looked at him blankly. He wrote the instructions down on a piece of paper and pressed it in to her hand.

"Mrs. Neville, you shouldn't be alone now. Can I ring your neighbour and ask her to bring the children back and get her to sit with you for a while?"

The two officers left when Alison, with her mother in tow, arrived with the children. It was obvious they had an inkling about what was happening so they felt it reasonable to tell them that Nat had had something of a shock and was taking it very hard. Could they please keep an eye on her but not ask too many questions - she'd been through quite enough for one evening. They promised faithfully to look after her and make sure she was alright.

iii.

She hadn't slept a wink all night. Torturous dark thoughts went churning around and around in her mind. Disbelief, denial, horror, self-blame, despair and ... finally, belief. The children too were affected without knowing why and didn't want to leave her to go to bed. They had never seen their mother so sad, they were frightened and she didn't have the strength to make up a convincing explanation, so she said nothing.

Alison returned first thing in the morning, saw that Nat was in no fit state, so she got the children up and dressed, gave them their breakfast, then saw them off to school. When she got back, she brought Nat up a nice cup of tea and a bit of toast and found her exactly where she had left her an hour before. What could she do to help, she asked?

Nat tried to rouse herself but found it almost impossible. It was as though every bit of energy had been sucked out of her body, leaving her deflated, an empty shell. She motioned to her friend to phone work on her behalf and tell them she wouldn't be in for a few days. She didn't care what she said, just make up any excuse. Alison reported back that someone called Simon had answered and had said not to worry, there was nothing important going on, they could hold the fort and they'd see her soon.

She then needed to speak to Charles in person. She forced herself into action. Getting through to his secretary, she haltingly explained that there had been some developments and she needed to speak to Mr. Kingsley urgently. She was put through to him and she briefly outlined last night's events and also that the police had asked him to attend with her for interview that afternoon. Charles said he would clear his diary and asked if she could come to his office beforehand to discuss things more fully, then they could go to the station together.

Alison was being a true friend. She told Nat not to worry about the children, she would sort them out and give them their tea when they got home from school. She knew what they were up to that afternoon, she told Nat, she'd seen the activities list blu-tacked to the fridge as she'd made the toast. Martin had swimming club and Juliet was going to gymnastics and they'd both be dropped off after by one of the mothers at about six p.m. No problem, fish-fingers, beans and chips ... her speciality. Nat winced but said nothing. Alison was being very kind and it wouldn't matter what they ate for once.

She assured Alison she was feeling a bit better, that she needed to get up and dressed. Satisfied that Nat was going to be alright, Alison cleared away the untouched tea and toast, told Nat that she would tidy around the house a bit then come back at about five o'clock. She had her keys, so to take as long as she needed.

Charles was quite taken aback when he ushered Mrs. Neville in to his office later that afternoon. He had considered her to be a very attractive lady, but the woman who stood before him now was a shadow of her former self. He was alarmed to note how she was carelessly dressed, quite dishevelled really, and had probably not even brushed her hair. Her face was gaunt and white, her eyes were blood-shot with black circles beneath. He quickly invited her to sit down and to tell him everything.

A raised eyebrow was all the response Natalie's revelation elicited from Charles. Privately, he thought it was worse than he could have possibly imagined, in fact it really was quite damning and would take quite a bit of defending in court. But neither could he reveal his repugnance for his client to his wife, so kept his manner business-like and professional. He took notes and prepared Nat for her interview with the police.

Before they left, Nat told him there was something else she wanted to discuss with him. She informed him that she wanted no further contact with her husband from now on. No phone calls, emails, letters, visits, whatever. She asked Charles how to arrange that in legal terms. Charles was disheartened and not best pleased but couldn't say he was really surprised. He did his very best to make Nat change her mind or at least reconsider. He carefully explained how it was always to the accused's advantage, his client's (and her husband's in this case), if his wife stood by him and supported him unconditionally. It would weaken his defence hugely if she, as his wife didn't publicly believe in and proclaim her husband's innocence. But Nat was not to be persuaded. She insisted that she would not tolerate any communication with her husband from now on.

Charles inevitably had to inform Nat that ethically he could not act for her in the matter. Her husband was his primary client and what she was asking could only prejudice the case significantly perhaps even catastrophically. He didn't think it would be appropriate for his chambers to represent her either as this would almost certainly be construed as a conflict of interest. Actually, he suggested, the solicitor who could best deal with the matter was probably Nigel Crowley, whom she already knew, he believed.

Nat was disappointed but saw the logic in what Charles was saying. Clearly he couldn't represent both Alistair and herself. Moreover she was aware that Nigel's speciality was family law. He probably dealt with situations like this all the time and that should undoubtedly serve her well. She was glad Charles had recommended Nigel and had even phoned him on her behalf and arranged an appointment with him for soon after. She felt more comfortable that she would be dealing with someone personally known to her and who also knew a significant amount surrounding the circumstances of her request. Both lawyers agreed that it would not be remiss if Charles were to accompany Mrs. Neville today as planned due to the short notice, but that would have to be the final intervention on her behalf.

12

While the interview under caution couldn't be said to have been a pleasant experience, neither was it as traumatic as she had been bracing herself for. Nat realized she was now equally as anxious as the police to get to the bottom of the whole sordid business and, to Charles's evident discomfort, was co-operating completely with them. Pennock and Parnell took her through the events of the previous evening and once again she confirmed that she had no knowledge of the cameras nor how they had got there. There was little more that she could add to what they already knew.

At least, thought Charles, he was hearing first-hand what the warrant had turned up in his absence, and it appeared that the latest evidence was even more damning than he had feared. He was beginning to seriously regret his arrogance at taking on such a risky client and the self-belief in his skills which assumed his ability to get an acquittal.

His faith in his client's consistent denials of any wrong doing - which was not the strongest in the first place, he now admitted to himself - was becoming weaker and weaker, being crushed under the overwhelming weight of evidence against Alistair. It would do his reputation no good if he were to lose such a high-profile case - public opinion would turn against him and he would certainly lose business and, perhaps, credibility with regard to his good judgement. No, he would have to implement a Plan A and a Plan B. As Nat answered the questions the officers posed, Charles began to formulate an alternative approach to how he could now best represent his client. It was becoming apparent that he may have to somehow mitigate Dr. Neville's alleged criminal actions rather than all out defend him from the prosecution's accusations. He would prepare a strategy and consult with his client as soon as possible.

The meeting concluded with Pennock thanking her for attending and gently informing Nat that a date had been set for the children to be examined. To his surprise, Nat was accepting about what was going to happen. Rather than the distress he had been expecting to cause her, she told him she felt a sense of relief that, at last they would know for certain what had really happened to her children.

Parnell saw Mrs Neville out, but Charles was asked to remain. He was told that Dr. Neville would be arriving shortly for re-interview. He would be given some time to consult with his client, but of course, by now he was already aware what they would be questioning him about.

As Nat prepared to leave the police station, Alistair entered. He was surprised to see her there.

"Nat love, what are you doing here?"

Nat ignored him and attempted to push past. He took her by the arm.

"Nat, wait. Stop. What's going on?"

"Take your filthy hands off me, you bastard."

Alistair was horrified at the acid in her tone.

"What's happened? Tell me, Nat."

"You know damned well what's happened. I never ... NEVER want to see you or speak to you again. If you ever come near me or the children, as God is my witness, I'll kill you."

"What are you talking about, have you gone mad? What have they been telling you?"

Nat tried to get past him again but he blocked her way.

"Hold on, we can sort it out. Whatever's happened, you know it's a mistake, I swear on my mother's life, I've done nothing wrong."

"Swear all you like, Alistair, I don't care any more. I don't believe you. The only thing I do care about now is the well-being of my children and myself. So, listen up. You will NOT contact me directly ever again, if you need to get in touch, go through Nigel Crowley, he'll be handling any communication between us from now on. So, just stay away from us - understand? Now get out of my way."

With that, she forced her way under his arm and out of the door.

"That's telling him," whispered the duty officer, P.C Brown nodding to D.S Parnell who had witnessed the whole thing.

"It certainly is. Very interesting. I think we're clear about where she stands now," agreed Parnell.

He turned towards Alistair, and said warmly.

"Dr. Neville. Thanks for coming. If you'd like to follow me."

ii.

The two investigators had expected nothing but denials from Alistair and that is exactly what they got. He put on a good pretence of being baffled as to why there should be spy cameras placed strategically around his house, and professed to be totally inept with matters of technology. He told them he never knew there were even such tiny devices available that could be used without any wiring.

"So to re-cap Dr. Neville, just to be perfectly clear, and for the benefit of the tape," reiterated Pennock, "you claim you have no idea where these cameras came from, you insist you weren't involved with secreting them around the house, and you're so crap with technology, you wouldn't have a clue how to do that spy stuff anyway. Correct?"

"Exactly correct. But if you'd only just listen to me properly for a second - it's what I've been telling you all along. If I'm innocent - and I am, then the only explanation is that my computer has been remotely accessed and that's how the pictures got there and ..."

"Yes, be that as it may," interjected Parnell, "but that doesn't explain how your house was remotely accessed as well and all that spy-ware hidden there, now, does it Dr. Neville?"

Charles felt obliged to intercede on Alistair's behalf. He had to do right by his client.

"Sergeant, please allow Dr. Neville the courtesy of finishing a sentence."

"Sorry, Dr. Neville. So to sum up," continued Parnell, undeterred, "If we understand you correctly, you're accusing someone of breaking and entering into your house and planting the cameras. You're suggesting this someone is framing you for some unknown reason, some enemy who wants to destroy yourself and your family for ... what, Dr.Neville? To what end? Why would anyone want to do that?"

"I... I don't know," admitted Alistair.

"So, out of fairness, let's explore your theory a little bit. Do you have many enemies, Dr. Neville? Maybe a dissatisfied patient, a medical negligence claim that didn't pay out or something like that?"

"No, nothing like that and I don't think I've got any enemies as far as I'm aware."

"Good, I'm glad we've cleared that point up. So, as far as you know, there's no-one with a grudge against you? Some kind of vendetta or crusade?" said Pennock .

"No, I don't think so," said Alistair miserably, "but, it's the only explanation that makes any sense."

Pennock took his time apparently considering what Alistair had said. He replied with steel and some contempt in his voice.

"Well, Dr. Neville, that's where we'll have to agree to disagree. It's not the only explanation that makes sense. The only explanation that makes any possible sense to us is that you are a systematic and unremorseful paedophile. You have been preying on and grooming your innocent children, no doubt deluding yourself that they were enjoying the experience of being raped just as much as you, their father."

Alistair squirmed uncomfortably - confirming what the detectives were certain was humiliation at being discovered. Pennock continued,

"And when you unexpectedly got caught out, you've come up with this pathetic fabrication to put us off your trail. Good try, Dr. Neville, we'll give you that, with your almost plausible alternative explanation but, I'm afraid we just don't believe you. And with very good reason. Very good reason indeed. You see, when our computer lads tested the spy-ware, they discovered it was blue-tooth paired with only one device. Just the one. Do you know what device that was, Dr. Neville?"

"No," said Alistair with real fear in his voice.

"Well you probably won't be surprised to hear that it was only paired with your computer. Can you explain that why that could be?... No?... Nothing to say? No new theories? So, thinking about it logically, it was no wonder you wanted to get those images on to a memory stick as fast as you could. Download and delete them from your P.C but keep them on the pen drive to view over and over again at your leisure. Your own little porn movies, to be enjoyed whenever you like."

Addressing his colleague and also Alistair's brief, who by now had definitely decided to go with Plan B, Pennock added with feigned surprise,

"And this from the man who swears he knows nothing about technology. No, I'm sorry Dr. Neville, but we've got you banged to rights this time. We've given you chance after chance to come clean, it would go better for you, but you're being irrationally stubborn. But I can tell you one thing for sure - when your children are medically examined next week, that'll be it - you'll be looking at a twenty year stretch."

Alistair hung his head. What could he say? How on earth could he persuade them?

Parnell wrapped up the interview.

"That'll be all for now. If we have any further questions we'll be in touch. Don't go far Dr. Neville. We've been informed you're staying at a new address, that's ok for now, but keep reporting as required. And I hope I don't have to remind you to stay away from your children and the family home, or you'll be making things a lot worse for yourself."

Charles was at pains to assure them that Alistair did indeed understand. He escorted his client out quickly, and leaving him outside on the pavement, told him they would need to meet at the earliest opportunity to review matters and formulate a new plan of campaign.

Pennock and Parnell were pleased with the way the case was shaping up. It was an added bonus when Parnell told his boss about the altercation between Dr. and Mrs Neville in the reception area. To have lost their main ally would be a hard blow for the defence but was a great advantage to themselves. And they had both noted how silent Charles Kingsley had been during the interview, he had barely said a word or taken any notes. They had had dealings with him on several occassions in the past and had found he was frequently aggressive and vociferous in the interview room, quite the formidable litigator who revelled in his own power and importance. But not today, it seemed, today he had been unusually passive. This too, boded well they thought, a brief who wasn't totally on board with his client could only be excellent news.

Once the report from the Forensic Medical Examiner was in, the whole file could be sent to the C.P.S. They were well aware that the Crown Prosecution Service would often toss the files back to the investigators with an attached note saying that the evidence was too flimsy or just not solid enough, or that there wasn't enough evidence to ensure a conviction or a multitude of other reasons. Well that wasn't going to happen this time. They had no doubt that their evidence was double locked down, and the medical report would be the final key that would guarantee Neville to be put away for a very long time.

All in all, a good day's work. There was very little to be done now except make certain that every step of the investigation had been carried out in strict adherence to PACE regulations, that nothing had been over-looked, and that every last shred of evidence was correctly documented. Pennock may be being O.C.D about everything but they had to make absolutely certain there was no way there could ever be a mis-trial.

iii.

Pennock declined his partner's invitation to join him for a swift beer. It wasn't that he couldn't do with a pint - he could - but all he really wanted was just to get home to his wife and family. Both men deliberately lived some distance from the police station. Neither of them had ever relished the prospect of running in to some local villain whilst out with friends or family (exactly like what had happened the other evening when Andy Motson was lording it in the pub). No, it was far better to live further out, even though that entailed getting stuck every day in rush hour traffic for an extra half an hour each way. What it meant was that they could be surrounded by pleasant, hard-working, non-criminal neighbours most of whom didn't know them and who they didn't know either.

Anyway, Richard Pennock wasn't the type of policeman who routinely socialized after hours like many of his colleagues - the other night with Parnell was something of a one-off. He was always aware of the fact he was their senior officer and needed to maintain a healthy distance, so he pretty much kept his work and home-life separate and, quite honestly, he preferred it that way.

Parnell, on the other hand, often enjoyed a quick half with his work-mates at the end of a tough day. He didn't usually stay long but told his boss that it helped him to unwind and leave business behind after a hard shift. Neither man took the job home if they could help it - Parnell's wife, Hannah was still interested in her husband's work, but after many years of marriage, knew not to pry, knowing that he'd tell her if there was something he needed to get off his chest. What he was working on at the moment caused her some concern because she could see it was weighing heavily on him. She didn't voice her worries to her husband though, he would share it with her when he was ready.

Pennock's wife, Katherine knew better than to even ask - her husband had made it abundantly clear that his home was his refuge from the trials and tribulations of the job, so she rarely enquired. However, she could sense this latest case was taking its toll on him and it certainly had kept him away from the family far more than usual. She had seen the newspapers so could guess what case he was dealing with. It sounded obscene, beyond belief, if what she read really were true. No wonder he didn't want to talk about it - the whole ordeal must be harrowing for him.

Pennock had been back late so often over the last few weeks that he feared the family might have forgotten him. But as he opened the front door, the kids came flying out to greet their Daddy and it forcefully brought home just what a negative impact the case was having on him. He hugged his children tightly and told them he loved them. They squirmed out of his embrace and scampered off squealing that they loved him too. He found his wife in the kitchen, preparing something which smelled absolutely divine.

"It's only spag bol you idiot," she said laughing, "but I can offer you a rather elegant glass of Tesco's finest Chianti. And, by the way, do you love me as well?"

"More than you'll ever know, my darling ... you're a wonderful cook, a great mother, and a not half bad wifey ... what's not to love?!"

He jumped back as she flicked the tea-towel at him and he felt the tension of the last few days draining away. It was good to be home.

The kids squabbled and chattered the whole way through dinner and Pennock revelled in their nonsense. Another drop of wine helped mellow him some more. As they cleared up afterwards, he told his wife he would bath the children that night, to put her feet up with another glass of the Chianti and he'd be down in a little while. She was a little surprised but made no comment. The few times he was home before the children were asleep usually found Richard out for the count on the sofa after dinner, leaving her to bath and put the children to bed. Still, if that's what he wanted to do tonight then it was fine by her - she wouldn't say no to another cheeky glass and the chance to relax - naughty and on a school night too!

As Richard swished the water to make the bubbles so frothy that the children almost disappeared beneath them, he wondered if this was exactly what Alistair Neville used to do with his kids. True, his own were a little younger than Neville's but the principle was the same. Sponging down their little bodies, telling them to keep their eyes shut tight if they didn't want to get soap in them, he couldn't help but reflect on Dr. Tomasson's comment - that whilst Dr. Neville's actions with his children in the bath may be perceived to be ill-advised, it couldn't be said to have amounted to sexual interference. Richard questioned himself honestly - tried to put himself in Neville's shoes and see things through his eyes - but the truth was he certainly didn't feel anything other than paternal love for his little ones. He looked at his children and couldn't begin to comprehend how anyone could possibly be sexually attracted that way, although he was well aware that plenty were.

He wrapped them both up in soft bath sheets and carried them through to their bedroom. He dried them gently and thoroughly before telling them to get their p.js on quickly if they wanted a story. As usual it had to be an exciting police drama where their Dad was the hero and always caught the bad guy. That night their father spiced up the story telling them about the assistance of an invented police dog who had saved his life when a burglar tried to bash him over the head with a metal bar, but was brought down by the courageous pooch who was later awarded a medal for outstanding bravery. Typically the children were more impressed by the dog than by their hero father and wanted to hear more, but he told them that was for another night and it was time for lights out.

Later, Richard tossed and turned in bed, thinking about the story he had told the children. He always caught the bad guy, didn't he? But had he done so this time? He didn't know why exactly but lately he had started to feel a sense of anxiety about Alistair Neville's claims that he was innocent. They hadn't really given them any credence - it was an open and shut case after all, wasn't it. But could it be a thread that they should have investigated more thoroughly? Could it cause the whole case to unravel? Perhaps they had dismissed his denials too quickly in the light of the overwhelming evidence against him. Maybe he should review Neville's claims for the sake of completeness.

Richard gave himself a mental shake and told himself to stop second guessing, stop doubting the results of a painstaking enquiry and the professionalism of everyone involved which, all in all, added up to a job well done. He eventually dropped off to sleep when he realized that he had been wasting his few remaining precious brain cells unnecessarily all this long while, because the results of the medical examination on the Neville children would be the clincher. Game over for you, Alistair Neville.

Nat was feeling an incredible sense of isolation and guilt. She could really do with someone to talk to and offload her fears and anxieties. It wasn't as though she could discuss her problems with just anybody, not even - and especially perhaps - her mum and dad. Her parents had been marvellous and as supportive as they knew how, but they were ashamed and embarrassed by the whole situation. Their solidarity with her seemed to stem from a sense of denial of what had happened rather than a belief in Alistair's innocence. She had been horrified by her mother-in-law's stroke and feared inflicting the same kind of stress on her own parents who were both quite a bit older and more frail. She loved Mr and Mrs Neville dearly and they had always treated Nat like the daughter they had never had, but now a subtle divide had begun to form, caused by their loyalty first and foremost to their son and seriously exacerbated by the fact that she had got a restraining order against him, which implied that Nat didn't believe in his innocence. They still saw the grandchildren regularly but Nat wasn't invited in like before.

Everything was spiralling, free-falling out of control - two or three weeks ago they had been a normal, happy family. Yes, she would be the first to admit, they had the typical fall outs and arguments that all families have, but they were close and united. Perhaps, she thought to herself, when everything is just plodding along in its usual daily routine, you miss what might be simmering under the surface. Apparently she had - this had been happening right under her nose and she was none the wiser. Had she been swept along with the mundane tedium of everyday life without ever once lifting her head up to observe what was going on around her? She always thought of herself as a competent, loving and attentive mother, but clearly that was a delusion. She now recognized that she must have simply gone through the motions of daily living like an automaton - functioning but not really involved. She berated herself for her blindness - if she had been a stay-at-home mum instead of chasing after a career, this would never have happened.

Finally she decided to reach out to Ann. She, of all people might have an inkling of what she was going through. Ann was less than warm when she realized who was calling and why, but eventually, albeit reluctantly, agreed to meet in town for a coffee after school that afternoon.

Ann was frankly shocked when she saw her former friend approaching the table - the woman had lost so much weight, was so pale and unkempt - that she felt a moment's compassion for her. She quickly suppressed the sentiment, reminding herself of the damage this family had done to them. She coolly greeted Nat who thanked her for agreeing to see her. Without further delay, she then began to tell Ann an honest, unabbreviated account of what had been happening. When Nat reached the part about the children being medically examined, Ann clapped her hand over her mouth in disbelief and distress.

"Oh, Nat, how can you bear it? Your poor babies," she cried aghast, tears streaming down her face.

"Well, there's absolutely no choice about it. And, in the end, it will prove conclusively if he's guilty," she replied as firmly and as dispassionately as she could. She was really struggling to keep her emotions under control and take the positive out of the most evil scenario imaginable.

"But you don't actually believe that Alistair could really be guilty, do you Nat?"

"Honestly? ... At first I would have sworn on my own children's lives that it was impossible, but as time's gone on and more evidence has been uncovered, I'm just not so sure ... Ann ... I think he did do those things to Juliet and Martin ... I really do … and the only way to find out for certain is for them to be examined. I hate the thought of what's going to happen, but if we're going to get through this, we have to know once and for all. And then, when he's been put away, the children and I can begin the process of rebuilding our lives and healing."

"Oh my God, how can you be so calm and rational about it? You're living in a total nightmare."

"You're right, it is, but don't let appearances deceive you, there's no way I'm as calm and rational as you think, but I've had time to think it through carefully. And anyway I can't afford to go to pieces, I've got to be strong for the children. Then I'll spend the rest of my life making up for failing them when they needed me most, when they were so vulnerable, for allowing this to happen under my own roof." Tears dripped unchecked down Nat's cheeks, tears for her children not for herself.

"No Nat, you're wrong! This isn't your fault, you couldn't possibly have known. He's the monster. Nat, please, please don't blame yourself."

The two women talked on and Nat felt some of the weight that had been crushing her had lightened a little. Ann insisted that she would accompany the three of them on the day of the appointment - Nat as support for her children and Ann as moral support for Nat - God knows, she was going to need it.

13

The long-awaited doomsday arrived all too soon. Ann was as good as her word and had arrived in plenty of time and would be driving them to the hospital. Nat was so grateful for her friend's support, she was trembling with anxiety and knew she would probably be in no fit state to drive back home afterwards. Nat had prepared herself and the children as best she could - she didn't want to alarm or frighten them, but neither could she pretend it was an ordinary event. She had very little idea of what was going to happen herself, she had researched as much as she could, but found there was hardly an information available. She and Ann had discussed the best approach and decided that they would describe it as like a school medical, something you had to do and get it over quickly and then do something nice afterwards.

They had been told to attend in a part of the hospital that she had never been into before. It was eerily quiet with none of the hustle and bustle normally associated with a busy medical facility. The floor was carpeted and the walls were painted a restful moss green colour showing no signs of the wear and tear that could be seen in the main body of the hospital. In the reception, they were greeted by a pleasant middle-aged woman who showed them through to a waiting area, saying that the doctor would be with them shortly. The room reminded her of Dr. Tomasson's practice with toys and books to engage and relax the children whilst they waited.

Within moments the doctor arrived and introduced himself.

"Mrs. Neville, very pleased to meet you. I'm David Donaldson - the Police Forensic Medical Examiner. And you two scamps must be Martin and Juliet."

They acknowledged that indeed they were. Nat introduced Ann, grateful for his easy manner towards herself and the children.

"Now then children, I'm going to take Mummy away for a few minutes for a chat, so make yourselves at home. We'll be back shortly."

Ann nodded that she would be fine with the two children and to go ahead. He led Nat through to an inner office and invited her to sit down.

"So, Mrs Neville, I want you to be quite clear about the procedure today and if you have any questions, please do ask. I'm well aware that this is a very difficult time for you all, and I hope to make it as bearable for you as I can. Firstly, you may wish to know about my credentials. I've been Chief Forensic Examiner for the police for nine years and before that, I was a consultant general surgeon in this very hospital. As you can imagine, we deal with a great variety of examinations but today's business, I am sad to say is something I am all too familiar with. But your children are in safe hands, I promise and I shall also be assisted by a female colleague and upon completion of our examination, we will get the report to the relevant police department as quickly as possible. Speed is of the essence in cases like this, I'm sure you'll agree. O.k so far? Any questions?"

Nat shook her head.

"Good. Moving on ... In my experience, this is an over-whelmingly stressful time for everyone concerned, so with regard to the children, I would like to recommend that we give them a little sedative beforehand."

He raised his hand to forestall Nat's interjection.

"Let me explain just why this is helpful. We usually put it in a drink of squash, and whilst it's not enough to knock them out, it relaxes them and renders them quiescent. Moreover, we've learned that they have hardly any recollection afterwards of what went on. Of course, I would need your permission to administer the sedative."

Nat told him that this had actually been one of her greatest fears, and was immensely reassured that the trauma of the procedure could be minimized. She was also overwhelmingly relieved that he seemed so sympathetic, kind and caring.

Dr. Donaldson rang through to the secretary and told her that the drinks could now be given to the children.

"I must warn you that I have asked Detective Inspector Pennock to attend afterwards to give him my preliminary report and, of course you will be welcome to hear what I have to say at the same time as well. Is that agreeable to you? Excellent. Very good. Now the sedative only takes a few minutes to take effect, so let me escort you back to the children. If you could put on their gowns while you wait, I'll be ready for them in about ten minutes. Obviously, I can't say how long it will take, but try to make yourself comfortable in the meantime. I'll return shortly."

The children were called after a brief while by a friendly looking lady doctor who chatted easily with them on the way to the examination room. Clearly the sedative was working. They were taking it very well, better than Nat herself who was dreading what the next few minutes might reveal. They were brought tea and biscuits while they waited - tea thought Nat, the universal remedy for all problems - if only that were true.

ii.

The procedure lasted under an hour. The children returned a little subdued but not unhappy. Nat asked if they were ok as she redressed them.

"It wasn't too bad Mummy," said Martin. Juliet nodded her agreement.

"Can we play for a while now, Mummy?" Juliet asked.

"Of course you can. I've got to talk with Dr. Donaldson for a few minutes anyway."

Once again, she was shown through to the office where D.I. Pennock was already seated. He rose to greet her and then they both sat anxiously awaiting Dr. Donaldson. There was little to be said, idle chit chat didn't seem appropriate at a time like this, so they sat in an uncomfortable silence, each immersed in their own thoughts. They didn't have long to wait.

"D.I Pennock, Mrs Neville," he addressed them crisply, professionally, "I have carried out a thorough examination of both children and the results are unequivical. From what I understand with regard to the high level of police confidence in this matter, I must confess, I am left feeling somewhat perplexed."

He raised a hand to stave off any questions from Pennock at this point.

"Perplexed but relieved. The protocols for establishing whether sexual penetration/rape have taken place are clear both for males and females, so I'll come straight to the point. I have liaised with my attendant colleague and we agree that both children are "virgo intacta" which, in lay-man's terms, is to say that neither child has been physically sexually penetrated, that their virginity is indeed still in tact. I say 'physically penetrated' deliberately because, as you can both probably appreciate, sexual abuse may take other forms which may not involve actual penetration. That, of course is out of my remit to establish, although I understand that both children have recently been assessed by the RASA police unit as well as a specialist psychiatrist. Of course my report will be more detailed, but I thought you would both be anxious to hear my preliminary results. Mrs Neville, I know you must be feeling incredibly relieved at the news. Have either of you got any questions?"

Both Pennock and Nat looked totally shell-shocked, incapable of absorbing what had just been said to them. Slowly Nat began to come to her senses. She shook her head in confusion and disbelief.

"Are you telling me, that my husband is absolutely innocent of everything he's been accused of?"

Dr. Donaldson answered, acutely embarrassed.

"It would seem so ... I must reiterate however that I am referring solely to my findings today. The police investigators appeared to be confident they had cast iron evidence, but that premise would now appear to be flawed."

"So, my husband was innocent all along - he told us he was, but nobody would listen."

She stared hard at Pennock who interjected, mirroring Nat's disbelief.

"Dr. Donaldson, are you absolutely certain? Could there be some mistake?"

Dr. Donaldson was not offended, it was a question he was frequently asked by traumatized relatives. However he had never been asked such a thing when being the bearer of good news.

"Absolutely certain. There is no mistake. This is one of the reasons we have a second doctor present during the procedure - to verify and agree the findings of the lead surgeon and to ensure there is no ambiguity or element of doubt with those findings. My full report will be with you within the week.

So, if you have no further questions, I'll leave you both now to discuss the findings. Good day to you."

The two sat in stunned silence. Eventually Pennock turned to Nat.

"I'm so sorry," was all he said.

"I'm sorry to ... You wove me such a compelling case against my husband - you had me utterly convinced. He begged me to have faith in him, but I chose to believe he was actually capable of those things. My God, what kind of monster am I that could think he would do such a thing?"

"You're not a monster - you're a mother protecting your children in the only way you know how. Don't be too hard on yourself. I was 100% sure he was guilty too. Mrs Neville, something is very wrong here and I need to get to the bottom of it."

Gently he placed his hand on her shoulder. "Nat, I have to go now but I'll be in touch shortly. Will you be ok?"

She reassured him that she would be fine and he departed, leaving her to inform Ann of the terrible news ... News that the man she had taken a restraining order against, who had allegedly been the one to have destroyed her family and their marriage, the man she so readily believed was guilty, was in fact, completely innocent - an innocence he had shouted out over and over, but which she, like everyone else, had refused to listen to. She had thought today would have brought some sinister resolution to the whole affair, but instead it had thrown up more questions than answers.

iii.

It had to be said that Charles Kingsley was almost as taken aback as the wife of his client had been when he was apprised of the news the following day. He too, he had to admit, had been rather swift in reaching the same conclusion that his client was almost certainly guilty and had already begun preparing how to mitigate the situation to Alistair's (and his own) advantage and still come out at the end of the trial with his reputation in tact.

The relief he felt realizing that the game was back on was tremendous - and yes, he had to confess, the buzz and anticipation of a battle to be fought and won revitalized him as his combative legal adrenalin began to flow once more. It never ceased to amaze him how quickly the scales of the justice system could tip in favour for or against a defendant and how now, suddenly they had fortuitously tipped in their favour. This was a lesson he should have remembered and was to be learnt here - never say die, there is always room to manoeuvre if you are an excellent advocate such as himself. He began to consider options - first to get the charges dropped, then to bring an action for wrongful arrest, defamation of character, loss of employment, and anything else he could come up with along the way. He was due to meet with his client in an hour at the London Road police station, so he had better be well prepared.

That afternoon Alistair had been shown a courtesy that had been glaringly absent on his previous visits to the police station. He had been provided with tea and biscuits as he awaited the arrival of his brief. Nat had earlier contacted him with the news that the examination had conclusively proved that the children had not been molested, he was in the clear. Why he should feel such a sense of relief now confounded him - he knew that he had never, ever laid a hand on his children in that way. Could it be that what he subconsciously dreaded was, perhaps, that someone else may have done and that he was the one being blamed for it? But no, the children were officially fine. Nat said they had coped well with it and she thought there would be no lasting ill effects. The conversation had been terse and brief, laden with guilt and remorse, but God willing, he thought, they might be able to resolve and find forgiveness in the future.

For now though, he felt nothing but anger - anger that he had been falsely accused, anger that he had lost everything that had ever been important to him - wife, family, friends, job. And overwhelmingly, anger that he had been so impotent, unable to do anything to defend himself against his accusers nor been able to protect his children. He tried to remain calm and in control as he waited for Charles, focusing on planning the next steps. First, he presumed, the charges would be dismissed against him then he would be released - a free and innocent man. After that, he would pursue a remorseless case against the police for the destruction of his life and everything he held dear. Charles would know how to go about that, he was sure.

Charles Kingsley arrived at what he deemed to be a fashionable fifteen minutes late for the appointment at the police station - his aim being to assert his position of strength and exert intimidation. He had no intention of letting them off the hook, he wanted it to be quite clear that there would be serious repercussions to his client's wrongful arrest. Therefore, he was exceedingly miffed to discover that the police were not already waiting anxiously for him in the interview room. The impact of his grand entrance was seriously diminished. Recovering quickly, always intent on portraying himself as the consummate professional, he decided that being productive and being seen to be productive was the best use of the extra time with his client before they arrived.

Pennock and Parnell were playing the same game - there was no way they would let Kingsley wrong-foot them. It was true, neither man was relishing the prospect of eating humble pie, but they needed to maintain the upper hand, so they had decided to leave them and let them stew for a good long while.

Earlier that day, Parnell had told Pennock that he had something on his mind that he wanted to share with his boss.

"Listen Gov, we both know something's off with this investigation. Ok we have to accept that the kids weren't interfered with but that doesn't let Neville off the hook as far as I'm concerned."

"So what are you thinking, Harry?"

"Well, clearly there is a case to answer - the images prove that. But in hindsight, there was no conclusive evidence to show Neville actually physically doing anything, only visual and that was basically innuendo and supposition. We've both had enough experience to know when something's going on, and there is something going on here, I'm sure of it. Problem is, what I now think is … that it all hadn't happened quite yet. What I think is that we were a bit too quick off the mark."

Pennock was catching on fast.

"Yes, you could be on to something … you think he could have been grooming them. He'd set up the cameras, started taking photos, preparing them … But then, the cars got broken in to, stuff was nicked and we got involved before he could carry out his intentions. Unlucky for him but lucky for the kids."

"Exactly and not only that, but Forbes mightn't be so innocent as we gave him credit for. It looks to me like it would take more than one person to stage such an elaborate scheme."

"You may well be right, but let's not get ahead of ourselves - we could be stretching the bounds of credibility a bit far there - but it is possible, there could be someone else involved as well - we'll keep all the options open. At least we can go to Worth now with more than a *sorry, we made an honest mistake* sob story as our excuse - we need to keep this case alive and get a conviction, for the sake of those children."

Entering the interview room some time later they were instantly greeted with an angry tirade from Charles Kingsley.

"How dare you keep us waiting for over an hour! I am a very busy man and my client has been sequestered here for far too long already without good cause. Right gentlemen, you called this meeting, let's get on with it. I demand you ..."

"Hold it right there Mr. Kingsley. There will be no one making any demands."

Charles snapped his mouth shut in surprise.

"We'll let you know what is going to happen now," said Parnell.

Pennock took up the thread.

"I imagine you were going to ask if the charges were going to be dropped against your client, in the light of the new evidence. I regret to inform you that is not going to happen - this is still a live and on-going case and after consulting with the Chief Superintendent, we have firm grounds to believe that a crime has been or imminently would have been committed by Dr. Neville. We shall not be revoking the charges at this time, his bail conditions will remain in place while we continue to pursue fresh leads in the matter. Any questions?"

"That's outrageous. What fresh leads? That's a load of bollocks - you're just trying to save face, there are no new leads. I insist you withdraw the charges against my client immediately."

"Out of the question, Mr Kingsley. We'll be in touch soon to re-interview Dr. Neville. Now, if there's nothing else, you may go."

Charles was more taken aback than he let on. They were being unusually forceful - could they actually have some new leads? No…?? He didn't think so, it was almost certainly a double bluff. He would have the last word.

"Fine we're leaving, but you'll be hearing from my chambers very soon. You can't expect to get away with treating innocent members of the public like convicted felons and get away with it with impunity. Good day gentlemen."

iv.

"Phew, that went about as well as could be expected Gov, I was waiting for a right ear bashing from Kingsley. You almost had me fooled about the new leads as well."

"Well we've got to develop some new leads asap, or this case will be going even more to the dogs. Right, we'll carry on looking into the Neville/Forbes line of enquiry first of all. You get back on to forensics and get them to have a more detailed look at those images - tell them to look for anything suspicious or out of place. Tell them to do their bloody jobs and damned-well find the evidence. Same thing for the electronic devices - we need to know exactly whose finger-prints are on them - whose should be there and whose shouldn't, and that goes for those hidden cameras as well. Those forensic guys are quick but maybe they're not as thorough as they ought to be."

"In all honesty Gov, I think we're just as much to blame as they are about that." said Parnell, pained by the admission. "We'd found our villain and thought we had him banged to rights because the facts clearly spoke for themselves. Or so it seemed. So, we didn't bother looking any further. A rookie's basic mistake Gov, I'm embarrassed to say."

"You're not wrong, Harry." agreed his boss, ashamed as well, "But we can salvage this, I know we can. We've still got the Chief Super on board, so this is what we're going to do - we're going to have to go back to square one and review every step of this investigation so far and see what we've over-looked or ignored. Look at all the interviews again and go over the evidence with a fine-tooth comb."

"There's one line of enquiry, Gov, we've totally ignored ..."

"Yeah, I know what you're going to say, and I'd be the first to admit it's true ... That Neville has always maintained it wasn't him, and we didn't want to know about it. Well, we're going to have to look into it now. Whilst you're looking into the forensics, I'll start delving into that possibility, hopefully put it to bed once and for all. I just hope to God forensics come back with something useful to work with or we'll have wasted all these weeks for nothing."

14

Several days later, after hours of pains-taking cross referencing and examination of the evidence, Parnell was ready to throw himself in to revisiting all the forensics. He now had a clearer idea of where he wanted this investigation to go. He had identified various potential slip-ups in the collation of the evidence which may or may not be damaging to the case. He had a lot of questions and a list of things that needed answering.

Meanwhile, Pennock was going to reinterview all the original suspects. He had decided to take a more softly-softly approach this time. He would interview them all at home and would be accompanied by a female officer - it couldn't do any harm to have a fresh perspective from an impartial colleague. He had just the person in mind - D.S Sandy Parker was well qualified as a psychologist and was a fine investigator as well. She was already familiar with the investigation and would need very little bringing up to speed.

So, instead of subjecting them to an interrogation as though they were still suspects (which of course they were), he wanted to cajole them into offering up as much information as possible by drawing them in to, making them part of, and helping with, the investigation - in effect induce them to discover and reveal the evidence for him. He arranged to attend at the Forbes' home address first. They would be at home later that evening after a day's work and he would interview them both at the same time.

Their reception at the Forbes' was cool. Unsurprisingly their solicitor was also present. Pennock apologized sincerely for having to return for a second time, but as Mrs Forbes no doubt had informed her husband, there were new circumstances to be considered and he was sure they were as anxious as himself to get things sorted out. He introduced his D.S and told them she would be taking notes and recording the interview under caution.

"Now then Dr.Forbes. I'm going to ask you first, what do you make of all of this?"

"What d'you mean, *'make of all this'*? For crying out loud - it's patently obvious that Alistair's been falsely accused and there's not a shred of evidence against him."

"Quite so. But what about the images Dr. Forbes, how do you explain them? You saw them for yourself."

"I can't explain the photos ... I've got no idea how they got there but there's one thing I do know - there's no way Alistair would be involved in anything like that. Hell would freeze over first. We've been close friends for years and he's like a brother to me. He keeps saying he's being set up and I think he might be right."

"Yes, that's something we're now looking into. But, let's start with yourself, Dr Forbes. Obviously you have unwittingly become embroiled in all of this as well, due to your, to use your own words, *'close'* friendship with Dr. Neville. Is there anyone that you can think of that might have a beef against you, some kind of gripe or sleight you may not have been aware of?"

"No, I don't think so. I've been thinking about this a lot ever since Alistair suggested the possibility. Of course, when you work in a big hospital, you come in to contact with a huge number of people - patients, their families, colleagues. It's always possible I might have offended someone without realizing it, but if I have, I don't know who it could be. I imagine the same would go for Alistair."

"Well, we'll let Dr. Neville speak for himself regarding that one. What about yourself, Mrs Forbes?"

"Well, just about the same as my husband. I've tried to think of anyone who might be holding a grudge. As you know, I work in a large secondary school where there's always loads of internal politics and jockeying going on with your fellow teachers. Then there's the parents - they're a nightmare at the best of times, not to mention the students themselves. But like my husband says, I can't think of a specific incident or anyone particular who might have it in for us."

"Does the same apply with the children? Have you had any run-ins with other parents over grades or at sports day or such-like? Anything out of the ordinary?"

"No, there's really nothing I can think of. I'm sorry."

"Don't be sorry Mrs Forbes, it's a process of elimination of possibilities. O.k, I think that will be all for the time being unless you or your solicitor have any further questions? No? Good. But can I please ask you both, if anything occurs to you, anything at all, no matter how unimportant it may seem, please get in touch right away. You've got my direct line. Thanks for your time Dr, Mrs Forbes, we'll see ourselves out. Good night."

Not terribly productive the D.S had to agree with her boss. Their brief hadn't uttered a word and they had both seemed honest and open, willing to assist, but then they hadn't really expected much from those two. Tomorrow's interview with the Neville's, he hoped, would produce better results. It'd be interesting getting them both in the same room together if what Harry had said about their recent altercations were true - see if their stories tallied up, see if they still supported each other. He and D.S Parker would be meeting them at the home of Mr and Mrs Neville senior the next day.

ii.

The following evening, Sandy Parker accompanied Richard Pennock to the Neville's house, where they were greeted by a worried and distressed Mr. Neville senior. He quickly informed them of what had happened to his wife due to the intolerable amount of stress she had suffered and how he wanted to minimize any further anxiety. Pennock said he was sorry that his wife had been so unwell and promised to be as brief as possible, that he would only need to speak to Alistair and Nat and if he and his wife would be kind enough to wait in the lounge they would be as quick as they could.

Prior to their arrival at the house, Pennock had asked his D.S to take close notice of the two interviewees - observe their body language, responses, eye-contact etc ... All the usual psychological markers which he knew the D.S was specially trained to interpret, and which she actually didn't need reminding about. However, upon entering the kitchen where the couple was waiting it didn't take an expert to workout what the state of play was between the two of them. Their body-language said it all. They were sitting stiffly side by side but not close, attempting to present a united front but failing. They were both clearly on edge and uncomfortable. The tension in the air was tangible. By comparison, a relaxed Charles Kingsley was seated on the other side of the table.

"Thank you for agreeing to see us." began Pennock. "Just to remind you that you are both still under caution and, Dr Neville your bail conditions are still in effect. As you are aware by now, both the psychiatric and medical examinations proved negative ..."

"Of course they bloody proved negative," snarled Alistair, "because there was nothing wrong with the children in the first place."

"Be that as it may, sir. We have, however, still got several lines of enquiry to pursue and, as I told you yesterday, until I'm satisfied that those have been exhausted, this investigation will continue. So, one of those lines of enquiry is to thoroughly look into your claims. Now then, Dr Neville - in a previous interview, you put forward the theory that this whole affair could be a set up to discredit and ruin you. Have you had any more thoughts about who the perpertrator might be? If I'm not mistaken, you said as far as you were aware, you had no enemies nor that there was anybody with anything against you. Have you had time to revise what you stated or if you've got any idea who could possibly be trying to destroy you?"

Alistair was wretched. "I've been wracking my brains, but I honestly can't think of anyone. Of course at the hospital, there's the usual run-ins with people, sometimes with work-mates or patients or administration but it's always professional never personal."

"Could you give us an example, Dr. Neville?" said D.S Parker.

"Well ... as an example and maybe it's a bit of a weak instance really - but sometimes, if you're sharp with a theatre nurse for being too slow or clumsy, it can cause a bit of an atmosphere, but that's about the extent of it and I always make a policy of apologizing if I've been a little harsh in the heat of the moment. When the team is under pressure in the operating theatre, it's common to be a little snappy but it would never be enough to cause anyone to have a vendetta against me."

"Really? So, Dr Neville, are you describing an actual event rather than a hypothetical one?" Sandy asked.

"Is this really relevant, little spats in the operating theatre?" interrupted Kingsley, keen to assert his authority.

"It most certainly could be." replied Pennock tersely. "What might seem to be *'little spats'*, as you so eloquently put it, to you or I, could be a big deal to someone else who might perceive it as a criticism of their professional ability. So, Dr. Neville?"

95

"Well, yes. That does happen occasionally."

"In that case, we'll need the names of any members of staff you may have had an altercation with, so that we can eliminate them from our enquiries. O.k?"

Alistair told them he agreed with Charles that it was stretching things a bit to label it *'an altercation'*, but gave them the names of a couple of the theatre nurses.

"And now could you tell us about any other incidents?"

"Well not really, just the usual bust-ups with the board of directors when we try to secure more funding and they're trying to cut it ... Things like that. But like I said they're professional disagreements. It's just the run of the mill type of friction that happens at work."

"Is there anybody specific you could say you've upset, annoyed or offended?"

Alistair thought for a moment but couldn't put a name to anyone.

"Thank you Dr. Neville. So to sum up, apart from the usual aggro at work, there's nothing and no one, other than the names you've given us, that stands out particularly. Is that about right?"

"Yes, as I say I can't think of any one who might be holding a grudge against me."

"Yet you insist someone has," noted Pennock.

Charles interjected then to point out that his client had always maintained his innocence and the fact that he couldn't name that person was irrelevant - someone was framing him for reasons unknown.

He added.

"Inspector, in the light of the medical results which firmly exonerate Dr. Neville, should you not be investigating his claims more intensively? Also, is it not now universally accepted that Dr. Neville never had the technical expertise to have mounted those hidden cameras, nor has there been any evidence, as far as we are aware, that his devices received images from those cameras?"

Pennock was not about to concede that Kingsley was correct.

"If you recall, Mr. Kingsley. I mentioned that we are pursuing fresh leads. I am not at liberty to disclose those details, but rest assured, every line of enquiry is being thoroughly investigated."

Before Kingsley could continue, he turned to Nat.

"So, Mrs Neville, I'd like to ask you the same question. Do you know of anyone who might have a serious problem with your husband - enough to try to ruin him?"

"Just like Alistair, I've been trying to think of who it could be. Alistair's a decent man, Inspector, he hasn't got any enemies. I don't know of anyone or why anyone would do this."

"O.k. So, can you tell us about where you work - any problems there?"

The thought of work brought a smile to Nat's face.

"No, just the opposite - work's great. I've got a brilliant and loyal team - we all get on really well. In fact we were all at a charity function together just before all of this happened, along with the Forbes and Alistair and we had a wonderful evening. The company's doing very well. I've been with them for a long time and I think I've got a strong chance of promotion. I love my job. No it's all good."

"So work's fine. Nobody you've had to reprimand or sack, no internal bickering or in-house fighting?"

"Not that I'm aware of and we're quite a close knit team. No, they're a good crowd and we work well together."

"What about at home, maybe socially or concerning the children? Any trouble with the neighbours, other parents, friends?" questioned Pennock.

"No, I don't think so. We've had a bit of a falling out with the Forbes but that's because of all that's been going on recently. But other than that, everything's ok. No arguments with neighbours or anyone else for that matter. I genuinely have absolutely no idea who might be doing this to us ... to Alistair." she amended.

"Well, thank you both for your time. That will be all for now. Has anybody got any questions? Mr Kingsley? No? Fine then. However, what I want you both to do is to think carefully about what we've talked about this evening ... Is there someone out there who has it in for Dr. Neville, who is it and why? You've got my number, if anything occurs to you, anything at all, however insignificant you think it might be, please phone me at once. Understood?"

They both did and Pennock said he would remain in touch.

iii.

Parnell joined them at the debrief the following morning. He was curious to know if anything new had been uncovered, and they wanted to know if he had any update on the forensics. The three of them sat down and began with the forensics. Parnell informed them that he had been warned that such minute attention to detail could take some time, so essentially he had nothing fresh to offer them as yet, except that the lads had got the message loud and clear and would pull out all the stops to uncover something. They were a bit dejected with his report, but like he said, no news wasn't necessarily bad news. But the whole enquiry seemed to have stalled, in fact, had come to a grinding halt. What they really needed was something fresh to kick-start the impetus again.

They then moved on to the interviews. Both Pennock and Parker agreed that there was nothing new from the Forbes household. No enemies, no grievances, so nothing to get their teeth into - once again, a dead end. Sandy reported that she had to admit the Nevilles seemed quite sincere too. She thought that the names Alistair had furnished them with, whilst being possible new lines of enquiry for them, didn't smack of him desperately trying to pin the blame squarely in someone else's court or diverting the interest away from himself. She informed Parnell that the information had apparently needed to be prised out of him during the re-interview. She concluded, either it was genuine reluctance or masterful misdirection.

"Well, at least we've got something to be looking into in the meantime, meagre as it is. Harry while things are quiet, you and Sandy take the first one, and I'll take the other one."

"Should we bring them into the station for questioning, Gov ?" asked Sandy.

"Definitely. We need to get this thing wrapped up soon or the Chief Super will be coming down on us like a ton of bricks. Haul them in asap and squeeze out every bit of info we can."

It was true that the Chief Super was getting a bit angsty, but only because he was getting an ear-bashing himself from the higher echelons. They wanted a result and they wanted it now. But nobody was going to bully Chief Superintendent Stan Worth into doing anything until he was good and ready, and he certainly wasn't ready to pull the plug on his team's investigation just yet. Keeping to the side-lines Worth had been keeping a close eye on this investigation and in his gut he felt that his officers were on the right track, and the leads they had been following were solid, even though, he had to admit, they had hit some dead ends. He couldn't give them free reign for ever but he trusted them, they were all good, thorough detectives.

He had risen through the ranks himself over a twenty five year long career. In fact, he and Harry Parnell were peers - whilst not close, their paths had crossed occasionally and he knew Harry was old school - just like himself. Although Stan Worth had soon realized that life on the street wasn't for him and had actively sought a future in management, he still believed in the tenets of good old fashioned policing and rued the day the local bobby disappeared off the beat. He believed that had been the beginning of the end for community relations - both the police force and the public had since become faceless individuals, seemingly cold and uncaring.

He suspected Harry felt the same way and had been pressing him for years to take the sergeant's exams. He was delighted when Harry finally conceded and made sure he was posted to the London Road nick. Stan wanted not only good officers but good men and women around him.

iv.

The next day, theatre nurse, Kate Mulgrew, presented herself as summoned, at the London Road police station where she was shown into an interview room and greeted by Parnell and Parker and sat uncomfortably down. A plain, well-built, competent woman of perhaps 35, who one would easily guess was, and indeed looked every inch of being, a no nonsense nurse. She was anxious at being called to interview - never having had any personal reason to interact with the police before - but remained composed and attentive.

"Thank you for coming today," said Sandy pleasantly, taking the lead. "We've got a few questions relating to an on-going investigation we're undertaking at the moment which involves a paediatric surgeon by the name of Alistair Neville."

"Yes, I know Dr. Neville."

"Good. Then you probably know what this is in relation to. To begin with, Ms Mulgrew, can you describe your relationship with him, for us?" asked Sandy.

"Relationship? I'm not exactly sure what you mean by that, but I haven't got any relationship with Dr. Neville, well ... except in a professional capacity of course."

"I see. So, you're saying you don't socialize with Dr. Neville or his family? I don't know - maybe children at the same schools, church or clubs, something like that."

"No, not at all. I don't even have any idea where they live and I've never met his wife or children. I don't move in their circles - hoi poloi doctors and consultants tend to stick together. I'm not interested in social or professional climbing. I go to work, do my job and, at the end of the day, go home to my husband and family. If we go out, it's generally with neighbours or friends or our own relatives - you know - brothers and sisters and their families."

"Ok, thanks. Moving on - how would you characterize Dr. Neville? What sort of man is he like to work for?"

Kate Mulgrew pulled a bit of a face at the question and took her time replying. It was clear she was trying to phrase her response fairly.

"Well, he's a stickler for detail. Everything's got to be just right. He's a brilliant surgeon though, totally professional and demands the same from his team. If a procedure is particularly complicated, he can sometimes get a bit sharp especially if people are distracted or don't respond fast enough. He insists on 100% effort and, quite often, has banned people from theatre if he doesn't think they're giving it their best."

"Interesting. Have you ever been on the receiving end?" Sandy pressed.

"Oh yes, more than once or twice." Kate had to confess. "I've never actually been chucked out though and I'm pretty sure I've got the measure of him by now. Of course, I've been there a long time. The secret is to always be one step ahead of him, anticipate his every need and know what's coming next. He can have a vicious tongue and be quite nasty but it's like water off a duck's back to me now. I know I'm good at my job so I don't let it get to me like some of the others do."

"So would you say you've got an axe to grind against Dr. Neville and his unpleasant methods?" continued Sandy.

"I don't think so. Not any more. As I say I've got over taking offence at him. I realize he's not getting at me specifically."

Parnell intervened. "Ms Mulgrew, is there anything that might lead you to believe that Dr. Neville is guilty of the charges against him?"

This time, Kate didn't hesitate to answer.

"Categorically not. It's definitely some kind of wicked smear campaign. I'll admit I don't know him very well personally, we're not friends or anything, but I honestly cannot believe he would be capable of it. We've been working together for a number of years now. I just haven't seen any evidence that he might be. He's an incredibly dedicated doctor - he specializes in paediatrics for God's sake!"

"Yes, indeed he does," said Parnell wryly. "Ok, thanks for your time, Ms Mulgrew. That will be all for now. If we have any further questions we'll be in touch. But if you have any thoughts, please don't hesitate to contact us."

After Kate Mulgrew had left, Parnell and Sandy discussed their gut reactions. They both had to agree that the woman obviously didn't appear to have any gripe at all against Neville. She didn't much like him, that was clear, but still continued to work with him nevertheless. Other than the fact it helped give a more complete picture of Neville - it was like adding a few more pieces of a jig-saw puzzle, as Sandy compared it to - it seemed they'd reached another dead end with this one. It would make for another short report. Hopefully D.I Pennock would have more joy than they'd had.

They decided to break off from their report writing and watch the Gov's interview from the observation room. Theatre nurse David Wickes arrived promptly an hour later and was respectfully shown in by P.C Brown. First impressions were that Wickes, aged somewhere in his mid thirties, was a lean, athletic looking man, smartly but casually dressed, seemingly full of nervous energy. He movements were quick but controlled as he entered the room. With a swift glance, he took in his surroundings, noted the two-way mirror, and sat down apparently relaxed and unperturbed.

"Interesting," commented Parnell.

He was glad they'd taken the trouble to arrive before-hand and gain this potentially valuable first impression. Then to Sandy,

"Looks like he's familiar with the inside of a nick and an interview room. Could be promising. You ok to stay out here? I'm going to ask the gov if I can sit in on this one. No wait a minute, actually you should get on to the PNC and see what you can find out about this bloke's criminal record and anything else you can. I've got a gut feeling about this one."

Sandy was off before he'd finished the sentence, saying she'd be back as quick as she could.

D.I Pennock was all business and raring to get on with the interview after Parnell had apprised him of their initial observation of the male nurse.

"That's great. Let's hear what he's got to say for himself then. You know the drill. Keep your eyes peeled and ears open."

Pennock began the interview by thanking Mr. Wickes for attending, assuring him they would be as brief as possible and that the interview would be taped. He was briefly disconcerted to hear Wickes confidently respond,

"Frankly, I was beginning to wonder if you were ever going to get around to interviewing me."

Pennock quickly recovered and asked.

"And why would that be, sir? I haven't even told you what this is in connection with."

"Oh, come on, Inspector. We both know this is about saint Alistair Neville, our lord and master."

"Yes, indeed it is," Pennock confirmed, "but it's a bit odd you'd refer to him in that way. Care to explain why you call him *'Our lord and master?'* Am I detecting a note of irreverence in your tone, Mr. Wickes?"

"Ah, nothing gets past your policing skills, eh Inspector?"

Pennock didn't rise to the bait, and certainly wouldn't allow Wickes to hijack control of the interview.

"No, you're right, absolutely nothing gets past me, Mr. Wickes. Now, can we please begin? Could you tell us in what capacity you and Dr. Neville are connected?"

"I am a theatre nurse in the paediatric department and Dr. Neville is a paediatric surgeon."

"Thank you. And how long have you worked together?"

"Well, he isn't the only surgeon in paediatrics that I work with of course, or any of us for that matter, but possibly eighteen months or so."

"And how would you say you get on with Dr. Neville?"

"What, professionally?"

"Yes. First tell us about professionally and then socially," replied Pennock.

"Well, I'd rather start with socially as that is quickly dealt with."

"Go ahead ." *'You manipulating smarmy bastard.'* Pennock silently swore.

"Quickly dealt with because there is zero social relationship between us."

"Are you sure? So you have never met Dr Neville outside of work on any occasion?"

"Correct," came the curt reply.

"Thank you. Now, do you know Mrs. Neville or the children perhaps?"

"No, I'm pretty certain I've never met his wife nor the children ... unless, of course they go to the same school as mine, and we may have crossed paths at some time or another. What school do they go to?"

Ignoring the question, Pennock asked.

"Perhaps you could tell us where your children go and then where your wife works?"

The name he mentioned wasn't the same as the Neville children's school and was some distance away from it in any case. His wife, it seemed, was a part-time nurse and they had lived for a number of years in the same village as the local school where their children attended.

"So, if we can just recap for the record. Mr Wickes, you claim that you have no personal connection whatsoever to Dr. Neville or his family. Is that correct?"

"As far as I'm aware, it is," was the reply.

"Very well. Let's move on. Can you tell us about your professional relationship with Dr. Neville, please?"

It was evident to both officers that Wickes was struggling to contain his emotions. He took a deep breath and began;

"When you say *'professional'*, I take it you are referring to the operating theatre, where, I can assure you, there is only one professional and that is Dr. Neville himself, or so he constantly informs us. The rest of us are *'imbeciles'* and mere minions to attend to his every beck and call and massage his massive ego. Hence the moniker we all use *'our lord and master.'* His will is our command."

"I see," said Pennock. "Now you've mentioned about his attitude to the staff in general, but what about towards yourself specifically?"

"Well, other than having to deal with his usual obnoxious self, I tend to get away relatively lightly."

"And why do you think that is?" asked Parnell.

"That's obvious. The man's a bully and I hate bullies. The women nurses are easy targets. He'd never challenge me directly, he wouldn't have the balls for it because he knows I'd give him it right back. So he settles for the snidey comments and subtle put downs, things he apologizes for afterwards, saying it was the pressure of the procedure and so on, blah, blah, blah. But the other surgeons don't behave like that, and they operate under difficult conditions as well. The man's a psycho."

"So why do you continue to work for him?" asked Parnell.

"Various reasons really. Like I said, there are other surgeons that I sometimes work with as well, but generally I stay with Neville because, despite being totally obnoxious, he really is a fine surgeon, and the others always say it's a lot easier when I'm around, and they're a good lot. He's not so difficult or offensive to them when I'm there and the whole atmosphere tends to be lighter and friendlier."

Pennock took up the thread.

"You know what Dr. Neville has been charged with, I presume."

Wickes confirmed he did with a nod of his head.

"For the benefit of the tape, Mr. Wickes has nodded his head. Do you think he's guilty?"

In a flash, Wickes extinguished a flicker of pure vindictiveness and took his time answering.

"Well, I have to be scrupulously fair here. As I've already told you, I don't know Dr. Neville on a personal basis, so I can't comment on his private life. Having said that, I've heard the rumours going round the hospital and what people are saying about him - whether there's any truth to it ... I wouldn't like to say. Professionally, he's said to be a genius - a truly talented surgeon - which is one of the reasons why so many of us stick with him. But to answer your question, if the burden of proof was on *'the balance of probabilities'*, that would be one thing, but *'beyond reasonable doubt'*... well I'd have to let a jury decide."

"So, you're not prepared to put your neck on the line?"

Wickes considered his response.

"No, I don't think so. I know what I privately believe, but that's not the same as having all the evidence to make a decision now, is it?"

"Ok, thank you." said Pennock throwing Parnell a warning glance to take note. "Now then. There has also been some suggestion that Dr. Neville could have been framed for all of this, somebody with a vendetta against him. Someone who's gone to elaborate lengths to bring him into disrepute, destroy his family and career. What d'you think of that possibility, Mr Wickes?"

"Interesting theory," he conceded, *"'elaborate lengths'*, it could be possible, I suppose, but I don't really buy it. Of course, you may know something that I don't and ... I presume you're not going to tell me what that is ... so I'd have to give you the same answer as before - leave it to the jury to decide based on the evidence."

At that moment the door opened and D.S Parker entered. She whispered a few words to her boss and withdrew.

Pennock continued as though there had been no interruption.

"Mr. Wickes, thank you for coming in today, I think we've covered about everything. Your input has been very useful, possibly filled in a few of the blanks. However, it may very well be that we'll have to ask you to attend again and make a formal statement under caution. Would that be ok? Excellent. Oh, and it may be a good idea to bring your solicitor along with you. If you don't have one, then a duty solicitor can be provided. Do you understand?"

"But why would I need a solicitor if I'm only making a statement?" Wickes asked, disconcerted.

"Just normal procedure, Mr. Wickes. As you know, this is a very serious and complex case, and your evidence could prove crucial. We've got to dot the i's and cross the t's, always got to be thorough to get a conviction. Nothing for you to be worried about, I'm sure."

David Wickes looked less than happy as he departed the police station, but had agreed he would attend when summoned, pleased especially if he could help in some small way to put Neville away.

The two men were back in the D.I's office waiting for Parker.

"Well I think Wickes's position was quite clear, don't you Harry?"

"Whether he's actually involved in the whole thing or not, we don't know yet. But he's implied Neville's as guilty as hell without coming straight out with it."

"Exactly. Hey, that was perfect timing, Sandy," said Pennock, "we were just about going to have to wrap it up with Wickes anyway. So what've you found out?"

"Sorry it took so long, Gov. It was a bit more complicated than I thought. It seems that Wickes hasn't got a criminal record."

"That's impossible. You've got to be joking," said Parnell. "That bloke knew his way round a nick like an old hand. I'd stake my reputation on it, Gov. Everything about him screamed ex-con."

Sandy was enjoying drip feeding them the info, taking her time.

"Well he has had a couple of speeding offences and has recently completed a speed awareness course. He currently has 3 points on his licence."

"Ha ha,very amusing, Sergeant. Now get on with it," urged her boss.

"Yessir. Actually, it's true. Wickes hasn't got any criminal record ... as an adult, that is. I agree with Harry, that bloke has been round the block a few times, so I decided to have a look back through his juvenile records. Of course that's easier said than done these days and especially when the record has been expunged."

"Expunged?" exclaimed Parnell. "Why?"

Sandy continued, "Well it seems that more than twenty years have elapsed and as soon as that was up, Wickes made an application to the court claiming his prior convictions would jeopardize a job application he was making should that information come to light."

"Makes sense. I did wonder how he could have come to be working as a nurse on a children's ward if he had a record," Parnell conceded.

"Exactly, and the court agreed with him. I haven't been able to access his juvenile file yet, it's probably going to take a warrant to get it unsealed. The Chief Super will have to make the application, I suppose - it'll require someone really senior."

"Damn, that's going to take time. And if we can access it, will it be of any use?" cursed Pennock.

"Well there's nothing we can do but wait and see. I'll get on to it right away, Gov," said Parnell

"Hold your horses gentlemen, that's not the end of my tale. It seems that young master Wickes had quite a turbulent childhood." Stopping them in their tracks, she passed the two men a couple of photo-copied pages, then resumed her presentation.

"This info is from Social Services, just a summary, so probably incomplete and full of holes. It seems Wickes started getting into bother around the age of twelve. What that bother was, obviously we don't know yet, we'll have to wait to find out. But it would appear to be the usual story - family break up, allegations of child abuse, drink, poverty etc etc. So, the children get taken into care. Wickes gets fostered several times but, as you can see, he proves to be too much of a hand-full and gets returned every time. So, he sees out his time in an orphanage till he gets kicked out at sixteen and told to make his own way in the world. His brother, Andrew, is luckier. He's a good few years younger and the family he's fostered out to decide to adopt him. He's not a perfect kid - probably scarred by his childhood I'd imagine - but the family stand by him to adulthood."

Pennock speculated. "The two Wickes brothers, could be an interesting combination - that is, if they stayed in touch with each other."

"Actually Sir, not two Wickes, just the one … Andrew took the surname of the family that adopted him." She referred to the notes. "It's Motson now."

"Motson?" questioned Pennock. "Where have I heard that name recently?"

"I've no idea Sir, it's not a name I recognize." said Sandy.

"But I do," from Parnell, "he's that halfwitted car-park attendant at the hospital."

"Bloody hell, you're right Harry - Andy Motson - now there's an interesting coincidence, wouldn't you say? What with them both working at the hospital and all."

15

Life at Natalie's house had settled down into an uneasy pattern. She was doing her best to maintain a routine, but nothing was the same. The house she loved so much seemed alien and cruel and even though the hidden cameras had been removed, she couldn't shake off the sensation of being watched.

The children still missed their father terribly - and so did she, if she were totally honest. An uncomfortable truce had been declared between the two of them since the outcome of the medical examination, but a reconciliation was unlikely to happen any time soon, if ever. The wounds that had been inflicted ran deep, perhaps fatally so. She could not imagine Alistair ever being capable of forgiving her for her disloyalty and lack of faith in his innocence, nor would she blame him. She had sworn him her unconditional support and had reneged at the first sign of trouble. She had always believed their marriage to be rock-solid, the envy of all their friends. How fragile it had proved to be, bursting into brittle bits at the first challenge.

She tried to take solace in her work, but that too was different. There had been a subtle shift in the dynamics of the operation, with Maria and Simon being given more authority and she side-lined to a behind the scenes administrative role. Nat didn't feel the timing was right to complain to her bosses about this apparent demotion, after all she had taken days off work, been distracted, brought shame on them. Maybe the rejigging of personnel was intentional, to give her a chance to get back to peak performance, or maybe - and this was her private fear - they were going to quietly squeeze her out. The team still worked well together with only a few minor tensions. They were a close knit unit, but it just wasn't the same anymore.

Nat's parents were being fantastically supportive, they had really come through for her. She found herself going home a lot more often than before. She knew it was partly because she didn't want to be in the house alone and partly because she needed them to tell her that everything was going to be alright. The kids too were thrilled to be seeing more of their grandparents and being totally indulged and of course, the grandparents loved having them as well. It mightn't be such a bad idea to consider relocating nearer to them after this was all over. She had to be realistic, the likelihood of a reconciliation with Alistair was remote and she really needed the support now from her mum and dad. Perhaps she could start house-hunting the next time she was down there, she thought.

To be fair, Alistair's parents were being marvellous as well. Their initial hostility towards her after Alistair's arrest, had waned. They seemed to have accepted they were all in this together and even come to accept why she had taken out the restraining order. This came after Nat had told them everything, about the secret cameras, the photos, her fears for Martin and Juliet, all of it. They had listened in shocked silence, eventually finding room in their hearts once more for both their son and daughter-in-law. Since the outcome of the examination of the children, a pressure valve seemed to have been released - finally, the outcome they had all prayed for - the son and husband could be presumed innocent.

But for Alistair life was in limbo. He was spending most of his time at his parents' these days, only bearing to go back to his digs to sleep. His mother continued to make a steady recovery and, to stave off boredom, Alistair was making himself useful around the house, doing small D.I.Y jobs that his father could no longer manage. The thing he hated most was not being able to see the children. When they were due to come round he had to make himself scarce before Nat dropped them off. Then, he and Nat would meet somewhere neutral and try to talk civilly. The gulf between them was still pretty wide, conversation was strained as they found themselves being overly polite to each other. He couldn't help still feeling bitter that she could think so badly of him, and believed the faith that had once existed was now probably permanently ruptured. However, after the other evening at the police station, Alistair seemed more hopeful that, at last, they were taking him seriously and investigating what he had been claiming all along. Please, please God they'd find the true perpetrator he fervently prayed.

ii.

The team was back in the Incident Room and the evidence board and log book were looking a lot healthier than they had done a few days before. All the proceedings to date had been entered on the computer and pictures of Wickes and Motson (both were ancient and would have to be updated) had been added, annotated and cross-referenced with all the information they currently possessed. They had discussed whether it was worth while following the second line of enquiry - the alleged set-up to incriminate Neville - and were all on board, agreeing that it needed thoroughly investigating and they probably now had some prime candidates. The frustration that they had all been feeling had been replaced with renewed vigour and enthusiasm. This new line of enquiry was the injection they needed, they'd got a few irons in the fire at last.

Andy Motson had slipped through the net alright. They hadn't even thought to interview him. Parnell had begun to access his records but decided they wouldn't call him in until they got the warrant executed to uncover his brother's past history and consider it's relevance to them both. They needed to build up the fullest possible picture about Motson in the mean time. It looked as though he had a fairly lengthy petty criminal record - petty in so much as he had never actually done any prison time - handling stolen goods (whose value had been too low to attract a custodial sentence), something about a gambling syndicate that had been broken up in the back room of a pub, a bit of class C drugs. Not a model citizen, but not a hardened criminal either. He obviously didn't have enough serious previous convictions to stop him landing a job at the hospital. The question was, had his brother assisted in his recruitment? Had he given Motson a glowing reference? Endorsed him as a suitable replacement for poor Sid? With no evidence they were related, no one would suspect a connection between the two of them. Interesting.

Pennock was back in his office when his mobile rang.

"Hello Inspector, it's Natalie Neville speaking."

"*Well, well,*" thought Pennock, "*everything's happening at once.*"

"Mrs. Neville. How are you? What can I do for you?"

"Fine thank you. I'm phoning because you said to give you a call if something occurred to me however insignificant it might seem."

"That's right, I did. Have you had any thoughts?"

" Yes, I have but … well, I feel a bit silly really even mentioning it ... And it's probably nothing, and I don't want to get anyone in trouble ..."

"Mrs Neville," said Pennock mildly, "just tell me what's on your mind and let me be the judge. Ok?"

"Yes, of course, thank you. Well it sounds a bit pathetic really when you say it out loud, but there's this chap at work and I think he's got a crush on me. He hasn't ever done anything innappropriate or anything like that, but he's a bit too touchy-feely and I always feel a bit uncomfortable around him. It's not anything I can put my finger on specifically, but it doesn't feel quite right."

"Ok," said Pennock, a little disappointed, he'd been hoping for more. "Why do you think it could be significant?"

"I don't know if it is or not, Inspector, but you did say to mention any small detail."

"Yes, I did and you were quite right to have contacted me, Mrs. Neville," Pennock agreed politely. "Now if you give me his full name, I can assure you we'll look into it straight away, and I'll get back to you. Thanks very much for the call."

A little deflated, Pennock returned to the Incident Room and had just started entering the call details into the computerized log, suspecting this would be another wild goose chase, when Harry Parnell burst through the door looking very pleased with himself.

"Good news, Gov. The forensics are in!"

Pennock was delighted and told Parnell to find Sandy and join him in his office straight away.

"Actually sir, one of their boffins is on his way in to present the results in person. Says it's a complex matter. He'll be here shortly."

"Excellent, sounds promising. We'll meet up in the conference room then when he arrives, ok?"

Finally, this was proving to be a really productive day, hopefully another turning point of the investigation.

James Church arrived less than an hour later and was shown into the conference room where the three detectives were keenly awaiting his arrival. He was a stout fellow, middle aged and bespectacled, with a slight stoop, presumably, deduced Sandy, from hunching over so many forensic objects for hours at a time. Oh yes, she always knew she'd make a great detective.

"Thank you for coming," began Pennock. "We're hoping that's because you've uncovered something significant you want to show us personally."

"Quite so," answered Church, "but before I begin, I would like to emphasize that my department fulfilled the brief we were originally tasked with, which if you remember, was to look at the mobile devices, laptops and computers and discover if they held any sinister content. Which we did, and then reported our findings back to you. Correct?"

Pennock, a little bemused, concurred that was indeed the case. Church resumed.

"Therefore my department cannot be held negligent for the revelations that have come to light as a result of the second brief, which was to uncover anything at all that may be relevant to your case. I believe you asked us 'to go over everything with a fine tooth comb'. Which we did."

Church handed out three files outlining their results. He discussed at length the electronic devices, which, in a nut shell, had proved once again to hold no further significance than they had done before. He assured them they had just about been taken to pieces in an effort to discover something, but no joy. They were clean, and were conclusively not connected to the surveillance equipment.

He then moved on to the hidden cameras which had subsequently been discovered. This was fascinating, simply fascinating, he said. Whoever had installed the spyware, had not only been meticulous in the locating of them - after all, the family had lived there for, one assumed, quite a considerable length of time without ever suspecting their presence, but had also done a superb job of covering the identity of the end user. They had tried everything, he told them, to reveal the I.P address but without any success. Their conclusion was, inevitably, that this person had a significant amount of technical knowledge, which may well be relevant when considering their list of suspects.

Eventually he came to the crux of his presentation. Slowly and with infinite detail, he drew their attention to each photographic image, covering in depth their findings. Finally, he summed up.

"The conclusion we have reached, is that these photographs have all been masterfully, digitally produced and doctored. I believe the phrase in common parlance is photo-shopped, which certainly doesn't do justice to this level of workmanship. We believe the techniques the suspect used to alter these images was most sophisticated. He or she has most convincingly added photographs taken from the family's digital albums and blended them with images drawn from the hidden cameras involving a process which would have required access to state of the art equipment to produce such painstaking work of this calibre. This, combined with the level of expertise displayed with the use of the spyware, indicates the perpertrator to be an individual of significant ability in computer manipulation. Frankly it is of no wonder the alterations were not spotted in the first instance, and my department should not be held accountable for this oversight."

Pennock sighed, he didn't blame them, he really didn't, they'd all been far too ready to believe the evidence of their own eyes from the very beginning. Like Harry had said, 'a rookie's basic mistake'. He was sighing because of all the man hours they'd wasted chasing up the wrong leads. He thanked Dr. Church, assuring him that their own shortfalls in the investigation had contributed just as much to this outcome, but that nevertheless the forensic results were invaluable and had totally altered the complexion of the case.

Before Church left, one final question was left and Pennock had to ask it for his own peace of mind.

"Dr. Church, based on your familiarity with the evidence, do you think Dr. Neville was capable of this type of sophisticated set up?"

"An excellent question, D.I Pennock. Indeed, it is a question I have been asking myself. Looking at the age and usage of Dr. Neville's machines, I suspect not. The software they contain is of the most basic variety - most young people today would consider it archaic. It certainly would not be sophisticated enough to have produced quality results like these. But these are the machines that were in everyday use, and which we know about. If Dr. Neville had access to superior software at a different location which we are, perhaps, not aware of, who is to say what could be the case? That is what you are here for detectives, to solve the mystery. However, on the balance of probabilities, I would still say he doesn't possess the necessary expertise. I hope that is of some use to you."

They all nodded that they concurred with his assessment and Church departed, leaving them in agreement that there was indeed an even greater mystery to solve.

iii.

Returning to the evidence log and the whiteboard, the three detectives minutely reviewed the case to date. It was generally agreed that Alistair Neville could probably be presumed innocent and was perhaps being framed for something he didn't do. But none of them was prepared to eliminate him totally from their enquiries, deciding to put him on the back burner for the time being. Wickes and Motson were clear front-runners now in the investigation - in fact, were the only two suspects they currently had.

That was until Pennock suddenly remembered Mrs Neville's recent call. He briefly outlined the gist of what she had said to the others and noted that their faces reflected the same scepticism he had felt during the conversation.

'Time to bolster the troops,' thought Pennock. "Listen up, you two … there's going to be a bit of a hiatus until we get the complete files on Motson and Wickes, but we've got stuff to be getting on with. We need to see what kind of life-style Wickes leads and what interaction he has with his brother, if any. And then someone's got to follow-up with an interview of this bloke Natalie Neville's being going on about."

"I'll take Wickes," said Sandy, getting in first.

"Looks like I'll take lover-boy then," said Parnell disgustedly, he hadn't been quick enough off the mark to nab the better suspect. "What d'you think, at home or at work?"

"Good question. Let's not embarrass Mrs Neville by showing up at her place of work. Harry, go this evening, arrive unannounced and catch him off guard at home. Get yourself invited in and with any luck you'll be able to have a shifty around where he lives and, maybe - if you're really lucky - find loads of hi-tech gear just lying around, get a confession from him and be home in time for dinner."

"Right Gov, in your dreams, like that's going to happen," Harry grumbled.

"What about you, Sandy? Any thoughts how you'll proceed?" asked Pennock.

"Yes, Gov. I've got a couple of snouts down at The White Hart. I'll see if I can find out what the word is on the street about Motson. He shouldn't be too difficult. Wickes, I'm not so sure about. Either of you got any ideas?"

"Ok, let's work together on Wickes. Some good old fashioned surveillance, I think. That ok with you, Sandy?"

For her part, Sandy didn't exactly look enthused, however Parnell was delighted. It looked like he'd just dodged a long stake-out.

"Let's find out his routines and associates. Build up a picture of the man. If the files prove promising we'll be getting a search warrant soon enough. Sandy, you go with Motson for the time being and I'll take Wickes."

Sandy was pleasantly surprised. Usually the newby drew the short straw, but not this time it seemed. The Gov really was a fair boss, always pulled his weight. He was generous as well, not hogging the best for himself. Harry, too, realized he probably hadn't got the rough end of the stick after all - he hated surveillance. All that hanging around in dingy places wasn't his cup of tea. So, lover-boy it was.

They would reconvene the next morning with the latest updates.

16

Before dropping in on '*lover boy*', Harry pulled up his record. He was a disappointed but not really surprised to find that he had no criminal convictions, not so much as Sandy's proverbial speeding fine. It was a bit optimistic to have hoped to discover a catalogue of stalking offences along with a long list of cyber crimes - but it would have been nice. He'd probably have to leave that revelation up to the Gov and Sandy to uncover.

The scant information that was available indicated that he lived in a decent neighbourhood but offered little else of use. For crying out loud, he thought, you didn't really need to be a police officer to find out those skimpy details. He, or anyone for that matter, could have discovered that from the census. On these types of occasions, Harry often wished that more personal information could be permanently stored on their data bases, legally available to law-enforcement officers at any time. So what if it was an invasion of your human rights - if you had nothing to hide then you had nothing to fear, wasn't that right and what they always told their suspects? Of course, he didn't really believe that, but it would make his job a hell of a lot easier if information were more readily accessible.

So, armed with nothing more than his long professional experience and an address, Harry rang the doorbell. As usual, first impressions always counted with Parnell and he was alert to the reaction his arrival would have on this individual. Would he be shocked at finding the Old Bill on his doorstep - caught unawares? Would he cast furtive glances back into the property in case there was something incriminating on show? Would he refuse entry to his home? Or would he be super cool and disarming?

The man who answered was none of those things. A fairly tall, brown-haired, medium built man, clean-shaven and smartly casual, stood before him. First impressions - he seemed fairly non descript, instantly forgettable in fact, not your typical idea of an evil, crazed stalker.

After the initial surprise of finding a policeman at his front door and having scrutinized Parnell's warrant card, Harry was warmly invited into the man's home. Parnell's reluctant initial impression was that he appeared to be both open and sincere.

"Please, have a seat. How can I help you, Officer?" Simon Bates asked.

Before answering, Harry took in his surroundings. He would be the first to admit that he wasn't exactly a connoisseur of fine living, but it looked to him like the place had been decorated by a professional designer. Minimalist but comfortable furniture was tastefully coordinated with cool and calming taupe painted walls accessorized with matching soft furnishings and lighting - the whole effect could almost be worthy of a feature in a home design magazine, thought Parnell.

"I'm here in regard to an on-going case involving a Dr. Alistair Neville. I believe you are a colleague of Mrs Neville, is that correct?"

"Yes, that's absolutely right. Are there any more developments?" he asked anxiously.

"Well, how about a nice cup of tea first and then we can discuss things?"

Harry was instantly on his feet the moment Simon disappeared into the kitchen to prepare the tea. He quickly crossed the room and risked a fast look into the bedroom, but it was in darkness. Pity. He returned to the sitting room, glancing around and continuing to observe his surroundings. A laptop was open on top of a small dining room table with a mobile beside it. Neither looked anything special nor state of the art to his untrained eye. But he reckoned his own mobile was newer than that one despite the fact that his grandkids were always ribbing him about being a technological dinosaur. Looked like this bloke was even more tech-adverse than himself. The laptop was a bog-standard gizmo that looked as though it could still just about do its job, but could probably do with being replaced as well.

The t.v, glowing quietly in the corner, however, was a different story. It looked like a brand new 65" model with all the latest apps and 4K or whatever it was called. There was a frozen image of what looked to be a nature programme - apparently he had interrupted Bates' evening viewing.

Harry could hardly believe his eyes when Bates returned with a tray laden with a tea-pot, cups, saucers, milk, sugar and biscuits.

"How do you take your tea, Officer?"

"Milk, two sugars, please."

Bates poured and passed Harry his tea offering him hob-nobs as well. Taking two, Harry asked,

"Do you live alone, Mr. Bates?"

"Yes, I do. I've been here for a couple of years and I'm very happy, it's a nice place to live."

"Mind if I have a look around, maybe use the bathroom?"

"Oooh." Simon was taken unawares. "No, not at all, help yourself. But you'll have to take me as you find me, I wasn't expecting visitors."

'That was the whole point,' thought Harry as he left the room.

The place was immaculate and, as Bates had just confirmed, exhibited no evidence of anyone else's presence. The bed was neatly made with no dirty socks or jocks on the floor. The towels were carefully folded in the bathroom, the sink and bath both gleaming. The kitchen was show-room pristine, with not even any sign of the recently made tea. Harry wondered if this pathological tidiness and cleanliness could be classified as OCD behaviour? And if so, could such an obsession be transferred and directed towards a person - someone like Natalie Neville, perhaps?

Returning to where Bates awaited, Harry commented.

"Mr. Bates, you seem to be seriously house-proud. Your place is spotless."

Bates laughed, unembarrassed.

"A strict upbringing Sergeant. My parents were sticklers for *'a place for everything and everything in its place'*. It wasn't until I bought this flat that I realized the value and expense of everything and began to appreciate how right they were all along. It's not such a bad philosophy after all."

Harry wasn't totally convinced, but one thing he was sure about was that it beat some of the horrible dives he'd had to visit in the course of his job. Plus, he wasn't often offered tea and biscuits - hob nobs at that. But, come on, he reminded himself, time to get down to business.

"So, Mr Bates, there have been some developments in our enquiries and I've got a few questions I'd like to ask you."

Simon's response did not appear to be disingenuous.

"Go ahead. If there's anything at all I can do to help."

"Mr. Bates. Simon. How would you characterize your relationship with Dr. Neville?"

Simon thought about how he would reply.

"In all honesty, until very recently, I hardly knew him. As you know, it's Natalie, his wife I work with. Obviously we speak about our families and stuff at work, and we've all met up for a drink in the pub now and again, so I suppose I have a bit of a sense of who he is, but it wasn't until the fund-raising evening that Natalie and her friend organized, that I actually got to know him a bit better."

"And what were your impressions of him?"

"He seemed like a decent enough man. He was a little stand-offish at first, seemed like a bit of a cold fish, but after a few drinks, he let his hair down - relaxed - and we all had a really good time."

"Is he the type of person you could see yourself being mates with?"

Simon thought about that one and responded dubiously,

" ... Possibly. Our paths don't seem to cross very much and Natalie's family life is private and quite separate from work. So is mine, for that matter. But he was certainly much more fun than I'd thought he'd be."

"Thank you. Now, what about Mrs. Neville?"

This time Simon's response was swift and sincere.

"Natalie? She's great. She's a good and fair boss who's built up a close team working for her. She's an excellent manager too. It's a real shame she's going through such a hard time."

"Would you say you're close to her?"

"Oh yes, I'd say we're very close. In fact we're a very close-knit group. '*All for one and one for all*' and all that. We always look out for each other's backs."

"Mr. Bates … disregarding the group dynamics for a moment … what about Mrs Neville specifically?"

Simon looked a little confused.

"I don't really understand what you're asking me, Sergeant."

"Well, I suppose what I'm really asking is if you could have romantic feelings for Natalie?"

Simon appeared totally nonplussed.

"Romantic feelings? For Natalie?… No, I don't think so … You see, Sergeant, I'm gay."

ii.

The following morning, Harry, red-faced and abashed, recounted the saga of his meeting with Simon Bates. Widely known among his workmates as a good raconteur, this time the truth more than spoke for itself - he didn't even need to embellish his tale. Both Pennock and Parker were in stitches.

"Leave your gaydar at home, did you Harry?" teased Sandy.

"So how're you going to enter that one into the evidence log?" chimed in Pennock. "Lover-boy turns out to be lovey-boy. Oooh ducky, nice one, Harry!"

"Alright, alright you two, put a sock in it," Harry responded with good humour. "I did what I was asked. Safe to say, I think young Master Bates can be eliminated from our enquiries."

"Agreed," laughed Pennock. "Pity though, it might have been the break-through we sorely needed. Ok, that's enough hilarity boys and girls. So, what about you, Sandy? Anything new?"

Sandy composed herself and consulted her notes.

"Not much to report, Gov. My snouts pretty well confirmed what we already knew. Motson's a creature of habit. The White Hart is his local of choice and he's in every evening, has three or four pints. Causes no bother. According to my sources, he uses the place to do some off-course race betting with varying degrees of success - but generally loses more than he wins. He regularly receives, what is almost certainly, knocked off gear, which he off-loads down at the second hand market. He takes his commission which pays for his beer and so, round and round it goes. Ah, the circle of life - what a wonderful thing."

Pennock glared at her to get a move on.

"Sorry Gov, getting a bit carried away." She continued, unrepentantly. "Seems there's sometimes a card school but he doesn't play very often, apparently he doesn't have the aptitude for it. All in all, a bit of a lonely old saddo."

"What about family, wife and kids?" asked Parnell.

"Seems that there used to be a family with, maybe a couple of kids, nobody seems to know for certain. Word is that the wife got fed up of him gambling away his wages every month, borrowing to cover his losses and getting the family further and further into debt. The house and car were repossessed, they were forced to sell everything of value. And one day she just packed their bags, took the kids, and has never been seen since. They say Motson is still very bitter, thinks she was very unfair and never gave him a fighting chance to prove himself."

"Yeah, right. Wise woman's what I say," said Harry.

"What about any contact with his brother?" Pennock pressed.

"Well, they couldn't say for sure that it is Wickes who comes into the pub, but, occasionally a non-local man joins him for a drink and spends an hour or so chatting with Motson, like socially. He isn't a regular, but comes in often enough for them to recognize his face. Interestingly, recently though, when he has shown up, it seems they've been deep in conversation more often than not. Neither of my snouts had any idea what they've been discussing, but agree it seemed to be hush-hush."

"Well, well, that is promising, but we don't want to put two and two together and make five, like we did at the beginning of this investigation. But it'll make the files from social services all the more interesting . That's if they ever bloody-well arrive."

Harry interjected. "The Chief Super applied straight away for Wickes' file to be released. If they pull their fingers out, we should have the complete records for the two of them fairly shortly."

"So, what about Wickes, Sir?" asked Sandy.

"Bit like yourself. Not much to report. I've got to say though, he lives in a very nice part of town. I wonder if he rents or was somehow able to afford to buy. His house overlooks Jubilee Park and the lake, on a quiet dead-end street, all well maintained and exclusive. He drives a flashy, three year old Golf GTI which he leaves parked in the drive. Fully taxed and insured. After he got home, he stayed in all evening. It appears that he lives on his own, at least I didn't see anyone coming or going. Whether that means his wife was working a shift or that they're separated, I don't know. In hind-sight, I think maybe surveillance is a bit of a waste of time until we've got something to be going on with."

Harry agreed, "It's not likely he'll get up to any dodgy business now he knows we may want to reinterview him. Let's work with what we've got and see where it leads us, Gov."

Charles Kingsley hadn't been idle either. He was gradually building, what he considered and knew to be a strong case on, so far, eight grounds against the police on behalf of his client. After Dr Neville had requested a meeting with him, he had been appalled to learn that what Alistair had maintained throughout appeared to be true - he was indeed the victim of an elaborate set-up, but the police still hadn't dismissed the charges.

At yet another appointment made with D.I Pennock to discuss the matter he was furious to learn that the police were still not prepared to retract any of the charges against him. He told Pennock in no uncertain terms that he would be making an application to the court to have the bail and reporting restrictions lifted at the very least, and was rather surprised when the officer said to go ahead and that the police would not oppose the application at this time. Charles wondered what they were playing at. How could they refuse to withdraw the accusations against Alistair and yet agree to the lifting of bail restrictions which, in effect would allow him to move back into the marital home? What was he missing here, what were they up to? It wasn't until some time later that he remembered the restraining order that Natalie had taken out against her husband - there was no way Alistair would be allowed to return home.

"But why won't you let me move back in, Nat? The police have no objections and I miss you and the children terribly. Please, I just want to get back to our normal life."

Alistair had called her with the good news of his successful appeal, but Nat was not to be persuaded. Alistair knew he was begging and it was degrading but what he really needed now were the stability, support and safety of a family routine.

Nat felt despicable, in her heart of hearts, she was now certain that Alistair was innocent and would undoubtedly be exonerated, but *'our normal life'* was undoubtedly a thing of the past. Also, the court's restraining order had, luckily, taken the decision out of her hands, certainly up till this moment, so she still had that excuse to fall back on. She knew he loved his children and would be incapable of harming them, but something was holding her back - it was the fear of not being able to go back - there was no going back - it could never be the same as it was.

"Al, let's take this one step at a time. I think it would be for the best if you were to move back in with your mum and dad for a bit. She's recovered enough now to have you and the press have lost interest and moved on. It shouldn't be a problem for them. Look, in a little while, if all goes well, I promise I'll bring the children round every day. We can have a few trips out and try to rebuild our family."

"What about the restraining order, Nat? Will you have it lifted?"

"We'll have to see, Al. We'll have to see." Evidently she wasn't going to commit to agreeing.

It seemed that everyone believed him - but not quite. No one was prepared to let him off the hook just yet - not even his own wife. When this was all over, he vowed, they would all pay dearly for destroying his life.

It was clear he would have to make do for the time being, but assuming his parents would have him back, he should start to make plans for his future. Obviously his reputation was in tatters and he supposed that word of what had happened would have spread like wild-fire through the medical profession by now, almost certainly precluding him from ever working for the N.H.S again. It seemed like he had two options. First, he could enter into private practice, although he had always vowed never to go down that route. He was a staunch believer in the N.H.S charter - it was a magnificent body envied and emulated throughout the world. While it may be straining at the seams caused by the overwhelming demands placed on it, nobody could deny the quality and dedication of the professionals that worked tirelessly to keep it running. But if he was no longer welcome among their ranks, perhaps he would need to investigate the private route. He firmly believed he had a wealth of experience to offer which would hopefully make him a desireable asset to a new employer.

Second, and this would be the worse case scenario, move abroad and start afresh - begin again with a clean slate where nobody knew him and where he could prove himself on his own merits. If he and Nat couldn't make it work, he might have to consider that possibility. But the thought of leaving his children behind was devastating, he couldn't begin to contemplate the prospect. Yet he knew, that even if he went for the first choice it would mean moving far away in order to be be incognito. Either way, he would have very little contact with his kids in the future - it was Hobson's choice.

iv.

Chief Superintendent Stan Worth may well have regarded his policing methods as old school, but that didn't mean he was old fashioned. The face of policing had changed over the years and the Superintendent had moved along with the times. His nick had the best technology his budget could afford and all his officers were highly trained in modern investigative techniques. That morning he had arrived early as usual, to spend forty minutes working out in the gym that he had had installed on the lower ground floor. He encouraged general physical and mental well being among the ranks and believed a gym was a great place to burn off the excess energy and frustrations the job brought with it. He was still a fit and robust man himself although now well in to his fifties. He believed it was important to be a good role model to his officers and kept himself in excellent shape. However, he preferred to work out when the gym was unoccupied and had his own key to the place - the troops didn't actually need to see him sweating and labouring to maintain his physique.

Upstairs though, it was a different story. He had an open door policy and encouraged his people to know he was always available. Government cut-backs had been brutal but he had tried to spare as many redundancies and lay-offs as possible, arguing that the area his force operated in presented a difficult and complex uniqueness requiring the extra man-power. So far he had managed to persuade the powers-that-be to leave them alone. As a result, he was well respected and liked by his officers - considered tough but always fair. Now, showered and dressed, he still reached his office long before his secretary arrived, switched on his computer and made himself a cup of coffee as he waited for it to boot up.

The ten minutes peace and quiet he had anticipated enjoying were shattered by the electronic arrival of the Wickes/Motson files. Of course, he should have remembered, they would come directly to him as the soliciting officer. Therefore the final decision to forward them to the team would also be his. He wouldn't normally have perused them so closely, but expunged records weren't an every day occurrence and moreover he was intrigued to uncover the background history of the two men - well, young boys as they would have been then of course.

The files made for grim reading but it was clear they were particularly relevant to the ongoing case and any doubts he may have had regarding the direction the enquiries were taking were now firmly put to bed. He would forward them to the team and attach a memo to say that he would attend a briefing from D.I Pennock and the others later that day, once they had all had the chance to digest the contents.

v.

The three officers were left bereft of words as they read both files. The two reports worked better being read individually first and then in parallel, so when combined together they presented the cause and effect of their story - what had happened to one brother directly impacted on the other. The files were lengthy for both boys, their stories complicated and harrowing. The background history began as a well worn and, sadly common scenario. A dysfunctional family where the bully of a father was the tyrant. He resented having to support a family of four and not have anything left over for his own entertainment. His wife was cowed down by his constant verbal as well as physical abuse which she tolerated to deflect the father's attention from the children. The report detailed how Mr. Wickes was never one to spare the belt or his fists.

The story began, so familiarly, with an unplanned pregnancy which had resulted in a shot-gun wedding - hardly an auspicious start to married life. Neither side of the family had approved of the other, but, with a baby on the way, it had the effect of uniting them. Surprisingly, however, it seemed that upon the birth of their child, a son named David, Mr Wickes Sr. had become totally enamoured and had absolutely doted on his first born. The union of the three of them was relatively harmonious in those early years. The two Wickes males went fishing, watched football, played cricket - all the typical father/son activities undertaken by a happy family.

It seemed that the perfect bubble had burst when Mrs. Wickes fearfully announced another unplanned pregnancy some years later when David was five. Mr. Wickes had been incandescent with rage and that is when the beatings had begun. He convinced himself that his wife had deceived him into deliberately getting pregnant because of the jealousy she felt being excluded from the close relationship the father and son enjoyed. She had done it to spite him, so that she could have something to love of her own. The second son never stood a chance.

119

Andrew was born and the whole dynamic of the family disintegrated. Wickes accused his wife of being an unfaithful whore, but, in truth, even he could see the boy was his - the similarity between the two was irrefutable. This wasn't enough, however, to forge a bond between the two of them. He irrationally hated the child and took every opportunity to punish him while rewarding and lavishing love on David at the same time.

The case of the two boys took a sinister and cruel turn when the company Wickes worked for was forced into foreclosure during the economic crisis. Now redundant, washed up at the age of thirty, he loitered around the house more often and tensions grew. He started to gamble on line, encouraged by the wealth of betting organizations that were now allowed to advertise on t.v. As money got tighter, he became meaner, and little Andy became the regular butt of his father's booze fuelled wrath. Smacks and six of the best progressed on to beatings and unprovoked assaults. Mrs Wickes would try to intervene and got regularly bashed for her pains as well. Both Andy and Mrs Wickes were so often black and blue that David had to be sent out for their meagre bits of shopping. Soon enough, David was caught shop-lifting some basic foodstuffs. The police were called and they cautioned but did not charge the lad. The Wickes had at last come to the attention of Social Services. Shame was brought on the family for which his brother was duly punished.

David was close to his brother despite his father's disapproval, and stood up for him, often saving Andy from a worse than usual beating. He knew he got preferential treatment and was beginning to hate his father for the favouritism he enjoyed and brutality against his mum and little brother. Their father had gradually slipped in to a cycle of apathy and self pity. He was unable to secure new employment and after a while didn't even bother looking. He was ashamed that his wife had to resort to going out cleaning other people's houses but was too lethargic by now to motivate himself. To punish his wife for his humiliation, he forced her to beat Andy with his belt as well. When she resisted, they both got lashed all the harder.

 David came upon such a beating one day and rushed forward to prevent his father from hurting them further. Mr. Wickes unintentionally caught the boy full in the face as he raised his fist and David was hurled across the room his head crunching grotesquely against the mantlepiece. The gash on the back of David's head was deep and bleeding profusely and the boy concussed. In A&E Mr Wickes concocted an unlikely explanation which didn't fool the staff for a minute. They could see the fading bruises on the wife and other child which told the real tale. Social Services were once again called, but with resources stretched to breaking point, the family still didn't get the intervention it needed.

David was a bright lad and knew he had to get some qualifications, after which he dreamt of getting a good job to be able to take his mum and brother far away and make a fresh start. In the mean time he was stuck at home. He tried to stay out of bother, but with such little money coming in, it was inevitable that he would be caught once again for shop-lifting. This time, there was no caution and the juvenile magistrates gave him a three month probation order. Social Services did what they could but the extent of the brothers' crisis went unawares. Their father had become increasingly violent - Andy had now had visits to A&E for a broken arm, leg, and ribs. His mother too with a broken jaw and ribs. The neighbours were aware of what was happening next door and had repeatedly contacted the police who proved to be ineffectual. Any of their direct approaches to Mr. Wickes was met with such frightening aggression that the neighbours soon retreated.

The day that Wickes literally broke his son's back was when Andy had been too unwell and sore to go to school, so David had gone alone. Wickes had forgotten his wife was out cleaning, and when she failed to bring him more beer when he shouted, he went looking himself. Hearing a sound upstairs he found his lazy, good for nothing son, lying in bed fast asleep. He thought he'd teach him a lesson alright - and, snatching up the cricket bat which was leaning against the wall, he strode across the room and thwacked it down with all his might onto the back of the recumbent boy. The sickening crack of the vertebrae shattering instantly brought Wickes out of his alcoholic fugue. He leaned over in horror, checking to see if the boy were still alive.

So he never saw who attacked him. David, coming home at lunch time to check on his little brother, had witnessed the whole thing. Convinced that his father was about to finish his brother off, he had run over and grabbed the discarded cricket bat. He had whacked his father with it over and over again until he was certain he was dead.

However, Mr Wickes apparently survived the assault, and while Andy lay immobile for several months in hospital, enveloped in a plaster body cast, David was taken into care and Mr Wickes into custody. Wickes was charged with attempted murder but finally pleaded guilty to the lesser charge of Assault Occasioning Grievous Bodily Harm. When the antecedents of the family and witness statements were taken into consideration, combined with his lack of remorse, Mr Wickes received a lengthy custodial sentence. David was also charged with G.B.H, but when the juvenile court heard those same antecedents and witness statements, their compassion and duty of care to rehabilitate the young offender/victim persuaded them against custody and to recommend a substantial probation order instead. The family court later ordered the boys to be taken from their mother and to be fostered while searching for suitable adoptive parents. Andy had been adopted by his first and the only foster family he had lived with and had taken their surname, while, regrettably, a suitable family for David had been unforthcoming and he had remained in a group home until he was sixteen.

The reports concluded that although the mother was still living, contact with her was sporadic at best. As far as it was known, there had been no contact with Mr Wickes senior at all. However it noted, that at the time of writing, the brothers saw one another occasionally and remained reasonably close.

Sandy was the first to comment upon the report.

"Well, as our American cousins say, Gov ... *'they've got motive, means and opportunity'*."

121

17

The trial date had been postponed until the New Year Alistair had been informed in a brief letter from the court, he would be advised when it would be relisted. Although he resented still not being exonerated of any wrong-doing, Alistair felt a spark of optimism that the tide was at last turning in his favour. The police were following new leads, so that had to be good. Thankfully his parents were pleased to have him for Christmas and he was relieved to be able to move out of that flea-pit and back into the sanctuary of the family home. During the last few weeks, he had never felt more vulnerable in his life, incapable of controlling or commanding events as he was used to, but things were definitely looking more positive now.

Mrs Neville was a real trooper. Thank God she had survived her stroke as well as the shock of her son's false allegations and was now determined to put a brave face on things and make the most of a bad situation. Now fully restored to good health, she had obviously been given a new lease of life too and had been flat out baking mince pies and a Christmas cake as well as making the turkey stuffing and bread sauce. She insisted on putting on the full works this year, pleased to have her little family reunited again. Bottles of sherry, port and advocaat sat on the sideboard, and Alistair suspected his mother may have already been enjoying a tipple or two in celebration.

She had commanded Alistair to go up into the loft to bring down the Christmas tree and decorations. It was a tradition she reminded him they had shared over the years - to have the tree up and the house decorated before his father returned from work. His father had long-since retired but had made himself obligingly scarce saying he had some last minute shopping to do. Opening the boxes, he saw that his sentimental old mother had kept some of the handicrafts Alistair had made years ago in primary school. They were hardly valuable and very tattered but she looked at them, one by one, through teary eyes before hanging them lovingly on the tree. The decorations and nearly bald artificial tree were definitely past their best, but he couldn't deny how they brought him back such happy, vivid childhood memories, so much so that he didn't have the heart to suggest chucking them all out and starting again.

For the first time in his married life, Alistair had been forced to brave the Christmas crowds and choose presents for all the family. That had always been Nat's domain, but it was proving to be quite a novel experience for him. It gave him something positive to do and, much to his surprise, discovered that he enjoyed himself. He'd thought long and hard about what to buy, and hoping he'd made some good selections, had wrapped and placed them all beneath the tree.

The Christmas good spirit seemed to be holding when Nat phoned him to say that she would pop in briefly with the children on their way to her parents and that he could spend some time with them. He hadn't seen his little ones for some weeks now and couldn't wait to see them or thank her enough. Whilst she still hadn't applied to have the restraining order lifted, it seemed, and he prayed it to be true, that Nat was thawing slightly. She had allowed him to speak to the children occasionally although under her strict supervision, but had not permitted a visit as yet. This would be the first time. Technically he was breaking his bail conditions, but what the hell? It was the best Christmas present he could wish for.

The children and Nat arrived mid-morning for an early lunch, the day after the schools had broken up. She had explained that she wanted to get to her parents' house in good time and before all the holiday traffic became a total misery, inevitably spoiling what should be a happy time. She had made certain that Mr. and Mrs. Neville would both be present when they came round, primarily to oversee the occasion and also to offset any tensions that might arise between herself and Alistair.

Juliet and Martin were beside themselves with joy at seeing their father again after such a long time and threw themselves into his arms. For Alistair, it was like seeing them anew. Holding them at arm's length, he could swear Martin must have grown a couple of inches taller. His handsome, sandy haired boy, the spitting image of his mother, was filling out and had become quite responsible during his father's absence. His baby girl was as sweet and innocent as he remembered. Tall for her age, she had her father's same athletic, stocky frame and the same determination.

"When are you coming home, Daddy?" she demanded, "We're really sad without you. Mummy cries a lot and my hamster misses you too."

Smiling at his daughter's naive logic, Alistair risked a glance at his wife before answering, noting that Nat's face was carefully neutral. He didn't have to be an empath to realize that there was not going to be a touching reunion for his family any time soon. Still, it was the season of good cheer and it did no harm to be optimistic.

"Soon, my darlings, soon. I promise. I think by the New Year the police will have caught the bad man and I'll be home before you know it."

"You said that last time, Dad," complained Martin accusingly. "Don't you love us any more?"

Alistair's heart was rent in two and the tears glistened as he saw fear and confusion reflected in his son's eyes.

"Now, listen to me both of you. Of course I love you - more than words can ever say. But the police say I can't come home until they've solved the case. I'll be able to come back then and we'll do some lovely things together and be a family again."

Nat, too was moved, her eyes shining with unshed tears. The bond between Alistair and the children was deeply touching and she was profoundly affected by their closeness. The feeling soon turned to amazement when he guided them to the Christmas tree and proudly presented the three of them with their presents. She had bought nothing for him, not even anything ostensibly from the children, it simply hadn't occurred to her to do so.

Martin and Juliet were thrilled with their gifts which she had to admit were thoughtful and appropriate without their father overcompensating for being absent. He shyly offered Nat her present, a Fit Bit watch - now that she had so much more running around to do, she might as well be counting her steps at the same time, he joked. He told her not to be embarrassed about not getting him anything, just them being together was more than enough.

The lunch was a happy, festive affair for the children and their grandparents with tearful goodbyes all round at the end. Alistair and she had, perforce, been reasonably cordial for both the children's and the grandparents's sake all of whom were watching them like hawks, on maximum alert trying to determine if anything were amiss between the two.

It was quite a strain to be civil, but making sure they sat well apart at the table meant they didn't have to interact with each other too much. The meal had been delicious - with many compliments and thanks toasted to Mrs. Neville for her sterling efforts. The children had deflected any potential awkward moments with their constant chatter and excited enthusiasm. Both Martin and Juliet whinged and begged to be allowed to stay longer, but Nat had the perfect excuse prepared in case the Nevilles pressed them as well - they needed to get on the road as soon as possible if they wanted to arrive at their other grandparents' house in good time.

Afterwards, she had to ask herself if what she was planning to do was going to be fair to them or just to herself? He was their father after all and they were so close. The Christmas lunch had shown just how much he loved them and they him. She had to mentally admonish herself not to second guess and be so ridiculous - her primary concern was to assure the safety and well-being of her children. Of course it was the right decision.

ii.

The Christmas break brought a brief but welcome break in the investigation. Officers and partner agencies were on holiday and nothing constructive could be done until the New Year. Pennock and his team had undoubtedly needed time away from the investigation too, but his fear was that the whole enquiry may well have stalled altogether, losing total impetus in the meantime. The clear-up rate was woefully slow on this case, they were lucky the Chief Super was still on board but they couldn't count on it for too much longer.

Their progress so far was frankly unacceptably slow - they had targeted a prime suspect who had pretty much been shown to be innocent; while other persons of interest had been proved to be anything but interesting and now they were chasing after, what could once again prove to be, two red herrings. He asked himself if what they had been doing could be said to be policing at its worst - making the facts fit an already, and erroneously, established theory (i.e that Dr. Neville must be automatically guilty) rather than solid, fact-based decision making? Their reputation for being the A team was being sorely tested, their progress was under the microscope and results were needed, and soon.

But while they were no other viable leads at that moment, Pennock knew Wickes/Motson was the best chance they had and they would have to investigate every time-and-labour intensive detail for the sake of completeness and maybe, just maybe, a conviction.

The three C.I.D officers met up to thrash out a plan of how to proceed. They agreed Sandy and Pennock would take Wickes and Harry and a uniform, Motson.

A discreet call to the hospital revealed that neither man had returned after the Christmas break as yet. A nice bonus for them to be able to catch the brothers in their respective homes and get to snoop around at the same time without a warrant. They were contacted and both men reluctantly agreed to a police visit later on in the day.

Pennock and Sandy drew up in front of a large modern semi, located in a good neighbourhood, actually not too far from the Nevilles. It seemed the Wickes preferred to live away from the hospital too. The house looked well maintained and tidy with the Golf G.T.I, as well as a small hatchback parked on the drive. The inspector had assumed, incorrectly as it turned out, that Wickes lived alone.

Mrs. Wickes, a compact, obviously capable woman somewhere in her mid thirties, answered their knock. She had clearly been expecting them and invited them into the lounge where her husband was waiting, albeit somewhat less welcoming than his wife. She went into the kitchen, returning a few minutes later with a tray bearing tea, Christmas cake and mince pies. During the first moments of chit chat they learned that Mrs. Wickes was also a nurse at the same hospital and worked shifts on the neo-natal ward. They had two young children who were having a sleep-over with their cousins at Mrs. Wickes' younger sister's house, and that she came from a large close knit family all living nearby.

They observed that the inside of the house was comfortably furnished but not extravagantly so with, sadly, no sign of computers or much technology at all for that matter, other than the usual t.v. flickering silently in the corner of the room.

Sandy asked Mrs. Wickes if she would mind showing her around the house. Mrs.Wickes, somewhat bemused, agreed, asking half jokingly what it had to do with the Dr. Neville investigation? Sandy deftly side-stepped the question asking how long they had lived there and what the area was like? She soon discovered that Mrs. Wickes also knew Dr. Neville, probably just as well as her husband did, it turned out. As a paediatrician, Sandy was informed, he was a frequent visitor to the neo-natal department, usually to attend to critical cases.

"So how do you get on with him?" asked Sandy. It would be interesting to discover if the couple's opinion of Dr. Neville tallied.

"Well, he's a real task master who likes to keep us all on our toes. Of course I only know him from being on the ward. He doesn't usually deign to consort with us minions. I don't think he even knows my name, he usually just refers to me as *'nurse'*. But from what I've seen, he's good and caring at his job. David tells me he's an outstanding surgeon. There's not much more I can tell you, I'm afraid."

The two returned a few minutes later and settled down. Sandy threw Pennock a quick glance with a slight negative shake of the head, indicating that she hadn't seen anything around the house to arouse her suspicions.

Pennock, meanwhile had thanked David Wickes for seeing them at such short notice and asked if he would like his solicitor present? Wickes asked why he should need his solicitor if it was just routine? No, he didn't think that would be necessary. So Pennock began.

"Mr. Wickes, further to our conversation before Christmas, we'd like to ask you some follow up questions."

Wickes nodded his assent to continue.

"And are you happy to have your wife present during the interview?"

"Why shouldn't I be? I've got nothing to hide," he responded, relaxed and reasonably pleasant.

"Very well. As you know, we've been investigating some extremely serious allegations against Dr. Alistair Neville, and, as a result of our interview before Christmas, our enquiries have lead us to look into your history more closely."

"My history? What connection could I possibly have to the case?" Wickes asked still showing no signs of tension or worry.

"Well, you see we've discovered a possible link between yourself, your brother and Dr. Neville."

In the ensuing silence, a now pale Wickes, looked gobsmacked.

"His brother? No. There must be some mistake," interjected Mrs. Wickes. "David hasn't got a brother. He's an only child."

"Shut up, Marie," warned Wickes. "What kind of link? And how did you find out I had a brother?" he demanded.

"As a result of researching Social Services files on your brother, Andrew Motson …"

"Andrew Motson? Not … Andy Motson … isn't he the car park attendant?" queried Mrs. Wickes.

"I said be quiet, Marie," snarled Wickes, glaring at his wife who shrank back in horror at his harsh tone. "And just why were you looking at his files, would you care to tell me?" he asked snidely.

Pennock replied vaguely. "Some evidence came to our attention regarding Mr. Motson which lead us to your file."

"My file? My file? But my file is sealed and my record's been expunged. I know that for a fact. How did you get hold of it? What right have you got to do that? You can't just go sticking your noses into people's ancient offences. I've got a right to my privacy. They told me no one would ever be able to access those files again." Wickes ranted.

"What file and what record are you talking about, David?" wailed his wife.

"I said shut up, Marie. Well? Answer me."

"For the most part that's true, Mr. Wickes," responded Pennock reasonably, "but when the police have strong grounds to believe a serious crime has been commited, they have the power to overturn the order to expunged records, pariculary if they believe there is a connection to that crime. You see, the truth is, previous convictions are never really wiped out, there's always a record of them held somewhere."

Wickes was almost apoplectic with rage.

"Get out! I want you to leave right now. Get out! I've got nothing more to say to you! Now, get out of my house!" he screamed.

Pennock and Parker had anticipated the interview would end badly, but perhaps no quite so badly as it had, so before the door was slammed in their faces, Sandy thrust a pre-prepared summons into Wickes' hand which instructed him to attend the following day at the London Road police station, and suggesting he come accompanied by legal representation.

iii.

Harry and a uniformed constable, pulled up at Andrew Motson's place.

"Des res," commented P.C Brown, who had been reluctantly plucked from the available pool of officers and who was hardly delighted to be involved in the interview himself. "Why do we always draw the short straw?"

Harry couldn't disagree. The building was well known to him and everyone else at the London Road nick for that matter. P.C Brown, too remembered many a visit to this very property. Many of their 'clients' used this address when on, or hoping for, bail - including Dr. Neville, Harry reminded himself.

The whole area, as well as the block of flats, had seen better days - an atmosphere of neglect, despair and abandonment pervaded the empty streets. Even most of the street lights had blown out bulbs. Nearly all of the shops were boarded up, those that remained in trade appeared to be either off licences or betting shops, interspersed with a few charity shops. Entering the building, the two officers took care to tread carefully - fearing the dangers of exposed needles or other offensive waste materials. Litter was strewn all over, walls covered in grafitti and worse, threadbare, torn lino on the floors and staircase - a truly dismal place.

Receiving a less than warm invitation to enter his flat, the two officers could quite understand why Motson spent most of his time down at his local boozer. It was a sad and sordid little hovel, which, it was clear, the current tenant had spent little effort improving. It comprised a dully lit kitchenette cum lounge/diner, the cooker so grease-laden that it had become a kind of permanent baked-on feature of the electric rings; the pattern on the sticky floor had been liberally added to with food debris that had fallen on to it, trodden in and never been swept up. A small fridge groaned noisily beside the sink that still held mismatched crockery onto which the remnants of many a left over meal still clung.

Off the main room was a small bedroom and a miniscule shower room. The bedroom held a rickety bed topped with a flimsy mattress covered in sheets that may have once been white but were now grey, stained and threadbare. The only other furniture to grace the room was a scarred bedside table with a shade-less lamp on top and an apparently redundant clothes rail, as most of the clothes seemed to be flung carelessly on the floor. The air freshner in the bathroom couldn't mask the underlying odour of urine, quietly seeping from the pan, nor improved the sight of the grime ridden hand basin and a shower tray, surrounded by a mouldy, half pulled down curtain. The whole flat was furnished with tatty second or third hand stuff well past its sell-by date and decorated with even older wallpaper whose original pattern was being constantly modified by the nicotine and tar trails emanating from each new tenant's cigarettes.

They sat carefully down.

"Nice place you've got, Mr. Motson," said Dickie Brown tongue in cheek.

"Well, if you like it so much, how about we swap houses?" Motson shot back.

Harry raised a restraining hand, and began, "Thanks for agreeing to see us, Mr. Motson."

"Didn't have much choice, did I?" he begrudgingly replied.

"No, I suppose not. D'you mind if Constable Brown has a look around while we have a talk?"

Motson didn't mind. "Take your time, I've got nothing to hide."

Moments later, the constable returned, He had clearly found nothing of interest.

"How long have you lived here, Mr. Motson?" asked Harry

"Two, no three years. I'm still trying to get back on my feet after the divorce. She skinned me for every penny I had. But you know how it is ... I just think I'm getting ahead and some unexpected bill comes in and I'm back to square one."

Harry and Dickie knew exactly what Motson meant - gambling debts.

Changing the subject, Harry asked.

"We'd like to know if you have a laptop, P.C or mobile phone, Mr Motson."

"Not really, except for a rubbish mobile," he replied. He showed the officers what really was a rubbish mobile, with no internet access and just about capable of receiving a call or sending a message. It didn't have a camera either, they noted.

"Anything else, laptop, iPad?"

"Well, I've got an iPad my bro ..." Motson stopped himself quickly realizing his mistake.

"An iPad your brother, Mr David Wickes gave you?" finished Harry helpfully.

"How do you lot know about Dave?" Motson said, confused.

"Oh, there's quite a lot we know about the pair of you Mr. Motson. So, tell us, just why did your brother give you an iPad?"

"He was getting a new one and said I could have the old one. Said I needed bringing into the 21st century."

"But you don't have any internet connection here, do you?" asked P.C Brown.

"That's right, I can't afford it. So what I do is hack into the hospital's connection and use it when I'm at work."

"So can we see it, please?"

"Duh! It's no good to me here now is it? It's in the cupboard in my hut at work."

"Ok Mr. Motson. Here's what we want you to do. We'll need you to come down to the station tomorrow at 3pm. Go to the hospital and bring the device with you and bring a solicitor as well, if you've got one."

"But why do you want me down the nick. I haven't done anything wrong."

"Perhaps not. But the Inspector wants to ask you and your brother some follow-up questions about the Neville case. Nothing to worry about, probably." concluded Harry.

"We'll find our own way out thanks. See you tomorrow, Mr. Motson." said P.C Brown cheerfully.

18

Chief Superintendent Worth joined the team before the arrival of the two interviewees. He had decided it was time to take a far more proactive role in this investigation. He didn't intend to interfere, but he did need this wrapping up asap. The evidence board and logs were filled in and annotated and the Super brought himself up to date, speed reading the latest input. Apparently the brothers would be seen individually and then, possibly together.

"What d'you think, Sir?" asked Pennock.

"It's the best we've got but it's certainly tenuous," came the reply.

Pennock was relieved that the boss had used 'we', that meant he was still with them, but he was right nevertheless, 'tenuous' was the word.

The brothers arrived within five minutes of each other and were shown into a waiting room prior to interview, but where they could be observed nevertheless. The two hugged each other warmly. Interesting, they were obviously closer than the team had realized. The officers could see Motson gesticulating nervously and mouthing something worriedly but then clearly being put at ease by his brother's response and reassuring hand on his shoulder. Motson seemed to calm down and take strength from his brother's presence and leadership.

David was dressed in comfortable weekend clothes, but still looked casually smart and very much in control. His brother, on the other hand, looked as though he'd turned up unshowered and in the same gear he'd been wearing for the past week, which he almost certainly had. David was accompanied by a solicitor that none of the officers recognized, but who was evidently known to Motson as well. They knew all the local briefs, so this one must be from out of town. They would soon learn that he would be representing both the brothers, having been their legal representative for a number of years it seemed.

Pennock entered the room briskly and introduced himself to the solicitor, a Mr. French. He informed them that they would be seen separately with Mr. Motson going first. They had previously reasoned that it would be far easier to crack Motson than his brother and use whatever information he revealed along the way during the following interview. Making sure Wickes was comfortable in the meantime, he, along with Parnell, accompanied Mr. French and his client to Interview Room 1.

"Thank you both for attending today," Pennock began, addressing them courteously and proceeding to give the Miranda warning and advise Motson he was being interviewed under caution. Motson's acknowledgement made it clear that this was not the first time he had been in this situation.

"Now then, Mr. Motson, or may I call you Andy?" Pennock continued after Andy's agreement. "As you know we are investigating a serious case and some information has come to our attention which may connect you to it."

"Oh yeah? Like what?" responded Andy annoyed.

Pennock was the one who did the asking - he wasn't the one to answer questions, especially from suspects.

"Well, before we go into that, I'd need you to answer a few questions first. You work as a car park attendant in the hospital. Is that correct?"

Andy confirmed that he had been there for the last eight months, since poor Sid, the previous attendant had suddenly died.

"And did you apply for the job or did your brother put in a good word for you?"

Andy reluctantly admitted that it was a bit of both. He had been out of work for some time when his brother had discovered the job was available and had put in a good word, acting as a referee to guarantee it for him.

"Good. Now tell us a bit about your family history. I have to inform you that we've seen the files from Social Services, so we know something of your circumstances. Take your time. In your own words."

Andy froze and looked like a deer caught in a car's headlights, petrified at the prospect of having to relive and recount the trauma of his childhood once more. He would rather have been anywhere than having to go through all this again. He cowered like a whipped dog as he stumbled and stuttered about those unhappy days, but essentially confirmed everything that they had read in the report.

"And do you have any children of your own, Andy?" asked Parnell, his voice carefully neutral.

"Yeah. Two daughters, but I haven't seen them for a few years. Their bitch of a mother took them away and has never let me see them again. I don't give a toss about her but I would have liked to see my girls grow up." Motson replied bitterly.

"And why did she do that, Andy? Why did she take them away? Was she worried about their safety? Worried that history might repeat itself - what happened to you could happen to them at your hands?"

Andy was horrified by the accusation. "Are you out of your tiny minds? No way. I'd never lay a finger on those girls, I loved them and was a good dad to them."

"Then why did she take them?"

"Well, it's like … well, I had a few money troubles for a while and just couldn't get ahead. Only temporary like. Things got a bit difficult, so she upped and left. No staying power, no loyalty."

Both officers knew this was a rewriting of history, that the poor woman could undoubtedly take no more of bailiffs pounding on her door, threatening all kinds of action against them. She had cut her losses and made her escape. She was indeed a wise woman.

"Andy, I'm going to be honest with you now," said Pennock. Andy's look said it all.

"Yeah, that'll be the day," he responded cynically.

"No seriously. Further investigations have revealed that Dr. Neville is actually innocent in all this. He's being framed by a person or persons unknown and for what reason, we have still to ascertain."

"Yeah, you're kidding right? That bloke's as guilty as hell. It's obvious." Motson's expression showed nothing but incredulity at the police's theory.

"No, he's not - he's been set up. Really. It's true. Now my question is this … Are you and your brother the prime movers here? Did you and he plan to set Neville up all along?"

The solicitor intervened at this point, warning his client.

"Don't answer that, Andy. Inspector, if you have any evidence to implicate either of my clients in this investigation, I should be grateful if you could let it be known."

Pennock held up a hand to stave off the solicitor's request.

"All in good time, Mr. French. Now Andy, could you please answer the question?"

Motson looked more perplexed than guilty as he replied.

"I swear to God, we've got nothing to do with any of this. You're wasting your time with us. You should be out there looking for the real villains, because it's not us."

"That remains to be seen, Mr. Motson. Let's continue. Now, it's no secret that Dr. Neville is not an easy man to get on with, nor is he well liked. We understand from several sources that he can be condescending and insulting to his staff, shouting at them and often reducing them to tears in front of their colleagues. In fact he's a bully … a situation, as you've just told us, you're very familiar with."

"I only know what I've heard from my brother and one or two of the nurses who have a little chat when they're leaving the car park. They say he's a real bastard, quick to criticise and slow to praise all their hard work. They can't stand him. He lords it over them, belittles them, yeah, he's a real bully. God knows why they stick with him."

"And is that how your brother feels about him, would you say?" asked Parnell.

"Pretty much. Can't bear him, but he also thinks the bloke's a bloody genius. Well that's what he tells me anyway."

"Andy, did you and your brother conspire together to bring Dr. Neville down a peg or two? Did you set out to discredit and destroy him?"

"Whaaat?? You must be having a laugh. Can't find the real culprit, so you want to pin it on us. Bloody marvellous. I don't hardly even know the bloke. I saw more of him when he was at the hostel than I did at work. I'm not exactly in his elite social circle. I only see him as he whizzes out of the car park. I haven't got anything personal against the bloke."

"Be that as it may, Mr. Motson," pressed Pennock, "but your brother has, and he may be holding a grudge against Dr. Neville which he's acted on with or without your assistance."

"What a load of cobblers. No way," Andy insisted.

"Well, we'll see what your brother has to say now."

Suspending the interview at that point, they left Motson to stew for a bit, and meanwhile invited Mr. French into Interview Room 2 where Wickes awaited.

ii.

Alistair whistled tunelessly as he put the phone down.

"You're sounding chipper, son. What's going on?" Asked his dad from behind his paper.

He hadn't really been reading the local rag, only in so much as to assure himself that he and his family didn't feature anywhere in the newsprint. He had been thinking of the impact his son's return had made on him and his wife. He could scarcely bring himself to forgive his only child for the stress wrought on them, particularly on Pat. That stroke could have finished her off, then where would they be? But on the other hand, he hadn't seen her this happy in years. She was fired with a new purpose, eager to get going every morning. At last she had the motivation and a reason to be up and at it. He supposed their retired life together had slipped in to some kind of monotonous routine that had probably needed a good shake up - however not quite to the extreme that had occurred - he had concluded.

He was partially to blame for their lethargy, that he knew. Since his retirement, their pace of life had slowed considerably. Not that they had been such gad-abouts, but they had certainly enjoyed a rather richer social life before than more recently. Frankly, he was happy to put his feet up and take life easy. He had never even considered that they were slipping into old age before their time, and it had taken this trauma of such monumental proportions to make him realize that they had less days to live ahead than the years behind. He supposed some good had come out of the sorry situation and, to be perfectly fair, Alistair was totally innocent.

"Things are looking up, Dad. Pete and Ann have just agreed to meet me for a drink this evening. New year, new opportunities to mend broken bridges."

"Good luck then, son," was his father's only comment.

133

Indeed things were looking up, thought Alistair. Things were falling into place, just as he'd hoped. That wasn't a question of luck but good management.

Christmas had been a quiet but relatively pleasant affair. He had enjoyed being an only child again, the sole object of his parent's lavish attention. His mother continued to go from strength to strength and there was a new vitality to her, now that someone new (i.e himself) depended upon her, and that her only son was no longer under police investigation, but a victim of a cruel plot. But he'd had enough now though and could really do with getting back to the old grindstone.

Nat had allowed the children to speak to him daily, although, strangely enough, he now realized, she hadn't spoken more than a few words to him personally. During one of those brief moments, he was delighted that she had agreed to come to court and support him from the public gallery. He knew it was vital for the judge to see a loyal wife, it would reinforce his not guilty plea no end. He would have to bridge the gap of their remoteness as well, he supposed, feeling positively optimistic at his prospects.

Most importantly though, the police had shifted their attentions elsewhere, searching for the real perpertrator who had set up the sting against him - just as he'd always been telling them was the case. The Old Bill might be slow, just so long as they got there in the end, he supposed. However, he had to admit to feeling some anxiety that the police hadn't yet dropped the case against him though. The trial date was nearly upon them now and he wasn't looking forward to it at all.

And now Pete and Ann were back in communication. He had braced himself for a backlash of recriminations from them, but surprisingly, the call had been better received than he had expected. He could only assume that it was because they had got wind of the fact that the police were now pursuing different leads and he was no longer considered the main suspect but the victim.

During the brief dialogue, Alistair had gleaned that his old friend was back working at the hospital. It transpired that Pete's reputation hadn't been tarnished beyond saving at all. It seemed that people's capacity to condemn a person on the flimsiest of evidence, was matched by their ability to forgive and forget just as quickly. Ann, he had been told, hadn't been quite so fortunate. She was also back at work, but no longer felt comfortable at that school. The whole business, falsely implicating her involvement with children, made her feel as though her colleagues had her under the microscope, scrutinizing her every interaction with the students. She still believed she had a role in teaching but that her position at her current school had now become untenable. It was such a pity really, Alistair thought - but she'd be ok - he easily consoled himself. Something would crop up, she was a good teacher after all.

Yep, it was all going to be sorted very soon, everything would be fine, things were definitely coming together. He was convinced and determined to be upbeat. He and Nat would make a fresh start, maybe have a family holiday, put it all behind them and bond together once more. Life would soon be as it was. Yeah, what a good idea, a nice holiday far, far away. He'd ask Nat the next time he got a chance. She was coming back today and hopefully she'd let him see the children. As he got ready, he smiled to himself and began to whistle once again.

iii.

Chief Superintendent Worth and Sandy Parker had observed Motson's interview from the other side of the glass. It hadn't made for entertaining viewing. Pennock and Parnell emerged, stoney-faced. There was little to be hopeful about. Worth's face was grim as well.

"Inspector, you'd better pray you get something more out of Wickes."

"Yessir," responded Pennock trying to keep the pessimism from his voice. He was desperately trying to take something from the interview but knew, in all honesty, they were clutching at straws. "The warrants are being executed as we speak. Motson's handed over his phone, iPad and house keys and Mrs. Wickes has been advised to expect the forensics team shortly. If there's something there, they'll find it."

"Let's hope so," The Chief Super growled. "And by the way, Mrs. Neville phoned. She wants to know if anything came of the tip-off she gave you?"

Pennock looked blank for a moment. What tip-off was she talking about? A slightly awkward silence ensued before Sandy helpfully filled in the info.

"She told us about Simon Bates, her colleague from work. Said he was a bit dodgy, remember?"

"Oh yeah, thanks," answered Pennock vaguely. Then he did remember, "but he turned out to be gay, didn't he?"

"That's right, Gov. Waste of time. But I don't think we ever got back to her. Want me to speak to her?"

"Thanks Sandy, appreciate it. Let me know what she says. Come on Harry, let's put the thumb screws on Wickes."

And, instantly forgetting Natalie Neville, D.I Pennock stepped into Interview Room 2.

"Thanks for being so patient, Mr Wickes," began Pennock. "Let's get straight down to the reason you're here."

"I know why I'm here. My brief's just been filling me in. Well you're barking up the wrong tree, mate. Neither of us had anything to do with setting Dr. Neville up."

"Well I'll be the judge of that. Right then, let's get on. We've been reviewing your files and it seems that you and your brother had a very traumatic childhood. Mr. Motson has corroborated Social Services' version of events, so we won't be delving too closely into all of that. First of all, I'd like to ask you why you applied to have your file sealed?"

"That should be pretty obvious. When I eventually finished school I decided I wanted to go into nursing. Of course I was a mature student by then, 24. They don't look the same way at adults as children, so there's no way I'd have been accepted with my past history. But, at a chance meeting with Mr. French, I was told about the possibility of sealing the files. The court agreed. Then later, I discovered that after so many years I could have them expunged, so I did. Inspector, I'm a different person now, I've got a wife and family, a good job and a good life. I never thought that it'd be possible for those bad times to come back and haunt me."

Pennock could almost feel a modicum of compassion for the bloke, but this wasn't the time or the place.

"Mr Wickes, as I think I mentioned to you before, there's no such thing as truly expunged files, but it's fair to say that they would never have seen the light of day if you hadn't become implicated in this investigation."

"Implicated? What's that supposed to mean? I'm not implicated. The only connection I have with Dr. Neville is that I occasionally work with him in theatre. That's it."

"But that's not all, is it? You, yourself told us that you often change shifts with your colleagues, so they don't have to bear the brunt of Dr. Neville's caustic tongue. You're able to stand up for yourself, isn't that right? He wouldn't dare take you on, would he?"

"Damn right, he wouldn't. There's not many male staff in theatre and he gets away with bullying the female nurses all the time. I can't just let him get away with it."

"I understand what you're saying. But what we'd like to know is, just how far you'd go to stop him from taking it out on your co-workers. Would you, for example, be prepared to set him up for a big fall, a total public humiliation if you like, bring a shameful end to his career?"

Taking his time in replying, Wickes pondered. Mr French shot him a look to be cautious. Finally he responded with a sly smirk.

"No. No, I don't think so. I don't think I would. That would definitely be taking it too far. The bloke doesn't deserve that. But then again ... clearly someone else disagrees."

Back in the incident room the atmosphere was subdued. There was no denying it - all their bridges were now well and truly burnt - unless, by some miracle, forensics came back with something positive, but no one was holding their breath on that one.

Pennock had never felt so deflated. He was used to being the best and worked tirelessly towards that goal. Suddenly, the golden boy with the fastest clear-up rate the station had ever known, had jack-all, no suspects, no leads and no direction. But his own dogged determination simply wouldn't allow him to give up. A crime had been committed and it was his job to bring the culprit to justice - somehow, someway.

Furthermore, Chief Superintendent Worth was not at all pleased.

"This has turned out to be a complete bloody farce. A total waste of police time and resources. That's it boys and girls, time to pull the plug. I've already had too many officers assigned to this case and it's run on way too long. I can't justify allocating any more police time to wild goose chasing. We've got nowhere and got no prospects. Inspector, I understand the trial is due to start in a couple of days. I'm formally advising you to withdraw the case before we have any more costs lodged against us."

"But Sir…," began Pennock.

"But Sir, nothing," responded Worth firmly. "It's over. If you choose to pursue the matter, you do so on your own time, understood?"

Pennock did indeed understand. The Superintendent's hands were tied, but Worth had tacitly granted him another 48 hours grace to get a result.

"Yes Sir. Thank you, Sir."

19

The trial date dawned dull and dreary but nothing could dampen Charles Kingsley's good spirits. He was going to have an absolute field day. He would shine brightly on this dismal morning. The press interest, which had understandably waned over the Christmas period, had been renewed. The scandals and gossip of the rich and famous had quickly tarnished like so many cheap Christmas tree baubles and the papers were now hungry for some fresh pickings. Indeed their interest could almost be said to be approaching a frenzy once again. The timing of the trial couldn't have fallen more conveniently, both for them and himself. There was always that New Year's lull with little news after the manic holiday festivities and extravagances, so a juicy story which combined a public figure in an ugly and deviant scandal was just what the doctor ordered, '*If you'll excuse the pun.*' he thought to himself. Quite witty really, considering his client's profession.

He would dress with care, soberly but not enough to become forgettable. Perhaps a bright coloured tie and a jaunty pocket handkerchief would do the trick. He wanted to be memorable, be in demand and assure that glittering future for himself.

"Bring it on," he said aloud.

Alistair wasn't feeling quite the same exhilaration as his lawyer. He had genuinely believed the case would never come to trial and, despite all Charles's assurances there was nothing to worry about, could not help that desperate sinking sense of anxiety in the pit of his stomach. The post-Christmas optimism he'd briefly enjoyed had been seriously dampened even though Charles had reiterated over and over that the pre-trial disclosure was beyond weak, pathetic really, and would never persuade a jury to convict.

That didn't help much now that the dreaded day had arrived. Alistair had been cleverly coached in what he was to wear during the trial, how to appear innocent and appealing and how to convey, through his body language, that he was obviously a maligned man torn unfairly from his family and career. Well that much was true, he thought self-pityingly. The idea that the whole problem would magically disappear was no longer a possibility, he would have to face his accusers after all.

As Nat got ready, she too was feeling anxious. She had promised her support and she would never break her word. She would sit in the public gallery shoulder to shoulder with Mr. and Mrs Neville in a show of solidarity but she felt like a charletan knowing full well that the moment the trial was over she would be moving far away taking her children with her.

She was now 100% convinced her husband was innocent and that the jury would also recognize that and, please God, he would never be convicted. However, that knowledge wasn't going to be enough to save her marriage, no matter how much Alistair beseeched her to give it another go and just how tempting that offer might be to her. It was over, there could be no coming back now, the trust between them had been broken, more on her side than Alistair's, she had to admit. He strongly believed they could still salvage their relationship, but she knew better. They might survive for a few weeks or even a few months but, eventually the recriminations and blame would start and all the pent up hurt he had to be feeling, would come spewing out. Their lives together would soon become toxic. No, it was better to make a clean break now while things were still relatively harmonious between the two of them. She didn't want to end up hating him, he didn't deserve that.

She put the blame squarely on the police. How hard was it to solve this kind of crime? They had proved to be total shambolic imbeciles. For heaven's sake, they were supposed to be professionals, but they didn't know if they were coming or going. And now it seemed that they didn't have any leads either. They had dismissed her tip about Simon, telling her that, as far as they were concerned, he had been cleared of any involvement. Actually, upon reflection, in many ways this was a relief. Nat was genuinely fond of Simon and he had been a constant and true friend, a loyal confidant who had always been there for her. But in other ways, it meant that Alistair would never be fully exonerated if the police couldn't find the real culprit. The case would undoubtedly go cold, be buried in some basement archive and Alistair would be left in a kind of limbo; not guilty but not quite innocent either.

ii.

Entering the Crown Court later that morning, Detective Inspector Richard Pennock felt the same sinking sensation that Alistair had been experiencing. He was not looking forward to the discussion he was about to have with the Crown Prosecutor. The trial was scheduled to start shortly and they, well he, had a big fat zero to show for it.

"Morning Peter."

Peter Banks Q.C pointedly ignored him and wouldn't even make eye contact with Pennock. He was seething with anger. Finally he spat.

"You've made me look like an incompetent fool, Pennock. We've got nothing, sweet f.a. You swore you'd come up with the goods in time. Now we're going to have to put a motion to withdraw. How in God's name did you persuade me to go against my better judgement and continue when there's clearly no case to answer? You've brought us both into disrepute this time Inspector."

"I'm sorry, Peter. I was certain we were so close. I take full responsibility, put the blame on me. It's my fault."

"Don't you worry, that's exactly what I'm going to do. I'm not carrying the can for your incompetence. Getting a conviction is hard enough as it is, even when the disclosure is compelling, but this was the worst kind of brinkmanship I've ever encountered. You find the suspect then look for the evidence. Shame on you Pennock. I shouldn't be at all surprised if you're not referred to the complaints committee."

His furious diatribe was interrupted by the arrival of His Honour Judge Braithwaite who entered and tapping his gavel, brought the court to order. Before him the newly elected jury of twelve honest and true citizens sat expectantly, enthralled by the occasion, proud to serve their Crown and be part of such a high-profile trial. They could see that the public gallery was full of reporters, family and other interested spectators - some of whom looked as though their interest was rather more salacious and unhealthy than judicial - but, like them all agog to see how the trial would unfold.

Soon Alistair was brought up from the cells and took his place in the dock. He looked, and was, nervous and afraid. No coaching could truly have prepared him for this. Overwhelmed, he trembled slightly as he tried to take stock of his surroundings. But it was all a blur, his brain was struggling to assimilate the scene before him. Finally he caught Charles's eye and felt relief wash over him to see his counsel so confident, collected and prepared. He breathed in deeply and tried to compose himself.

Pennock realized Peter was probably right. His career would be over, a reprimand or worse on his official record would guarantee that. It would be no more than he deserved, he knew. Had he been too arrogant, too self assured that he would solve this case in time? The honest answer was yes, he had. He could have withdrawn the prosecution in a timely manner, just as he had been instructed to do by his superior. He could have continued the investigation in his own time, maybe with Parnell's help and, most importantly, wouldn't have risked his rank and whole career in the process. Whatever the outcome a review might recommend, he now swore to himself that he would find his culprit and bring him to justice. But for today, his mortification was about to be completely compounded as he shamefully had to endure Peter Banks Q.C slowly rising to his feet and announcing somberly that the Crown would be offering no evidence.

Both the Judge and Defense were taken aback at the declaration. It also took the jury a moment to process that the trial would not be going ahead and their disappointment was palpable. Charles too was caught unawares, his surprise quickly turning to peevishness at not being allowed his time in the lime-light. However, he soon rallied. Time to bring Plan B out, ahead of schedule true to say, but an opportune moment nevertheless. And jumping to his feet, proclaimed.

"This is outrageous, Your Honour. Offering no evidence? The prosecution is offering no evidence? Wait until the eleventh hour and then do this? Unbelievable. Truly unbelievable. For months my client has been a pariah, both in the workplace, socially and at home. He has been denied access to his children and his reputation has been brought into the worst kind of disrepute. He has been tormented and ostracized, his marriage has broken down and his mother has suffered a stroke as a direct result of the stress this matter had engendered. Your Honour ..."

"Thank you Mr Kingsley," interjected the Judge smoothly but firmly. And looking sternly at the prosecution table, he continued, "Whilst the Court understands and sympathises with your client in what can only be described as a serious abuse of the criminal justice system, this is not the time nor the place to seek that kind of legal redress. However, let it be noted that this Court is most unhappy with today's proceedings or lack thereof, and makes an order against the C.P.S for Wasted Costs and strongly recommends that you pursue the proper channels in order to acquire the appropriate compensation Dr. Neville deserves."

"Thank you, Your Honour."

Satisfied, Charles sat promptly down. His point had been made and quickly taken. The mission to get the judge to agree in open court that a travesty of justice had occurred had been his primary intent, and secondly, that the reporters covering the case should have it clearly spelled out that there had indeed been a flagrant miscarriage of justice.

Turning to the defendant, the Judge continued.

"Dr. Neville. If I can explain. The prosecution does not intend to offer any evidence against you. Therefore, there will be no trial. This means that you are free to go."

Alistair, bewildered, looked to his lawyer for confirmation, but a beaming Charles was already on his feet and moving towards him. The usher opened the side door to the dock and invited Alistair to step down into the body of the courtroom. Charles shook his hand warmly, giving the press photographers ample time to capture the scene before firmly leading him out of the court and into an adjacent anteroom.

"Well that was short and sweet," Charles commented. "Thank God they came to their senses. But it's not over, not by a long chalk. The fact that the prosecution chose to offer no evidence doesn't mean they believe you're innocent. You're not off the hook yet. It's all rather unsatisfactory really. However, we'll discuss where we go from here in the coming days, formulate a plan. But now's not the moment. I suggest I go and find your family and give you a bit of space with them while I speak to the press." And with that Charles rapidly departed.

Alistair, his parents and Nat wept with relief that the ordeal was finally over. Upon Charles's return, they talked quietly together, still too much in shock to allow the anger to set in.

"Will I be able to return back home now?" Alistair asked hopefully.

Nat stiffened instinctively and this wasn't lost on Charles, who in a rare moment of sympathetic intuition, wondered if the woes of these two were now over or just about to begin.

"I'm sorry Alistair, but you'll have to stay at your parents' for a bit longer. At least until I can have the charges against you formally withdrawn. In theory the bail conditions still apply and we don't want any over-enthusiastic plod carrying out the letter of the law now, do we? It will only be for a few days, I'm sure." he concluded, staring hard at Nat who was limp with relief.

"Alright, I suppose so. If it's only for a while. After what we've been through, a few more days can't hurt, right? I'll soon be home, eh Nat?"

iii.

If the wheels of an internal investigation turned as slowly as the wheels of justice, then Pennock believed he still had a week or two in his current position before the sword of Damocles fell. Returning to work the next day, he walked the long walk of shame back into the Incident Room.

Some officers wouldn't meet his eye, anxious to distance themselves from any association with him and his sullied reputation. Others whispered pointedly amongst themselves. But Sandy and Harry made a public show of solidarity with their governor and Pennock very much welcomed and appreciated their loyalty. Thanking them, he began.

"Before we all get redeployed, I want to arrange for Dr and Mrs Neville to come in for a debrief. I owe them that much,"

"I'll see to it, Gov," Sandy volunteered.

"So what now?" asked Harry.

"Well the important thing is not to get you two implicated in my mismanagement of the case. I was the S.I.O and you two were simply following my orders, alright? And as soon as the Superintendent instructed, you both moved straight on to the next case. That's what happened. Is that understood? No need for you two to carry the can as well, it's my head they'll be after."

Both Sandy and Parnell nodded in grim agreement with their boss's assessment. They would always support their governor, but the truth was there was no need for them all to be reprimanded. He had been the Senior Investigating Officer and they had been following orders. It stuck in the craw, nevertheless.

They were interupted by P.C Brown from the front desk who informed them that a Dr. and Mrs Neville were waiting downstairs and would like to see them.

"Show them in to Interview Room 1. We might as well get this over and done with straight away." Pennock commented. "Sandy, it seems they've saved you the trouble. Can you get the paper-work drawn up to lift bail restrictions and to have their electronics returned to them, please?"

A few minutes later, Pennock and Parnell entered the interview room and were greeted by the stony faces of the Nevilles who were sitting wide apart. After their offer of refreshments had been declined Pennock took the initiative.

"Thanks for coming in today. First of all, I want to apologize for the anguish you've been going through these last few weeks. I take full responsibility for dragging the case out and putting you both through such an ordeal." Pennock raised his hand to forestall Alistair's interjection and continued in a conciliatory tone. "Dr. Neville, if I can just explain my rationale and get you to see that my motives were honest, I hope it will go some way towards you understanding why I didn't drop the case."

Alistair's face glowed with misery, anger and incomprehension. "This had better be good, Inspector. My life's in ruins. I strongly doubt I'll ever have a career in paediatrics again. And you've seen what it's done to my family."

"I know and I sympathise, truly I do. But unless and until we find the real culprit, isn't it fair to say your life will still be in ruins and you'll continue living under a cloud of suspicion for ever more? I, for one don't want that to be the case, and I'm sure you don't either. I believed, and still do for that matter, that the true perpetrator felt secure whilst you were the only obvious suspect. He or she felt immune and invincible - their job done, framing you for a heinous crime against your children. For what purpose we still have no idea. I had hoped to bring that person to justice before the start of the trial, but the leads we were following all proved to be dead ends. In short, I ran out of time. I did my best, that I can promise you, and I won't rest until I discover who it was and why. I give you my word that this will not become a cold case, whoever is responsible will be prosecuted with the full force of the law."

Slightly appeased, but by no means happy, Alistair asked, "And where does that leave me now?"

"Well we're drawing up the paper-work at this moment to have your bail restrictions lifted and your possessions returned. You'll no longer have to report to the station and will be free to return home. With regard to any legal redress, you will have to liaise with your counsel as to the appropriate way forward."

"You said that you haven't got any other leads, Inspector. But, what about Simon Bates?" interjected Nat.

Pennock permitted himself a small smile.

"Ah, well he proved to be one of those dead ends. We thoroughly investigated your tip-off but found nothing remotely suspicious. He admitted to us that he's gay apparently and therefore couldn't have any kind of romantic crush on you. He regards you as a true friend, nothing more. We couldn't determine any other incentive he might have. Furthermore, he fully co-operated with my officers who concur that he simply doesn't have any motive."

"Gay? Simon's gay? I don't think so, Inspector. I would have known, he would have told me." said Nat, unable to hide her surprise. "He's had girlfriends, I'm sure of it. Well, maybe not recently, but I'm convinced that he's as red blooded as the next man."

Pennock regarded her dubiously. The poor woman really was delusional, clutching at straws and pointing the finger anywhere but at her husband. Frankly he believed Harry's instinct over Mrs Neville's any day. Having read the report carefully, he'd agreed with Harry and didn't believe that line of enquiry was worth pursuing any further. But in order to satisfy the woman before him, he reluctantly promised.

"Really? Are you sure? I'm certain he told Sgt. Parnell in those very words, that he was gay. But don't worry Mrs Neville, I'll review the log again and take any appropriate action. I can assure you there will be no stone left unturned. Have you any further questions? No? So, once again, I'd like to offer our sincerest apologies. We'll keep you informed of any future developments. Now, if you'll accompany D.S Parker downstairs, she'll process the paper-work and then you're free to go".

Pennock was relieved that his encounter with the Neville's had gone as well as it had, it could have turned very unpleasant, and frankly he wouldn't have blamed them. Sandy and Harry concurred, although they had all noticed Mrs. Neville looked deeply unhappy.

"Some tough times ahead for that family," observed Sandy upon her return. Pennock and Parnell couldn't help but sadly agree with her. It was clear that the trust between the Nevilles had been shattered, probably irrevocably.

Pennock and his team, like all the officers in the Incident Room, had a back-log of cases clamouring for their attention. There was never enough hours in a day to do justice to them all, and Chief Superintendent Worth had been perfectly correct when he said that the Neville business had taken up a disproportionate amount of police time. It went unsaid, the implication understood between the three of them, that Pennock would continue investigating the matter, but on his own time. But Harry, true to form, said.

"Any time you need a hand, just let me know, Gov."

"That goes for me too, Sir," echoed Sandy.

"Thanks you two. I appreciate it." And he did. No one could have ever asked for a better team

20

As it turned out, Sandy and Harry were separated and assigned different cases with other colleagues in the department. They barely had time to even say hello to each other over the next few days, one usually coming in just as the other was on their way out. Pennock was called to account on the third day after the non-trial, fiasco, debacle, cock-up, take your pick - which Chief Superintendent Worth did, managing to employ all those epithets and a few more choice, colourful and profane ones as well, when he hauled his Detective Inspector over the coals. The dressing down delivered, Worth continued.

"Right then. Enough said. You can expect the Spanish Inquisition to descend any time now. It's not going to be pretty, but I'm behind you all the way and appreciate what you've done to minimize the fallout for Parker and Parnell. Just to let you know they're in the clear. I understand Internal Affairs have looked at their involvement and agree there's no case to answer against them. You're a different story, they're out to make an example of you. Make sure your paper-work is thorough and complete and you've got your story straight. By the way, I don't want to know if you're still going to pursue the Neville business, but, if you do, it's on your own time and on your own head. I don't want any more mud sticking on the department nor on me. Got it? But, it might be good to get to the bottom of it all, if only for your own satisfaction and peace of mind. Meanwhile, you're still one of my senior officers and I need you on the Boutin case. If you get that cleared up sharpish, it could go some way to restoring your reputation a bit."

"Yes Sir, thank you, Sir," responded Pennock humbly.

Worth looked at him suspiciously but could detect no hint of insubordination in his officer. Opening the door and ushering him out Worth said loudly for the benefit of detectives outside who were pretending they had important things to be getting on with but who were all actually on tenderhooks with what was going on in the Super's office.

"Get out of here, Pennock and do your bloody job and get some bloody results for once."

Back in his office, Pennock opened the Boutin file, but his mind couldn't focus on its contents. It was a high profile case. The dwelling of a famous premier league footballer, recently and expensively transferred from PSG, had been burgled and a considerable amount of valuables stolen. That in itself wasn't what made the crime noteworthy - lots of famous people were done over all the time. It was because he had unfortunately been at home at the time when three masked men had broken in, bound and gagged him, trussed him up like a turkey, leaving him otherwise unhurt, but very shaken up by the ordeal. The press were in their element stirring up accusations about foreign gangs and organized crime, maybe even terrorism. Apparently the French footballer believed their voices were Eastern European and now the national rags were spewing out their xenophobic rhetoric, demanding results and action.

'*God give me strength*,' he thought. It wasn't that he wasn't sympathetic, of course he was, but it was all so trivial. It was common knowledge that the footballer was often seen doing the rounds of the clubs and casinos. His wag wife was a well-known wannabe socialite, attention-seeking and keen to be in the lime-light. They both dripped gold and diamonds on their nights out. No wonder they'd got done over.

He called in his newly allocated sergeant, Frank Casey, to ask what progress had been made so far.

"Not much Sir, but it's early days."

There were a few leads he was told and that the officer was about to head out to interview a promising witness who'd been walking his dog at the time and may have seen the whole thing going down. Pennock told Frank that he would accompany him and that he wanted to be fully briefed on the way. Maybe some time away from the office would clear his brain fog and get him enthused for the new case.

They had only gone a couple of miles when Pennock realized that they would be going straight past Natalie Neville's place of work. He hadn't been quite honest with Mrs. Neville when he had told her that he had reviewed the log, in fact it had completely slipped his mind. The details were vague. This might be a golden opportunity to catch - what was his name? - on the hop. Oh yeah, Simon something. He remembered Harry and Sandy had made some kind of saucy joke about it - Bates, that was it. He instructed his surprised sergeant to drop him off and come back for him after the witness interview had been done.

It was a bit of luck to discover that Simon was at work and that there was no sign of Natalie. Belatedly, he thought she might have been embarrassed at him turning up unannounced to interview a suspect she'd recently pointed the finger at. But fortunately it was a moot point. Approaching, he asked if Bates could spare him a few minutes, that he had a few follow-up questions. Pennock could detect no discomfort or anxiety in the man as he was shown into an office, rather bemusement and polite compliance.

"Is this your office?" Pennock asked, and was told no, it was Nat's. Simon decided not to mention that he hoped that very soon it would be his. He pointed out his own workspace located in the body of the room. As far as Pennock could determine from where he stood, it was a bog standard table, perhaps slightly larger than the others, laden down with monitors, modems as well as the usual desk-top paraphernalia. Nothing dodgy going on there, he surmised. Way too visible.

"Mrs Neville not at work today?" he asked, putting his disappointment aside.

Simon looked pained, clearly debating whether to tell Inspector Pennock the whole story. To his great satisfaction and pride he was in fact, the only one she had confided in so far, revealing that she would shortly be handing in her notice and be moving away to live closer to her parents. She had sworn him to secrecy, and although she hadn't said, in so many words, that it was over between herself and Dr. Neville, she had certainly never mentioned that he was going with them. So he'd drawn his own conclusions.

He had to admit he would miss her terribly, she was a wonderful friend and boss. They had so much in common and were each other's confidants in most things. But every cloud and all that ... her job would be up for grabs and he was quietly convinced that he was the number one candidate to succeed her. So, he would keep it brief, he decided, be economical with the truth - if Nat had wanted the Old Bill to know her plans, he was certain she would have told them.

"She's taken some leave. I don't know for sure when she'll be back. Is there something I can help you with, Inspector?"

"Actually yes, Mr. Bates, it was you I came to see. I know Sgt. Parnell took a preliminary statement from you recently, and I would like to arrange a closing interview with you, if you don't mind. I know you're at work now and I don't want to take up any more of your valuable time. Would it be convenient to come to your home address this evening?"

Simon looked somewhat disconcerted.

"A closing interview? I've never heard of one of those."

'Of course not,' thought Pennock, because he'd just invented it.

"Couldn't we do it now? I'm relatively free at the moment."

"Unfortunately not, sir. My sergeant is waiting for me downstairs. We're on our way to another case. I just popped in on the off chance I would catch you. So what time shall we make it? 5.30 suit you?" Pennock didn't want to dither or give Bates too long to get prepared.

"Fine. If I have to. I'll see you then," Simon reluctantly agreed.

ii.

Pennock had been waiting patiently in his car well before Bates got home and tailed him into the flat a moment after he had entered the building, slipping through the front security door before it latched closed. He stepped smartly into the foyer just as the lift doors closed on Bates. Pennock took the other lift up to the seventh floor and the doors opened as Bates was entering his flat. Perfect timing, Bates wouldn't have a chance to remove any incriminating evidence.

He knocked firmly and the door was opened by a rather taken aback Simon Bates.

"Inspector, you've hardly given me time to take my coat off," he complained. Then suspiciously, "And how did you get in? You're supposed to be buzzed in."

"That's strange, the door was open, so I thought I'd come straight up," Pennock lied. "Alright if I come in?"

Bates reluctantly allowed him in. Simon Bates's residence was exactly as Harry had described it - pristine. Compact and bijou in estate agent's parlance.

"Nice place, mind if I have a look around?"

And before Simon could object, Pennock was out of the room and heading towards, what he assumed was, the bedroom.

He returned a few moments later, annoyed but not surprised at having Harry's observations confirmed. There was no evidence of anything untoward in the flat at all, no high-tech gizmos, paedo magazines nor, sadly, any signed confessions. Undeterred, Pennock took a seat opposite Bates.

Taking his time, he looked around, taking it all in, just as he knew Parnell would have done. The flat was extremely comfortable, not in the sense of lavish decoration and furnishings, but rather, having some tasteful, choice pieces artfully arranged and/or restored, all displayed in a home that was immaculately clean. There wasn't a speck of dust to be seen, nor a thing out of place. Bordering on OCD if not a full-blown case, surmised Pennock. There were a few family photos in old fashioned silver frames showing Bates with, who Pennock supposed, were his mother and father. No photos of any significant other half on display though.

"Thank you for your co-operation, Mr.Bates. I've just got a few further questions for you, if that's ok."

"Go ahead, Inspector. As I said before, if there's anything at all I can do to help." Clearly Bates had recovered his composure and had decided to be amenable.

Pennock took out his notebook more for effect, knowing that Parnell's report had been thorough, but nevertheless in case Bates said something worth recording.

"Mr. Bates, may I remind you that you are still under caution?"

Simon acknowledged his agreement with a slight nod.

"Very well. Could you just tell me about your connection with the Neville family."

"Well, as I told your sergeant, I work with Natalie - Mrs. Neville that is - and have done for a number of years. I hardly know Dr. Neville at all. Probably just meet him a couple of times a year, that's all."

"And what's your job within the company?"

"My main function is I.T. although we all turn our hands to most things. It's still a fairly small operation, and we're expected to pitch in - but we're doing well. The directors of the firm believe in rewarding their employees which promotes a strong feeling of loyalty and belonging. They consult with us on ideas and innovations and really take on board any good suggestions. I think there's a good future for me with them."

"That's good to hear," replied Pennock politely. "Now, you say you've worked with Mrs Neville for a number of years. How well do you think you know each other?"

"Very well, I think." Simon paused to consider. "She's more than just a boss, I'd count her as a close friend. But having said that, we don't often meet up socially, just once in a blue moon.

Obviously she's got a young family and husband to get back to. Frankly I don't know how she juggles such a hectic life. Anyway, I suppose, you could say that we know each other mainly from in the workplace."

"So, it would be fair to say that she knows you quite well too?" Pennock asked.

"Of course. Nat's the mother hen of the office. Nothing gets by her. She keeps a look out for all her team, keeps everyone in line and productive. She's an excellent manager and good friend to us all. I'm certain the others would all agree as well."

"So you see, that's where we have a contradiction of opinion, if, as you say, *'nothing gets by her'*."

Bates looked confused, so Pennock decided to come straight out with it.

"Mr. Bates, I understand you told Sgt. Parnell that you were gay, but when Mrs. Neville was told, she disputed this and insisted that she's known you to have girlfriends and no way are you gay. So I'm a bit confused. Now you understand the contradiction. Which one of you is right?"

Simon had the grace to look embarrassed, but nevertheless took his time replying. Looking Pennock in the eye, he stated.

"I'm not gay, Inspector."

"Then why say you are?"

"You don't know what it was like, having someone, a policeman, come uninvited into your home, snooping around, touching your things and making judgements about you. When your officer started commenting on my lifestyle, I just said the first thing that came into my head. I felt like I was the one under suspicion."

"It's not part of my officer's remit to pass judgement on people's personal affairs, Mr Bates. My sergeant was carrying out a lawful investigation into a very serious crime, not prying in to your private life." responded Pennock officiously. Bates looked thoroughly abashed.

"I realize that now and I'm sorry. But it was said in the heat of the moment - no real harm done, eh?"

"Probably not, Mr. Bates, don't worry. I'm sure it isn't relevant to our enquiries. But, by the way, do you live alone or are you seeing anyone? There only seems to be family photos?" Pennock asked as an apparent afterthought.

Simon replied tiredly.

"No. I'm not going out with anyone, Inspector. I'm happy to bide my time at the moment - waiting for the right woman to come along, I suppose. So, there's just me and my dear old Mum. Dad died a few years ago - now it's just the two of us."

Pennock stood up and making a show of putting away his notebook, said.

"Well thank you for clarifying that for me, Mr. Bates. Sorry to have taken up so much of your time. Have a good evening."

iii.

The silence was shattering. The air literally vibrated with tension. Alistair was speechless with shock and incomprehension, his face gaunt and white. Slowly it dawned on him that she was serious, she really meant it. This was a living nightmare, worse than any of the horrors he had previously endured.

She had asked him to come round to the house while the children were at school, saying they needed to talk. Naturally he had taken the call as a good sign. New year, new resolutions and a fresh start. Maybe he would be moving back in by the end of the day. The children would be delirious with joy to have their Dad back once more. He was more than ready to return to the family home and he didn't doubt for a minute that his parents would be relieved to have their own house back to themselves again.

"You're leaving me? Moving away?" he was incredulous.

"Yes. Yes I am. I'm sorry. It's true." Nat knew there was no point in sugar-coating it. She wasn't going to give him false hope, it wouldn't be fair. She had to be cruel to be kind. "I spent the Christmas holidays looking for a new school for the children. In fact, they'll be going to my old primary school. It's got a good reputation, they're bound to do well there. And we'll move in with Mum and Dad in the meantime, till I can find myself a job. Then we can look for our own place to live in."

She couldn't look him in the eye as she delivered her speech. She couldn't bear to see the hurt she was deliberately but unavoidably inflicting on him. Presenting him with a fait accompli over something so important, something which concerned them all, was unfair, yet it was a decision she was determined she would have to take alone.

"No Nat, please don't do this. Once the furore's died down, we'll get our lives back on track. Things'll go back to the way they were. And anyway, you can't just go doing this without consulting me. I've got a right to have a say in what happens to my own kids."

His voice was full of anguish at what was about to happen but not with righteous anger as yet. Nat knew that emotion would not be long in arriving.

"Of course you've got every right to have a say in what happens to them. I'd never prevent that. They're your children and you love them and will always be a huge part of their lives. But no, Alistair, you're wrong about life getting back to normal. Things will never go back to the way they were. It's impossible. That's all in the past now, it's over and done with. Believe me, there's been too much pain, hurt, suspicion, accusations - you name it. Mainly caused by me, I admit it. You asked me to have faith in you and I let you down. Al, you may not hold it against me now, but you will, you will do one day, I know, and rightly so. I believed for a very little while that you actually were capable of it. What kind of wife does that make me? You'll never trust me again, nor I you, if I'm honest. Sooner or later it would destroy us."

"But we're aware of all that now, we can avoid it, get past it. I can't live without you and the kids. I don't want to be apart from you."

"Stop being naive, Alistair." Nat warned him. She'd had time to prepare for this moment, had thought the whole thing through. She had weighed up the situation and knew without a doubt that there was no future for them now. She had had the benefit of time to reflect upon it, Alistair hadn't. She had to remain firm, she wouldn't, couldn't be deflected by his heartfelt appeal. She strengthened her resolve. "We could steer a clear path for a while but all the hurt and anguish is bound to build up and overflow one day. It's only a question of time. It's true. In your heart of hearts you know I'm right."

Alistair remained silent. What she was saying did hold some truth. Much against his will, he had already begun to feel a sense of bitterness against her. Actually Nat wasn't the only one, he too had had plenty of time to reflect on the events of the last few weeks and months and although he had tried to put the negative thoughts to the back of his mind, in all honesty, he had never quite succeeded. The resentment had been quietly festering beneath the surface - simmering malignly - unawares he now realized. Confronting the reality, he had to face the fact that she hadn't been by his side the whole way through, had she? Why not? Because she wasn't commited enough, she had doubted him. She herself, had admitted it. She had only lent her full support once she was convinced he was innocent.

Added to that, she had been cool towards him for some time now. Maybe she thought he hadn't noticed that she'd avoided being alone with him, that she had subtley been distancing herself. They hadn't kissed or even touched each other for weeks. No, that was probably not a sound basis to move forward with their marriage, he had to acknowledge that fact. Nevertheless, he wouldn't give up without a fight. He would never admit defeat, nor ever be separated from his children.

"But Nat, it's so far away. I want to be able to see you and the kids all the time. Can't you be nearer?"

He knew he was begging but couldn't help himself.

"I've thought about that, but I'm going to need my parent's support to start off with. I think a fresh beginning is for the best, I really do. But more to the point Al, what are you going to do? Will you be going back to the hospital and staying here, or has the whole business made your position untenable? Do you plan to go somewhere else?"

"I don't know," he had to admit miserably. "It's all up in the air at the moment. I've got a meeting with the board next week. Charles says they've got no right to fire me, that legally they should reinstate me, obviously, as the charges were proved unfounded. But, he says I've got to face facts, that they're hardly going to welcome me back with open arms. He reckons that they'll pay lip-service to the letter of the law but get rid of me on some other grounds. Hopefully, they'll sweeten the deal with a cash incentive, but I'll probably be out on my ear. He says they're old hands at giving people the push without leaving themselves open to unfair dismissal claims. He's not hopeful."

"So, the chances are you'll be leaving the hospital? Will you have any trouble finding somewhere else to go?"

"I don't think I could stay on, even if they did keep me. It'd be too awkward." Alistair paused - an idea forming, taking shape. Then he thought he might as well test the water. He didn't think he had anything left to lose.

"Perhaps I could look at somewhere closer to where you and the kids are going to be? Could that be a possibility. Would you be ok with that?"

He was as happy as he could be under the circumstances, certainly happier than he had been for what seemed like a long, long time, when Nat replied.

"Al, I'd like that, and I know it would make the children happy too.

21

The next day, Pennock was reviewing the Boutin file but found he couldn't concentrate. His mind kept wandering back to the interview of the previous night. Something was nagging at the back of his consciousness, something he couldn't quite put his finger on. He remembered that nothing had seemed amiss at the time, so what was it that was bugging him now? He hadn't actually intended to take any notes but was glad that he had, albeit a bit scratty. He read through them again. No, nothing jumped out. It was all consistent with the report Harry had drawn up. Why then, did he feel there was something off? What was he missing or couldn't see? Or was he trying to force-fit the facts again, just as he had been accused of doing by the CPS? He knew he'd never fitted anyone up in his life and wasn't about to start now, but it was like trying to do a jigsaw puzzle, pressing in a piece that looked like it should fit but putting it into the wrong place.

He didn't have time to dwell on the problem when his sergeant came to brief him on the witness statement that had been taken the evening before. It had been very useful and, with a bit of luck, would lead to an arrest and conviction. It turned out that the witness was a member of the community watch group who had been observant and clear in his recollection of that evening, but more importantly, had jotted down the presumed get-away car's number plate.

"Thank goodness for nosy neighbours. They might be the bane of our lives, always calling with imagined crimes in progress, but sometimes they have their uses. Let's get him down here straight away to make an official statement. We want this to be done as cleanly and quickly as possible"

Pennock had to commend his officer's diligence and admitted to him that he couldn't take the slightest credit for the result, for his imput had been zero.

"Well done Frank. And do we know where the suspect the witness mentions, lives?"

"Yes Sir, and he's well known to us. I think you'll know him too, it's Pete Barnes. Got plenty of previous for shop-lifting, burglary, car theft etc. This seems to be an escalation for him though. Usually he acts on his own, opportunistic like, so being part of a gang is quite a departure for him. The car's also registered in his name to the same home address that we have on record. Looks like he was the get away driver. Clearly not the sharpest knife in the drawer. And as far as we know, he hasn't got any ties with Eastern Europeans."

"Right, bring him in, read him his rights and let's see if he coughs to the burglary. If he hasn't got any ties, maybe he'll grass up the others. Depends what hold they've got over him. Let's hope this isn't the start of an investigation into organized crime, or God forbid, terrorism. And Frank? You can take the lead in the interview."

Frank was delighted. "Thanks Gov, but I'd appreciate it if you were in there all the same."

"Will do. Credit where credit's due, Frank," he was told.

Frank swiftly departed with a couple of constables to pull in the witness and Barnes, while Pennock nabbed Parnell on his way out of the office.

"Got time for a cuppa, Harry?"

Harry looked at his watch.

"I'd prefer a beer, but I suppose as it's only 10 o'clock in the morning, tea will have to do. Alright, let's go down to the canteen. It'll be quieter there."

Pennock got straight to the point.

"Harry, I won't delay you. Just to let you know, I reinterviewed Simon Bates last night. Mrs. Neville was adamant he's not gay. She kept on pushing it. It was a loose end that I needed to tie up for my own peace of mind as well. Anyway, he admitted he's not. Said he made it up in the heat of the moment, that your presence intimidated him blah blah blah."

"Well he gave a bloody good impression of it," commented Harry.

"I agree, but the fact is, he's not. That apart, what other impressions did you get about him?"

Harry thought back.

"Well he seemed open enough, I suppose. Answered all my questions. He talked a lot but didn't really say anything much."

"Yeah, yeah you're right. He did talk a lot - but about a whole load of nothing. I agree."

"Gov, I've got to say he seemed kosher to me. A bit strange alright, a bit of a saddo. Obsessive about cleanliness and tidiness and a real mummy's boy, but then, that's not a crime, is it?"

"Probably should be though. Yeah, I'm sure you're right. I just had to be certain about him, that's all, double check with you before I put it to bed. Thanks Harry."

The two men went their separate ways, Harry to wherever he had been going in the first place, and Pennock to Interview Room 2 where Frank awaited with Pete Barnes.

ii.

Barnes immediately knew they'd got him banged to rights, when he was told about the witness. Just what he needed, some flaming do-gooder sticking his nose in where it wasn't wanted. He had never been the greatest criminal mind and knew now he should have stuck to the petty stuff. All his life he'd lived on the dodgy side of the law but had managed to get by without drawing too much attention to himself. Why, oh why had he agreed to do the driving?

"So you're denying your involvement in the burglary, Pete?" began Frank after giving the Miranda warning and determining that no, Barnes wouldn't like his solicitor present.

Barnes was righteously indignant, they weren't pinning that on him.

"Too right I am. I wasn't in on the burglary, I was just the bleedin' driver. No way you're fittin' me up for what went on in the house, I wasn't even in there."

"But Pete, being the driver makes you an accessory to the crime and therefore just as guilty."

"No way, man. They was out of control, tying the poor bloke up like that. Might have damaged his legs, finished his career. I wouldn't have never done nuffin' like that, he's the best thing that's happened to United for years."

Frank had to agree with Barnes on that point and also that he was probably telling the truth for once.

He continued.

"Tell us about the lads that did the burglary."

Barnes went silent, tight lipped. He wasn't about to give them up. Frank sat and stared at him until Barnes started to squirm in his chair.

"I'm not telling you lot nuffin'."

"Alright Pete, then we'll tell you something. You're an accessory to an aggravated burglary on a famous person."

If Frank were a betting man he'd wager that Barnes wouldn't know that it didn't matter if you were famous or not, an aggravated burglary was equally serious for all.

"Plus you've got previous as long as your arm. You're looking at a probable 3-5 years custodial. On top of that we have the terrorism side of it ..."

"What you talkin' about, man? I ain't no terrorist."

"Looks like you might be by association. Mr Boutin believed his assailants were Eastern Europeans. You can never be too careful these days."

"Eastern Europeans? What the hell's he talkin' about? They wasn't no Eastern Europeans."

"Are you certain? Mr Boutin was quite sure that the intruders had strong foreign accents, which he believed to be Eastern European."

"What's that stupid Frog talkin' about?" Barnes was rattled. Suddenly Boutin wasn't quite as hero worshipped as he had been a few minutes before. "They wasn't foreign ... they was from Glasgow."

"From Glasgow?" repeated Frank turning towards Pennock with raised eyebrows and barely able to suppress a grin.

"Yeah, they was a crew what come down on them *'Take away days'*."

Both Frank and Pennock looked blankly at him.

"Yeah, they come down, *'take away'* and go straight back up norf. Been doin' it for ages. Come down on the train, that's why they needed a driver to take 'em to Wagland."

"Right, let's see if we've got this straight. There's a crew who regularly come down from Glasgow on the train, they carry out a burglary in some exclusive part of the city and then take the train back home with the gear."

"Yeah, that's right."

"And how are you connected with them?"

"I ain't connected wiv 'em. Never even met 'em before. Got the word down the boozer that some Scottish crew needed a driver and there would be a bullseye in it, so I said I'd do it. They'd asked Motson but he can't drive, so Andy put them on to me. Wish he hadn't now."

Andy Motson, there was that name again. He seemed to be cropping up more than his fair share of the time.

"So you got paid £50? Not exactly a fortune. You're right Pete, it wasn't really worth it," commented Frank. "Ok, so Andy Motson put you on to the job - you can't tell us who they are because you don't know, but maybe you can tell us what time train they caught back up to Scotland?"

A defeated Barnes told them it was the 17.45 and seeing as he'd been so cooperative, could they be see their way to being lenient? Frank almost felt a genuine pang of compassion for him.

"I'm sorry Pete, but I'm going to have to charge you with aggravated burglary but I'll tell the CPS everything. I can't promise anything but we will let them know you've been helpful in the investigation. That's the best I can do for now. It'll go in your favour if we can spot the crew on CCTV and you can positively identify them, and we get a conviction. Understand?"

He did. Barnes was released on conditional bail and sadly left the police station to enjoy what little was left of his freedom whilst he still could.

Pennock was splitting his sides.

"Glasgow? Really? I've heard it all now. That's got to take the biscuit. Anyway, I think you've got this sewn up now, Frank. CCTV at railway stations is usually first class."

Frank winced at the unintended pun.

"Shouldn't have any problem with facial recognition, if they've got previous, which they likely will have. Otherwise why would they bother to come all the way down here? It can't just be for the easy pickings."

Frank agreed and said he'd get on to it straight away.

"Let's meet at the end of the day and see what progress you've made. I'll inform Worth that there's nothing to get worked up about re the terrorist angle and then you can give him a full report later on. Then we'll have to decide if Glasgow will make the arrests or if we should go up there and do it ourselves."

Both men were more than happy with the day's outcome and relieved that there was nothing more sinister involved and that they wouldn't have to bring in any outside agencies to combat the non existent Eastern European threat. Pennock was particularly pleased he could report back to the Super that the case was on the point of being closed. It wouldn't do his situation any harm to have a few collars under his belt before Internal Affairs closed in.

iii.

Driving home that evening, Pennock had to admit it had been a good day, despite the threat of disciplinary action being taken against him. He had advised Frank to close the case quickly and cleanly and that's exactly what had happened. Worth had been pleased too, his end of month figures would look good, despite the hiccup the Neville case had caused. Perhaps he would come out looking good too, or at least a bit more competent than the Review Board might think him to be.

As he waited in traffic Pennock let his mind wander back over the events of the last couple of days. Coincidentally, he realized, both matters he had been looking into involved verbal interaction and misinterpretation; the Boutin case where the language barrier had almost caused an international terrorist alert, all because of a misunderstanding of the origins of an accent, and the Bates business where there was apparently plenty of communication being exchanged without much information being conveyed.

Could that have been a case of misinformation or misdirection? Or was he still reading too much into it? Despite what Harry thought, and he had agreed with him at the time, there was something still niggling away at the back of Pennock's consciousness. Something that was itching his neurons but which he couldn't quite reach to scratch. In his mind he replayed the interviews that had taken place in Bates' work and at home. What exactly had Bates said that might be of value?

He had talked about his professional and personal friendship with Mrs Neville. Anything odd there, out of the usual? Nope, Pennock had to concede, nothing that would cause alarm bells to ring. What he had said was natural and consistent with what friends/colleagues might say about each other.

Then he had spoken briefly about his job. What was it again? Oh yeah, he was part of a small but growing company, that everyone was expected to turn their hand to any task, but he was the I.T guy. His desk had all the techie tools someone doing that job would routinely use, in fact all of the desks had P.Cs on them and there had been an industrial printer in the office and other stuff which he hadn't the foggiest idea what function they served.

And he had alluded to the close team atmosphere and encouragement of ideas by the management, promotion opportunities. It all fitted, had a ring of truth about it. They were a close knit unit who all looked out for each other. Pennock finally had to admit he was wasting his time on Bates. There was nothing going on there. Harry was right, put it to bed, it was time to let this red herring go too.

He arrived home, and for the first time in a while didn't dread seeing the look of fear on his wife's face. He couldn't bear to see her distress, being the cause of it yet not be able to do anything about it. But suddenly it didn't matter. It was going to be alright he was certain. Whether or not he solved the case, he knew he had acted honourably and decently in the Neville investigation. He had done his utmost. He was sure the Board would see it from his point of view once he explained everything. Anyway there was nothing he could do about it now except damage limitation. He wasn't going to let it get him down, he'd be well prepared when the time came, and face it when he had to.

Katherine was normally a steady and objective woman, well used to being the wife of a career officer and accepting of all that it entailed; the long hours, early starts and late finishes, burned or binned dinners, a snatched kiss as he flew out the door, a quick hug with the kids. She had known what she was signing up for and had supported her husband every step of the way. But now she was frantically worried that Richard would be demoted, or worse still, dismissed for gross incompetence. The force was his life, his vocation. She knew that he was a sound and thorough officer, one of the very best, but that might not be enough. Could he stay on in the same nick if he was reduced in rank? Would he want to, or would it be too demeaning? Might they even have to consider moving?

The timing really couldn't have been any worse. She wasn't just thinking about herself, that was bad enough, but she wasn't that selfish. No, the children were happy and settled, in great local schools and doing really well. They had a wonderful group of friends and plenty of activities on the go to keep them busy. She and Richard had acquired a solid friendship base with other parents from school, as well as with some of her former co-workers, when she was a solicitor's clerk, and some of Richard's present colleagues at work. She hoped his work friends would stand by him, that was going to be a test of their true loyalty. It would be interesting to see if they thought the bad luck might rub off and tarnish them by association. Somehow, she didn't think so. They were better than that. Nevertheless, she'd hate to have to give it all up.

Neither could the news that she was expecting their third child have come at a worse moment. What should have been exciting, had proved to be a burden to them both. Of course she hadn't expected to fall pregnant this quickly - Oh God, she had even been drinking wine right up until she'd done the pregnancy test - not the most auspicious start. Of course Richard had said he was thrilled, he had to though, didn't he? They had been planning on completing their family and this should have been perfect. But he had to be as worried as she was. Oh, he hid it well and promised everything would be alright, but how did he know for sure? She hated being so pessimistic but better that she reckoned, than burying their heads in the sand, and pretending it would all go away and everything would be alright.

So, she was very pleased to see him come in looking more relaxed than she'd seen him for ages. And putting on a bright smile, she poured him a can of his favourite Boddy's and told him to sit down for a bit. The kids were upstairs doing their homework and dinner would be in twenty minutes. She joined him on the sofa with a sparkling water and, with some trepidation, asked him about his day.

Dinner was an easy going, happy meal. The children had sensed things were not right and had been unusually quiet of late, but this evening was full of banter, chat and boisterous laughter. Mum was in a good mood, their Dad was home early for once, homework was done and dusted, so they all settled down to watch yet another re-run of the kids' favourite film. Good old Disney, as well as singing along to all the songs, they knew just about all the character's dialogues as well. It was the relief and distraction the whole family needed, to let off steam and forget their worries for a while. The evening was rounded off with raucous shrieks and squeals as their Dad chased the children upstairs, into the bath, then tucked them up soundly in bed with a quick and, as usual, true police story where the children were the investigating officers and he was the baddy destined to be caught by them.

As he and Kath settled down to watch some inane telly, he realized it was just the diversion he'd needed. He was fortunate to have a loving wife and wonderful children. With one more on the way. He couldn't help the smile that crossed his lips as he gently placed his hand on his wife's as yet non existent bump. He really wanted this child, boy or girl, he didn't mind. He knew Kath was scared of what the future might hold and that his blandishments were not convincing her as yet, but he had faith it would all turn out ok. Time would tell.

22

"Morning Gov," said Harry the next day. "Heard you and Frank got a collar in the Boutin case yesterday."

"No thanks to me, Harry. Frank had it just about stitched up before I was put on it. Anyway we're not quite there yet. We haven't formally charged them. We're off up to Glasgow in a bit, 11.45 train, to interview the suspects. Glasgow Central had them identified in double quick time from CCTV and has got them locked up in the station. Three brothers, the McKays, well known up there apparently. Regular little Robin Hoods - stealing from the rich but keeping it for themselves. Central was quick getting a search warrant, so they hadn't had time to offload all the gear and the idiot brothers still had most of it round their mum's house. Glasgow told us the older brother was actually wearing Boutin's Rolex, and his mum had on some pretty expensive diamond earrings."

"Amateurs," observed Harry disgustedly. "Well enjoy your day trip up to chilly Jocko-land. See you when you get back."

Pennock, Frank and Chief Superintendent Worth had met earlier that morning to consider how to proceed. They agreed there was no need for any posturing or guarding of juristiction. Glasgow was welcome to the prosecution. Worth had discussed it with his oppo in Central and he had concurred.

It might have been a different story had there been the terrorist edge to it, then they'd have fought tooth and nail for the glory of a conviction, but not over an aggravated burglary. They decided Pennock and Frank would go up and carry out the interviews and charge the trio, but that the trial - if there were to be any trial - would go ahead in Scotland, no need to go to all the expense of dragging them back down south of the border. Both forces could take the credit and London Road's costs would probably only be a couple of officer's return rail fares and a one way ticket for Pete Barnes.

It had all gone to plan. The Chief Superintendent at Central had been a decent bloke, made them very welcome and deferred to them under their agreement. One of his officers would be present during the interviews, to become thoroughly au fait with events of the burglary. The three brothers, in turn, knew when they were beaten - fools to be caught red handed with the goods. There had been no need to do the good cop/bad cop scenario.

They hadn't charged Mrs. McKay as an accessory, although she had undoubtedly been in on it. Pragmatism dictated that there was no point making a good result more complicated. The family was notorious in the area with the mother being the domineering matriarch of them all. All her boys would be looking at lengthy stretches, perhaps that would be punishment enough for her. Pennock and Frank took the return train back, tired but well satisfied with the result.

Police expenses treated them to a dinner in the buffet car and a couple of beers. After, Pennock just couldn't keep his eyes open any longer. Travelling always took it out of him, that plus the success of the day. Frank was already out for the count. Pennock dozed, head leaning against the steamed up carriage window. He let his mind drift. What was it with men and their mothers, he wondered? Some seemed destined to be mummy's boys forever, such as the likes of the three McKay brothers and Simon Bates - all kept firmly under the maternal thumb.

That niggle at the back of Pennock's mind startled him rudely awake. Could that be it? He recalled the family photos, the family of three, and then more recently, just the two of them, ones of just Simon and his mother. But what he could not remember seeing, as he reviewed the landscape of Simon's sitting room in his mind's eye, was any evidence whatsoever of technology in that flat. Ok, not quite true, there was the obligatory t.v and a mobile phone, but what young man these days doesn't have a laptop or P.C, an iPad, a Play Station, or other types of boys' toys? Especially someone who lives alone. What does that person do for entertainment? That wasn't normal, was it? What young man, who also happened to be the company I.T whizz kid, didn't have I.T at home as well? Well there was a conundrum, to be sure - and Pennock, for one, didn't like puzzles he couldn't solve.

ii.

There was always a brief lull after a case was closed, before the allocation of the next pressing matter fell on the desk. Pennock left Frank to write up the report which he'd review and sign off before finally allowing his sergeant to submit it. He took the opportunity to seek out Sandy Parker.

"You busy at the moment?" he asked casually.

She regarded him speculatively, finally answering.

"Nothing I can't put off. What you got in mind, Gov?"

"Fancy a little ride out? Get some fresh air?"

"See a man about a dog?" she completed the refrain.

"Actually, see a woman about a dog, as it happens," came the cryptic response.

"You've got me intrigued. What's it all about?"

"I'll explain on the way. I need you as female liaison, if that's ok with you?"

"Give me five minutes. I'll just sort this and let my Gov, the new Gov that is, know that I'll be gone for a bit. I don't think he'll ask any awkward questions. He's alright as it turns out and knows we've still got some unfinished business."

"That's a relief," remarked Pennock. He could do without anyone asking those awkward questions.

As Sandy drove, Pennock outlined his theory, explaining exactly how and why he'd come to the conclusion he had. From Sandy's perspective, the saga he recounted lurched from one train of thought to another, the supposed leads and logic apparently random and disconnected. Sandy wasn't convinced, commenting it all sounded a bit far fetched. She reminded him how they'd been up a few blind alleys before, and, to her, this smacked of yet another waste of time.

She didn't want to accuse him of making the facts fit again, but she knew her old boss would never let it rest while there was a chance he could be correct. She didn't know if she was doing the right thing, sticking by him, or was she hammering the last nail into her own career coffin? One error in professional management might be forgiven, but two would seem like an unacceptable pattern.

"Listen Sandy, I've got a gut feeling about this. And if I'm right, I'm going to need you alongside, fighting in my corner."

She was beginning to regret her promise of loyalty and support. There was a very real danger of her being dragged down too. She gave herself a vicious mental shake. What was she thinking? This was a man she admired and respected. He'd taught her everything she knew and had given her a chance to develop professionally. He was selfless and generous. Why was she doubting him now?

Sandy considered her response before answering carefully.

"Sir, if you really think you're on to something, I think we should get Harry out here as well."

Pennock debated with himself, clearly in two minds whether to involve his former sergeant. If he was wrong Harry would never survive the fallout either. It could be all of their careers down the pan.

But she was probably right. Hell, he was convinced now that he was definitely right. Harry deserved to be there too.

"Make the call," he instructed.

iii.

They waited in the car around the corner, out of sight of the house, taking in the neighbourhood in the meantime. A pleasant, middle-class, residential street. Little groups of semis, all boasting well-maintained properties with immaculate gardens. Most people were out at work, it seemed, for there were very few cars on driveways and no sign of twitching net curtains as yet. It looked like a close knit community where all the neighbours knew and cared about each other.

As he waited, Pennock logged in to his police laptop to see what he could trawl up regarding the family. Not much, it transpired. He hadn't been expecting much, but discovered that Mrs. Bates had lived at the same address for over thirty five years and confirmed that Simon was her only child. There appeared to be two death certificates, first for a three day old baby girl, deceased two years before the birth of Simon and another issued four years ago, presumably for Simon's late father Edward Arthur Bates. A retired accountant was recorded as his occupation. There was nothing else of note, no criminal convictions, no county court judgements - not so much as a speeding ticket or parking fine as far as he could ascertain. Well, he supposed, even that lack of information told him something about the family.

Harry arrived within thirty minutes. He'd come up with some cock and bull story to escape the office but suspected nobody had been fooled. He'd been caught on the hop by the sudden summons and had never been any good at improvising. Inspector Pennock, Sandy Parker and now, himself would be conspicuous by their absence. It wouldn't take long for Worth to hear about it. He hoped to God he wasn't laying his career on the line, just when he'd been given a *'get out of jail free card'*.

Pennock had said very little, only to get himself over to this address asap, and that he would explain everything when he arrived. He parked up behind Sandy and got into the back of their car.

"What's going on, Gov?" he asked nervously.

Pennock related once again the theory he'd expounded to Sandy Parker. This time it sounded more coherent. He'd got his jumbled thoughts into some kind of order, more focused and detailed. He told Harry with brief, factual clarity what he suspected and what they would be looking for. Pennock said he was hoping for cooperation from the house holder, but told Harry, that he was sorry to have dragged him all the way over, but please get back to H.Q to organize a search warrant, just in case, then to get himself over to Bates' place of work and bring him back to his mother's house.

Harry set off straight away while Pennock briefly outlined to Sandy how he wanted to deal with Elizabeth Bates.

A surprised Mrs. Bates opened the door to their ring, looking at her watch. It was clear she had been expecting someone else.

"You're early, love. Ooh sorry, I thought you were my son."

"No, we're sorry to call without warning, Mrs Bates. We're police officers. Is it alright if we come in?" asked Sandy, taking the lead.

Elizabeth Bates closely inspected Pennock's and Sandy's warrant cards before leaning out to look up and down the street to check if anyone might have observed the police arriving on her doorstep. Satisfied, she allowed them into the house. She showed them into *'the good room'*, invited them to make themselves comfortable and with inherent good manners, excused herself to make some tea.

"A lot more homely than Bates' flat." whispered Pennock. "Of course, all this furniture dates from the seventies or eighties and Bates' pad is modern and minimalist by comparison. But this place is warm and cosy, a proper family home, it couldn't be more different."

They could both tell that, old as it was, the furniture was good quality and durable, but still serviceable. The same could be said about the furniture in her son's apartment, that it had been made to last. The difference being that his home held no warmth, no welcome, it was sterile.

Mrs Bates returned with a laden tray, bearing home-made cake and, what was probably, her best china. She sat down primly. She was of medium height, and slimly built. Possibly in her mid sixties. However, her grey hair was nicely cut and styled, she was what a woman of her generation might be called *'neat and trim'*. Her overall appearance gave an impression a woman who took care of herself without excessive vanity.

"I don't get too many visitors, especially not the police." she began. "Was it Simon you wanted to see? He's out at work of course at the moment. Actually he doesn't live here, he lives in his own flat now, but I'm expecting him round for his tea this evening. He doesn't usually visit on a Tuesday, but he said he had some important things to sort out and he needed to get them done tonight. Oh, why am I babbling on so much? I always gabble when I'm nervous!"

Mrs. Bates knew she was rambling. Why was it you felt guilty in front of police officers, even if you knew you'd done nothing wrong? For their part, Pennock and Sandy let her witter on. So often information was revealed through nervous chatter.

Pennock took up the lead, noting that it seemed the mother was as talkative as her son, and that hopefully she would let something significant slip.

"Don't worry Mrs. Bates. The police often have that effect on the public. Actually it's both of you we'd like to talk to. We can speak to you first before Simon gets home, if that's ok with you." He continued without giving Mrs. Bates the chance to agree or disagree. "Mrs. Bates, did Simon tell you about a case we've been investigating which involves one of his colleague's husband?"

"Yes he did. Dr. Neville and his wife Natalie. Such a lovely woman. Nice, polite children too. I've met them once or twice. A dreadful pity about what happened. I've been following the story in the newspapers, of course. I read the trial collapsed. Does that mean he's not guilty? I asked Simon what he thought, but he said it doesn't mean he's guilty but that he's not not guilty either. All very confusing. Of course, Simon is terribly discreet, I've asked him for the inside information but he refuses to tell me anything, says there's no point in speculation, that the police only deal in facts."

Suddenly realizing she was babbling once again, she enquired curiously.

"Anyway, what is it you wanted to ask me?"

"Mrs. Bates. We understand your son is a computer specialist. We recently visited him at his home. Do you often go there?"

The apparent non sequitors didn't seem to faze Elizabeth Bates one bit.

"Yes, that's what he does. He was always very clever when it came to computers. His dad and I didn't know where he got it from, we were both dinosaurs with technology. I still am really, but Simon was a natural. He's just as good with a camera as well, you know. He's got a real artistic talent, he could have been the next David Bailey I always said. We bought him the best camera we could afford in case he ever wanted to make a career out of photography. But it was only a hobby he said, his first love was always computing. His father had to use a computer at work, of course. He was an accountant, you know. I suppose he used it for spread sheets and projections and that kind of thing, but he wasn't interested in bringing the office back with him of an evening. He used to enjoy settling down to a bit of telly to round off the day. Of course, I've got a mobile phone now, which I can just about use. Simon insists I keep it with me all the time in case of an emergency. I told him not to bother with that internet stuff, but he convinced me I needed bringing in to the twenty first century, super fast broadband and all that. He bought me a laptop a couple of Christmases ago so I could facetime and email my friends, and I have to admit, it's been very satisfying staying in touch with people and being able to see them while you talk."

"And do you go over to his place very often?" asked Sandy interrupting Mrs. Bates seemingly endless flow of chatter.

"Not usually, dear. You see it's two bus rides, then a ten minute walk. Unfortunately I don't drive. Edward, that's Simon's father always said he never minded taking me where I needed to go. But I keep thinking to myself, *'Elizabeth, you're a modern woman, it's never too late. Go and get yourself some driving lessons.'* And I'm seriously thinking of doing just that. But, what was I saying? Oh yes. So Simon comes here instead, regular as clock work. Wednesdays and Saturdays. Except today of course, which is most unusual - he's such a creature of habit as a rule."

Elizabeth Bates seemed a little disconcerted and quite put out at her son's sudden change of routine.

"Of course, I've had to change my plans too. I always go to Zumba on a Tuesday. I love it and they're such nice people. It's just round the corner and we all go for a coffee afterwards. They'll be wondering where I am. I think I'll send a text to explain I won't be there this week. Then there's housework on a Monday and swimming on a Thursday."

"Quite a busy social life you've got there," Pennock quickly interjected. "Lucky for us then that we'll catch the two of you together today."

As Mrs. Bates sent her message, Pennock took the opportunity to check his own. He had felt the phone vibrate. It was from Harry.

'No chance of a warrant. Bates on way. Back asap.'

iv.

Harry got some funny looks as he rushed back into the department, but didn't slow down on his way to Chief Superintendent Worth's office. Worth was not amused and ruthlessly laid in to his sergeant.

"Parnell, what the bloody hell's going on? First D.I Pennock and Parker disappear without a word, then you. It's like the bloody *'Marie Celeste'* out there. Hasn't anybody heard about the chain of command? Am I always the last one to know what's going on?"

Worth ranted on some more before stopping long enough to let Harry get a word in edgeways.

"Sorry Sir. It was all a bit of a rush. I got a call from D.I Pennock asking me to get over to Mrs. Bates residence - she's the mother of Simon Bates, who works with Natalie Neville."

"Get on with it man, I don't need a bibliography of the whole case."

"Sorry sir. Well, Inspector Pennock's got a new theory. And sir? I really think he's on to something this time. He told me to get back here sharpish and get a search warrant, then go and pick up Simon Bates and take him back to his mother's."

All business now, Worth responded.

"Tell me what he's got."

Harry repeated it exactly as he had been told.

"And that's why he needs the warrant," he finished. Worth considered what he had been told before he replied.

"No can do. I'm sorry but those are not sufficient grounds. It's tenuous at least and the downright hounding of an innocent member of the public at worst. As far as I'm aware, this Simon Bates has already been interviewed twice and released without charge and there has certainly never been any suggestion of involvement by the mother. In all conscience, I can't take that to a magistrate, and the District Judge would never sign it off on the basis of what you've just said. It's just too weak."

"But, what if he's right, Sir?" asked Parnell quietly.

Worth was nothing if not fair, and if there was a remote chance that his D.I was right, he wouldn't want to let that slip through his fingers. But there was no way he was going to be the laughing stock again. *'Fool me once shame on you. Fool me twice, shame on me.'* He thought.

"Pennock's resourceful. I'm sure he'll be able to carry out the search with the agreement of the house-holder. Just make absolutely certain you operate within the confines of PACE. If you unearth something, I'll have a full warrant to you within the hour. If nothing shows up, all you'll have is egg on your face and this department won't have been brought into disrepute again. Understand? Now get out of my bloody office."

As disappointed as Parnell was for his former boss, he couldn't say he was particularly surprised about the warrant. As he departed, he caught sight of Frank loitering by the coffee machine. He sidled over.

"Fancy an outing, Frank?"

"What? You asking me out on a date, Harry?"

"Yeah, something like that. Thought we might take a trip into the town, maybe call in for someone on the way."

"Count me in. I've finished the McKay report, so not much going on at the moment. I could do with getting out for a bit, stretch my legs. My latest new Gov's down at the magistrate's court, so he won't be back for ages. I don't think anyone will miss me if I go awol for a bit."

The truth was, Frank had earwigged most of the conversation between Worth and Harry and he wanted in.

On their way out, Parnell told Frank what had transpired so far and that he should drop him at Bates' work then continue on to his mother's house. Parnell would travel in Bates' car, to make sure he didn't abscond en route.

23

The tea finished, it was time for Pennock and Parker to get down to the nitty gritties of their visit. Nothing Elizabeth Bates had said made Pennock think he was in the wrong once again. Far from it, without realizing it she was confirming everything he had begun to suspect. He could see dawning comprehension on Sandy's face too, controlled excitement that they could be just about to crack the case wide open.

He was now certain he wasn't making the facts fit the evidence, as Sandy had previously feared. He wasn't second guessing himself, he was acting on solid police detection, with a good dose of professional gut feeling added in.

"Mrs Bates. You said that Simon sometimes stays the night. Can we see his bedroom, please?"

"Oh, I'm sorry Inspector, but Simon's very strict about his *'personal space'*. That's what he calls it - *'personal space'*. Even I'm not allowed to go into his room. I've told him over and over, ' *Simon, love, I'm more than happy to change your sheets and give the room a quick freshen up,'* but he won't have it. He always says *'Mum, I'm a grown up now. I'll keep my own room tidy. I don't want you running around after me'.*"

Mrs Bates paused briefly to draw breath.

"I'll let you in on a little secret. The truth is he's actually very fastidious about his room. He likes everything to be just so. Everything in its place. For the life of me I don't know where he gets his compulsion for tidiness from. I mean, I keep my house nice, who doesn't? But within reason. So, what's a mother supposed to do? It wouldn't be any trouble. He's such a considerate boy, don't you think? He never wants to put me out."

Sandy and Pennock exchanged a glance conveying the thought, 'No, just *'keep'* you out. Really considerate.'

"Mrs. Bates. Are you saying you never go into Simon's room?" asked Sandy incredulously.

"That's right, dear. I haven't been in there since he bought his own flat, and that was a couple of years ago now, I suppose. But he says he likes to keep his room just as it was when he was a boy. Takes him back to his childhood, or so he says. Such happy memories. His Airfix planes hanging from the ceiling and the metal toy soldiers he'd spend hours and hours painting. The colours and dimensions had to be exactly correct. I should think they'd be worth quite a bit these days. Then there's his rare coin collection, valuable as well most probably. And his Hornby train set too, I shouldn't wonder. He was always such a stickler for detail, liked everything perfect really. So, I have to respect his privacy if that's what he wants. Oh ... and of course ... there is also a padlock on the door," she added as an afterthought.

Pennock and Sandy sat up straighter upon hearing this. Pennock, suppressing his eagerness, asked in a neutral voice.

"Mrs. Bates, I don't suppose you happen to have a spare key for the padlock, do you?"

Mrs. Bates reddened and grew a little flustered. She didn't actually possess a spare key but she did know where Simon kept one. Coming up the stairs one Sunday morning, she had seen him slip something behind the large family photograph her son had taken which hung on the landing. Later, after Simon had gone, she had taken a look and had discovered a key which she presumed was to his bedroom, but she had never been brave enough to open the door to see what was so important inside - so important that it needed to be locked away, out of her sight.

Elizabeth Bates was not very adept at lying, and especially not to the police.

"Well, I haven't got a key, but … "

"Mother, say no more. That's quite enough."

They had been so engrossed in their conversation that they hadn't heard Simon Bates letting himself quietly in, swiftly followed by Harry, and to Pennock's surprise, Frank Casey as well.

"Simon love, these police officers are here about Dr. and Mrs. Neville." His mother replied defensively. She hoped he hadn't heard her mention the hidden key.

"Yes, thank you mother, I'll deal with it from here."

His mother looked crestfallen and quite put out by her son's brusque tone.

Harry smoothly interjected.

"Mrs. Bates. D.S Casey and I could do with a brew if it'd be no trouble."

"I'll give you a hand and we can leave the others to have a quick word with Simon, can't we, Mrs Bates?" said Sandy, getting up and drawing Elizabeth Bates into the kitchen with her.

"Ok then dear. More tea all round," said Mrs. Bates, relieved to hand the interview over to her son.

Pennock wasn't about to allow Bates to get the upper hand and firmly told him to take a seat, that they wanted to ask him some more questions.

"But Inspector, you've already spoken to me twice. I don't think there's anything more I can add," complained Bates, reluctantly sitting down.

"Indulge me, Mr. Bates," responded Pennock mildly. "Now then, I have to remind you that you are still under caution and anything you may say may be used in evidence against you. Do you understand? Good. Then, if I can revisit our last conversation. There are a couple of points which still need clarifying. Simon, you told me that your job is in I.T, and you added that everyone is expected to turn their hand to whatever task needs attending to. Is that correct so far?"

Simon nodded his agreement.

"Good. However, and this is what I find rather unusual Mr. Bates, is that when I visisted your home the other evening, I found no evidence of any technology other than your t.v and mobile phone. When I say technology, I mean gizmos such as an iPad, laptop, P.C and so on. When I thought about it later, I realized this was very unlikely. I think it's most unusual and rare in this day and age for a young man who lives alone, not to have the typical consoles and other goodies for their entertainment, especially someone like yourself, who is so competent with modern technology. Wouldn't you agree, Simon?"

Simon took a moment to reply, looking genuinely bemused.

"Actually, I wouldn't Inspector. I think I must be one of those 'rare' people you just mentioned. Some other young men might be happy playing mindless video games all evening, but that's not my thing. I think it's puerile and only for the likes of morons who haven't got anything more constructive to do with their time."

Pennock was somewhat taken aback by Bates' response, but recovered to ask.

"And so, how do you spend your free time?"

"I read, relax. I listen to music, go to the theatre or cinema. Meet up with friends, have dinner. All the other 'usual' things a young person of my age might enjoy doing."

Pennock could feel his upper hand slowly slipping away. He needed to gain control of the interview and fast.

"Simon, tell us about your visits home."

"Tell you what? That I come to see my Mum a couple of times a week? Nothing 'unusual' there I don't think. Since Dad died and I got my own place, I like to pop over regularly to check on her, we have something to eat, have a chat and a laugh."

"And you often stay the night in your old room?"

"Correct. Another example of me being a responsible adult. If I've had a couple of beers or some wine, I wouldn't want to risk driving back home, so I stay the night. I think Mum enjoys the company, and, if I'm honest, I do too."

"Quite the dutiful son," commented Harry wryly.

"Simon, would you have any objections to showing us your bedroom?" asked Pennock.

"Whatever for, Inspector? It's only my old boyhood room. Nothing of interest in there, I can assure you."

"Well, I'll be honest with you Simon."

Pennock knew it was time to gamble and lay his cards on the table, in an attempt to draw Simon into the dilemma he was facing.

"I find myself in a bit of a quandary, so it's for my own peace of mind really. You see, I think something doesn't quite ring true where you're concerned. You talk the talk, and are certainly very persuasive, but something's off. Nothing's quite what it seems or should be. Until I'm satisfied as to whether you're connected to this investigation or not, I can't rest. I'm sure you can appreciate my position. I would love to eliminate you definitively from our enquiries. If you've got nothing to hide, it shouldn't be an issue, should it? So, I'll ask you once again, Mr. Bates, will you please grant us access to your bedroom?"

"I can't, Inspector," replied Simon in an abashed tone, "there are certain items in there that I'd rather you didn't find."

"Such as?" enquired Parnell.

"Well, let's just say some things that might not be quite legal."

Pennock was becoming exasperated.

"Mr. Bates. You have my word that we are not remotely interested in anything that isn't directly connected to this investigation. We don't give a damn if you've got a crack den, a casino or a hareem going on up there. You know perfectly well that's not what we're looking for. Well?"

"No."

"No? Are you sure? Last chance. Ok then. Harry, phone Chief Superintendent Worth and get a warrant. We'll have to do this the hard way. And you, Mr. Bates, you need to phone your solicitor."

24

The celebrations carried on well into the evening. Pennock had eventually returned and briefed his superior who was delighted with the result. Worth had instructed them to let Bates stew in the cells overnight. It was too late in the evening to begin questioning him in depth. By the time they'd got the warrant, arranged for forensics to attend, overseen the search, then got him back to the station to process him, they were exhausted. It would be better to come back the next day refreshed and raring to go. So they had charged him and briefly interviewed him under formal caution, arranging with his solicitor to reconvene at 10am the following morning.

For now, the whole department, well those that were still in the office that late, had been invited down to the local boozer for a pint, just the one mind, because Chief Superintendent Worth was treating them all to the first round and some of the team were still on duty and had work to do, as he was at pains to point out. And that included the former persona non grata who had since become the hero of the hour. He felt awkward and slightly embarrassed being the object of everyone's attention. He had never had so may pats on the back and *'well dones'* before. The same people who had refused to make eye contact with him just a short time ago were now his best mates, claiming they knew he'd break the case, that they'd never doubted it. He tried not to bear them any malice.

Chief Superintendent Worth called for hush. He was never one to resist the opportunity to grandstand and cash in on the success of one of his officers.

"Quiet boys and girls! I just want to say a few words of congratulations on behalf of the whole department."

The *'hear hears'* resounded round the pub.

"Inspector Pennock's diligence and unfailing professionalism are a credit not only to himself but to every police officer on the force. He has demonstrated that by dint of sheer determination and hard work even the most complex case can be solved. He has shown dogged resilience in the face of some tough moments and he and his team are to be commended for seeing it through to such a satisfactory conclusion. Please raise your glasses in a toast to D.I Pennock!"

"D.I Pennock," responded the chorus in unison.

Pennock accepted their congratulations, telling anyone who would listen, that it was team work. The praise belonged to them all. He was keen to escape as soon he reasonably could, but kept getting waylaid eventually having to force his way out. He told Harry and the others to stay and enjoy the rest of the evening. He'd see them in the morning. He had a few loose ends to tie up in the office before he went home. His poor wife, he had suddenly realized, would be wondering where he was as well. He'd better let her know what was going on. Then he'd better contact the Nevilles.

ii.

Who on earth would be calling at this time of the evening? A late night call was never good news. His parents had gone up to bed early and while he was relieved to have control of the remote - he'd actually had a life-time's fill of nature documentaries and cookery programmes - he had nevertheless found himself too lethargic to browse for something that would really capture his attention, instead settling to watch some gormless reality programme on the telly. The sound of his mobile was like a siren going off in the quiet of the house, and would surely wake up his mum and dad. Already irritated, he was even more so when he looked at the caller display. That incompetent, life wrecker, Pennock. Still determined to torment him, at all hours of the day and night. Would he never be left in peace?

"Inspector, what is it you want now? Do you realize what time it is?" he whispered down the phone, anxious not to wake his parents.

"I'm sorry to disturb you, Dr. Neville," responded Pennock, "but I wanted to let you know as quickly as possible that there've been some significant developments. Can you both get down to the station tomorrow afternoon at about 3pm? Is Mrs. Neville there with you now?"

"You know she's not, Inspector. As you're well aware, we are no longer together," he snapped, unable to keep the bitterness from his voice. Then, more controlled, "but I think I can contact her at home. Is it important for her to be there too?"

"I think when you hear what I've got to tell you, you'll want her to be there as well."

Alistair was suddenly on high alert. What the hell? What had they discovered, that it had become imperitive to see them both together? Pennock's tone of voice was giving nothing away. No indication whether this was good or bad news for him.

"Developments, you say? What kind of developments?" he asked cautiously probing.

"I'd rather wait till tomorrow to discuss it with you both in person. I'm not at liberty to say any more at the moment."

As intrigued, or perhaps anxious, as he was, Alistair had waited this long regarding his fate, another few hours one way or the other wouldn't kill him. Would it?

"Alright then, Inspector. We'll be with you tomorrow at 3."

iii.

Pennock was at his desk by 8am and was joined within minutes by the rest of his team. They got straight down to the report writing ready to present it to Worth who called them in to the Briefing Room promptly at 9.

"Morning everyone. So who's going to start? Sgt. Parnell filled me in to some extent yesterday when he asked for the warrant. I want to hear clearly and concisely exactly what happened." he began.

Harry commenced.

"Well, Sir. To quickly recap. After speaking to Mrs. Bates, we were led to understand that Simon Bates still had use of his old bedroom at the family home. And that bedroom was secured by a pad lock. Nothing illegal in that, obviously - just suspicious. We requested several times for Mr. Bates to grant us access to the room which he declined. At that point D.I Pennock asked me to arrange for the warrant. Bates gave us an implausible story about having something dodgy or illegal in the room that he didn't want us to see. He was stalling and trying to persuade us that there was nothing of interest for us up there."

Sandy took up the thread.

"Frank Casey and I interviewed Mrs. Bates under caution in the kitchen while we waited for forensics to arrive."

Pennock continued the saga.

"He still wouldn't unlock the door, so forensics opened it with the bolt cutters. Sir, it was an Aladdin's den like you've never seen before ..."

iv.

The small house could scarcely accommodate the number of people that had squeezed in. Outside, the cul de sac was full of police and specialist vehicles, a visual cacophony of blue lights silently whirring. There was no way the Bates' would be able to keep secret what was going on at their address. Inside, none of Pennock's team wanted to miss the grand finale. He left a disappointed Sandy and Frank downstairs guarding Mrs. Bates and Simon while he and Harry accompanied the four forensic experts upstairs.

With a snap of the breaking lock, the door to the room burst open and they all crammed in. Too many people. Pennock ordered everyone to wait outside except himself, Parnell and the lead forensic examiner. He needed to get a feel for the room before it was torn apart. They wouldn't touch anything, wouldn't contaminate the scene, but it was important to see it first hand, in situ as it were, to experience it through Bates' eyes.

The scene before them could not have been further removed from the image Mrs. Bates had painted of her son's childhood room. Where were the carefully crafted mobiles, the figurines, the adolescent posters, the football stickers? This was definitely not your common or garden teenager's bedroom. What they now beheld was more akin to something from GCHQ. Lining the widest wall was a bank of computer monitors, all in live mode. Each high definition screen showed different images - images of rooms that Pennock was confidently able to identify as being in the Neville household. The kitchen, lounge, both children's bedrooms and Mrs. Neville's own bedroom. They could see that the family was currently eating their evening meal, sitting around the kitchen table. The three officers were all startled to suddenly hear Natalie clearly ask the children if they'd finished their homework for next week because she wanted them to spend some time with their Dad before they went back to Granny and Grandad's on Sunday evening. The visual and audio quality was outstandingly good.

"What the hell?" demanded Pennock angrily. "I thought you lot had removed all the cameras and microphones from the Neville household."

"We did. We swept the whole house for bugs and sound equipment and, I can assure you that house was clean when we left it," came the affronted yet defensive response from the forensic team leader, Stephen Reid.

"Then how in God's name are we seeing them in front of us right now?" he pointed an accusatory finger towards the screens.

"I can't understand it," came the baffled response. "I'm certain we got them all."

"I think I can answer that one, Gov," interposed Harry. "Have a look at this."

A single bed complete with its incongruous 'Toy Story' duvet cover and pillow case seemed to have been pushed out of position, and was now flush against the smallest side wall on the left of the room, leaving space between the foot of the bed and the door frame for a huge ply board panel.

They could hardly believe what they were seeing. The board had been neatly divided into compartments and in each of which hung an imprinted plaster mould as well as its corresponding metal key. There was name tag to identify each box which were numbered from 1 to 10. 1) A.N car. 2) N.N car. 3) Front door. 4) Back door. 5) Conservatory. 6) Garage. 7) A.N Parents. 8) N.N Parents 9) Susan. 10) -

"Oh my God," moaned Pennock, "I don't believe it. What an imbecile I've been. It never occurred to me to tell them to change the locks, and they obviously didn't think of it either. That sick bastard's gone back in and planted his cameras and microphones all over again."

It was clear that was exactly what had happened. It may have caused Bates a minor inconvenience as well as some considerable expense, but the whole set-up had been recreated. They assumed he had simply reused the keys he'd already had cut and replanted the spyware.

Continuing their eyeball search of the room, they spotted a tall filing cabinet. Pennock donned his latex gloves and with one finger delicately slid the first drawer open. Each file had been clearly marked. He saw folders labelled - " Photos N", "Photos J", "Photos M". He didn't attempt to pull them out.

"I've seen enough. There's plenty of incriminating evidence in here to charge him. Get downstairs and read him his rights, Harry. I'll be down in a moment."

"With pleasure, Gov," Parnell answered happily.

Pennock turned to Reid.

"I'm sorry Steve. I should have known better than to jump to hasty conclusions."

"You and me both. For a minute I thought that we really had missed some of those bugs. This bloke must have money to burn to have replaced the whole lot as well as having this amount of quality gear lying around."

"Well, that is something I hope to find out. Right, I'll leave you and your team to it. Tear the place apart if you have to. But, can I ask you one favour? Can you let me know asap if you think it's Bates acting alone or if he's involved with anyone else?"

"What d'you mean?"

"Just, was he working solo, or in cahoots with Alistair Neville? Or was he part of an organized paedo group? Who funded all this technology? What was the ultimate purpose of it? We need to consider every angle."

"Got you. As soon as I know, so will you."

25.

Bates' interview began promptly at 10 a.m.

"For the benefit of the tape, present today are D.I Pennock, D.S Parnell, Mr. Simon Bates and his solicitor, Mr. Adrian Noble. Can I remind you, Mr. Bates that you are still under caution and that anything you may say may be used in evidence against you in a court of law?"

Bates had accompanied them under duress the previous evening. He had vociferously proclaimed his innocence of any of the trumped up charges against him. His lawyer would have him out in short shrift he insisted after he had been charged, finger-printed and swabbed for D.N.A earlier on.

"Shall we begin? Good. Mr. Bates, can you explain the surveillance equipment we found in your room at your mother's address?"

"I should think that it's quite obvious, Inspector," Bates replied with confident composure. "You asked me yourself, yesterday - why didn't I have any technology at my house? Well, now you know. I keep all my electronics at my mother's. Not surprisingly, when I come home from work I like to totally disconnect from my job. Looking at computer screens all day long is hard on the eyes and very tiring. When I get home, I like to de-stress away from the daily grind, so I limit myself to using my computers to a couple of times a week at mother's."

"You have some very impressive kit there. Did you buy it all yourself?" asked Parnell.

"I'm a single man, Sergeant. My social life is modest, so other than my mortgage and the usual out goings, I have a fairly substantial disposable income each month. And that's how I choose to spend my money."

Pennock kept his voice neutral. He wanted to keep Bates relaxed and responsive, so he kept the questions simple. He was going to tease the answers out of him.

"Let's move on then. Could you tell us about the moulds and keys? Why do you possess keys to the Neville's property, their families' houses as well as Susan's?"

"I know it looks suspicious, Inspector, but, I promise you there's a totally innocent explanation." came the slick and well executed reply. "Like most women, Natalie keeps all her keys in her handbag ... house, car etc. She lost her bag one day, well misplaced it as it turned out, and was frantic because she couldn't do anything without her keys. It made me realize how vulnerable she was. So I took her keys and decided to make copies of them for her in case that should ever happen to her again."

177

"Why didn't you just take them to the hardware store and have copies made there? Why did you have to take moulds of her keys and then have them made up?

"I didn't want to embarrass her or imply she was unreliable. So I took the keys from her bag, made mouldings of them and kept a spare set safe for her."

By this point Pennock had had more than enough of Bates' ridiculous explanations.

"Are you serious Mr. Bates? That out of the goodness of your heart, you made copies of her keys and then stashed them in your old bedroom, in case she should ever lose them again?" asked Pennock incredulously.

"Strange but true."

"They'd hardly be accessible at your mother's house now, would they? Wouldn't it be more logical to keep them in a drawer in her office in the workplace?"

"Perhaps, but less secure."

Pennock and Parnell let his explanation go. What he was saying was total drivel, they both knew that. However, they were more interested in what was going to come next. They were gradually moving towards the critical part of the interview.

"Let's talk about the photos."

Bates' jaw tightened, the only indication that he was feeling any strain at all.

"We found photos of the Neville family in your filing cabinet. All of them had been sorted and filed by name. Why do you have so many photos of the family?"

He relaxed, back on solid ground again.

"Inspector, you've failed to mention that all of my photos and discs are stored in the same place, not just those of the Nevilles. There are all sorts of photos archived in there, family holidays, friends and relatives, days out. Nothing odd about that. As you must have realized by now, I am very particular about having everything in it's place. I like to catalogue and annotate items so that I can easily access them should I need to."

"But why so many of the Nevilles?"

"No particular reason. Nat is a close friend, it's only normal that I've got pictures of her family."

Pennock had just about had enough of Bates' bullshit. Nothing Bates had said was a lie but none of it was true either. Slowly and clearly he asked,

"Mr. Bates. Tell us about the other photos."

"What other photos? I don't have any other photos. I don't know what you could be referring to." he answered, his voice rising an octave.

"Oh, but I think you do, Mr. Bates. I think you do. I'm referring to the images that you had secreted away between the two ply board panels holding the keys. In fact, these photos, and these discs."

Pennock produced a large envelope. Bates blanched.

"What? Did you think we wouldn't find them? Now then Mr. Bates, I caution you to think very carefully about what you're going to say next."

Bates looked panicked, turning desperately towards his brief.

Mr. Noble quickly interjected.

"Inspector. I need to speak to my client before I can permit him to answer any more questions. Could we have a few minutes to confer?"

ii.

It was pitiful really, their gratitude. He was embarrassed and knew he didn't deserve their heart-felt thanks after what he had unnecessarily put them through, bringing down upon them such disastrous results. But it would not be as pitiful as the explanation they deserved and which he was about to deliver.

Alistair and Natalie Neville had arrived separately, but promptly at 3 o'clock as agreed. They weren't sure whether they were going to be the recipients of good or bad news. Pennock had taken them through to the Family Liaison Room, offered them coffee and begun the debrief. He began the story at the point when, returning on the train having concluded another case, he had realized something was seriously awry with Simon Bates' interview and how he had eventually followed the trail to Mrs. Bates' home, and subsequently what had been uncovered there.

Pennock informed the Nevilles that once the evidence had been laid before him, Simon Bates had crumbled, anxious but almost proud to get the whole story off his chest. Pennock recounted in detail how Simon had kept saying that he knew the Inspector and the Sergeant would understand once he had told them everything, they would know he had been right, that his actions had been justified. The course he had taken was correct, there was no remorse to feel because what he had done was for the greater good.

His rambling, but coherent monologue had portrayed Alistair Neville as a superior, arrogant tyrant, who ruled his household with the same rod of iron and distain that he exercised in the operating theatre. Bates had scornfully described the rotas pinned to the fridge door in the kitchen, which obliged the whole family to comply to a strict agenda not to be deviated from. He spoke angrily of the military operation that surrounded the family routines, the repression they had to endure at the hands of a dictator. The diatribe continued as he outlined how he had built up supporting evidence against Dr. Neville through interviews held at the local pub where his colleagues habitually drank, all of whom, Bates insisted, universally loathed the man.

More calmly, he had revealed how his admiration and respect for Natalie had developed slowly into love. He readily admitted that Natalie had not reached the same depth of love as himself, explaining that her overwhelming fear of her husband had paralysed her into a physical and mental atrophy. He described their special, close relationship and how little it would take to encourage her feelings into becoming feelings of true love for him. He explained how, alone, Natalie would be incapable of breaking away from the man who held so much power over her and how he himself had taken the decision to liberate her from her shackles. Once free of her husband's hold over her, Nat would see for the first time how love should be with a man who worshipped her above all else.

His plan had been many months in the preparing and executing. Simon was not an impatient person he had told them, he was a thorough man who weighed up the pros and cons of all the options. The ultimate prize would be worth the wait. The one thing Simon was certain of however, was the solution had to be permanent - short of killing him that was. Although, he had confessed, he had briefly toyed with the idea of going to those lengths to be rid of the problem once and for all, but knew he would be unlikely to get away with it. He had to conceive of a plan that was so totally catastrophic and devastating that Alistair Neville would be totally obliterated and would never see the light of day again for many, many years.

 He had proposed and discarded several ideas because either the element of risk was too great or the chances of success too slim. Any vestige of connection with her husband would have to be quashed so irreparably and irreversibly that, having eliminated Alistair, Natalie would naturally turn to him for solace and support. Bates then told the two detectives how a plan had begun to form. It was so horribly vile that, if he were able to execute it, Natalie would assuredly be resolved that neither she nor her children would ever be inclined to have any contact with Alistair again. He would be indelibly exorcised from their lives for evermore. And that's where he would come in, to pick up the pieces and help them rebuild their broken lives.

He described how slowly, so slowly, he had begun to insinuate himself into Nat's life, both professionally and socially. He had to be subtle, he did not wish to alarm her, but to gradually become indispensable - a solid, reliable friend. He could tell she favoured him over the rest of the team, delegating him as her right hand man. She would see his true worth for herself soon enough.

Gaining access to her handbag couldn't have been easier, he told them. All the women in the company left their bags unattended. What was the need for security? They were all long term colleagues and it was rare for a stranger to come into the office and anyway, it was nearly always by appointment. He had entered her office one morning when he had a genuine enquiry and needed her advice. He had spotted his chance and removed the clearly visible keys, believing it was unlikely she would miss them in the short space of time he would need them. He took the crafting clay from his desk where he had secreted it, waiting for just the right opportunity and went into the gents where he carefully made impressions of both sides of each key before casually dropping them unnoticed back into her bag when he had reason to talk to her again. Then he had copies made up that same day.

After that, time was on his side, he could set the trap at his leisure. The family's whereabouts, so conveniently secured to the fridge, allowed him unrestricted access to the house with the keys he had had cut without fear of discovery. He had planted the cameras and listening devices and began to familiarize himself with their lifestyle and routines. Later, in his room, he had expertly and painstakingly photo-shopped pictures that he had removed and scanned from the family albums and frames as well as digital images from the P.C. He was meticulous, methodical and thorough in his preparation … he knew it had to be fool proof.

Bates described his fury when the police technicians had discovered his spyware, but how that was soon remedied over the Christmas holidays when the house had been empty. He was able to undertake his vigil once again at his own convenience, observing and listening to the family as well as remotely accessing the Neville's P.C. Listening in one evening, he had been alarmed to learn that Nat was planning to remove herself and the children down to her parent's neck of the woods and he feared that his master plan was about to be derailed. Upon reflection, however, he realized that this was probably a blessing in disguise. To have Nat far away from all the bad memories would give him the chance he needed to establish a new and genuine, loving relationship with her.

Finally Bates described how, on that bitterly cold November night, he had broken into several apparently random vehicles in the hospital car park, stolen some carelessly left items and returned home with them. He had gone through the haul, doctoring one of the lap-tops fortuitously owned, he was later to discover, by Dr. Neville's best friend, Peter Forbes. He told them that the following day he had gone along to the London Road police station and returned all the stolen goods - but planting one extra item - a pink memory stick.

From that moment on, how the saga would unfold would be out of his hands. He had to have faith that the police would do their job competently. What he had not anticipated was that they would be quite so tenacious. Once Neville had been charged, he thought he was home and clear. He had not counted on the possibility of a failed trial. The best outcome would have been for Neville to be convicted. Then he would have been permanently eliminated from their lives. However the prospect of it becoming a cold case would also serve as a good result. Not so clean, but the Neville's marriage was in shreds, a reconciliation would be impossible. Nat had told him that herself. For him it was a win, win situation. Or so he had thought. Neither, it seemed, had he counted on D.I Pennock's dogged determination.

iii.

Pennock had asked the couple to restrain themselves from interrupting during his debrief. He would answer all their questions at the end. He had to frequently stop them from interjecting by raising a hand to forestall their shocked comments and denials. He didn't want to get side-tracked but needed to get to the end of this tale, delivering it as he had been told by Simon Bates, before hearing their response. By the end, both of them were silent, struck dumb by the enormity, complexity and thoroughness of the plan hatched against them. And by how close it had come to succeeding.

Nat said angrily.

"Some of what he says might seem true on the face of it, but that's only to the casual observer. Anyone who really knows us, knows that's not who we are and certainly not who Alistair is. He's a good man and a good father. What gives him the right to make assumptions about us without even knowing us properly? He knows nothing about our lives and how we manage."

"Oh, but he does, Mrs. Neville. He knows plenty. But unfortunately his version of two and two make five. Simon Bates was utterly convinced that he was saving you from a monster, Natalie, and bringing you safely into the arms of the man who could protect and cherish you. That's why I thought you both deserved to hear his account from me, not from the papers which'll sensationalize the whole thing or in court where they'll sanitize his version of events."

Finally, Alistair commented,

"It's like he sees things through a different lens from the rest of us - delusional. As though he's out of phase with reality and makes up for it by forcing the pieces to fit his concept of the truth."

"That's exactly what he's like. His vision of the world is totally distorted, but he believes his impression is right and it's others who are out of kilter, not him," agreed Pennock.

Alistair was emotional, Nat too.

"Thank you, Inspector. We can't thank you enough for seeing it through. You said you wouldn't let it rest and you didn't."

"You're very welcome Dr. and Mrs. Neville."

He accompanied them as far as the exit of the police station, shook hands with them both and said goodbye, wishing them all the best. He continued to observe them as they slowly made their way towards the car park. United at this moment, no doubt relief flooding through them, bonding them, now that the ordeal was finally over. Although not really over, was it?

He turned sadly away, feeling strangely deflated. It had been a good result in the end, but at what cost? So many lives shattered including, quite possibly, his own, as he was about to soon find out.

He paused mid-step, a sudden lightning-bolt striking, then exploding into his consciousness.

'So many lives'... And what was it that had Dr. Neville had said? That Bates' world was distorted, out of phase with reality. Could it be that Dr. Neville wasn't the sole victim of Simon Bates' warped vision of the world? Could Bates have targeted previous victims? Suppose, just suppose, Alistair Neville was only the tip of the iceberg, perhaps one of many? It didn't bear thinking about. A cold shudder coursed through Pennock's entire being as he contemplated the possibility of other unknown, convicted yet innocent victims out there.

'Hey, just hold on a minute. Let's deal with first things first.' he cautioned himself sternly.

Steadying himself, he took a deep breath, squared his shoulders and made his way resolutely back upstairs to the department, steeling himself to confront his fate with the awaiting Internal Investigation disciplinary committee.

Printed in Great Britain
by Amazon